THE ALIEN CORN

FROM THE AUTHOR OF THE CHALKY SEA

CLARE FLYNN

CRANBROOK PRESS

A Lina Negri, amica da anni –
perché questo libro parla anche dell'Italia che amiamo

The voice I hear this passing night was heard
In ancient days by emperor and clown:
Perhaps the selfsame song that found a path
Through the sad heart of Ruth, when, sick for home,
She stood in tears amid the alien corn;

From Ode to a Nightingale by John Keats

THE HOMECOMING

ONTARIO. Canada, September 1945

THE FIRST THING he registered was the smell. It was just after dawn and the sky was still streaked with pink but the scent of ripe wheat told him at once that he was home. Jim breathed in a lungful of air and looked towards the distant horizon, across the shafts of wheat waving in the breeze. He had stood here in this same spot the last time he saw the farm. Back then his beloved dog Swee'Pea had been beside him and it was still a few short hours until he would discover his fiancée, Alice, in the arms of his brother, Walt.

It felt like a lifetime ago, but it was only five years. No, it was a lifetime ago. The Jim who had stood here then was naive, hopeful, uncertain whether to join up to fight Hitler, torn between his duty to his country and his wish to see his wedding plans through. The Jim who stood here now was battle-worn, tired, old beyond his years. The war had chipped away at him, cutting out the softer parts, sculpting him down to the hard rock that was now at the core of him, turning him into a man whom, he believed, could no longer be shocked by anything.

He wanted to whistle for Swee'Pea but it was pointless. His mother had written to tell him when the dog died. He'd been sad for a moment or two but the feeling had passed. Having looked into the damaged face of his dead brother, and with men dying around him every day, there had been little space left to brood over a dog who had lived a long and happy life and he hadn't seen in years. But now he would have given anything to have his old friend bound up to him, tail wagging, ready to follow in his footsteps wherever he went.

Jim pulled the grains off an ear of wheat, rubbing them between his fingers. It was a reflex action. A few more days until they'd be ready. He walked slowly along the perimeter of the field, breathing in the sweet, fresh smell of the crop. In front of him the ground dropped in a short, steep slope. Beyond, more fields stretched away, ending at a distant line of trees that marked the boundary of the farm. Jim stopped short, surprised to see that instead of another expanse of wheat the land lay fallow. Why hadn't Pa planted the bottom acres?

He walked on through more land covered with grass and wild flowers where wheat should have been standing tall. What had happened? His father would never have neglected planting in the past. A stab of guilt pierced him. The farm was too much for one aging man to manage alone. His father had said as much the night Jim left to volunteer for the army.

He glimpsed a splash of light where sunlight hit water though the trees. The creek. He moved down the slope to the strip of shallow water which deepened into a pool under a large tree. His throat constricted as he looked at the cottonwood tree with its branches bending low over the water. Home. All his childhood memories began in this spot.

He thought of his brother, Walt. Dead and buried in England in the Canadian section of the cemetery at Brookwood after the fateful Dieppe raid. Jim had visited his grave back in 1943 before he left for the front. The spot was marked only by a temporary wooden cross with a simple metal marker bearing Walt's name, a few rows away from the plot where Jim's friend Greg was interred. He hoped permanent tombstones would soon be erected.

Picking up a pebble, he ran it round in his hands, feeling its roughness, then tossed it into the stream and watched the ripples spread through the clear water. A tattered rope still dangled from the branches of the tree, too worn now to bear his weight. How many times had he and Walt swung from that rope as boys, hanging on as long as possible before letting go and plunging into the pool below?

The sun was moving higher in the sky and the air was already warm. Jim took off his jacket and dropped it on the ground, slinging his battered, army-issue, canvas holdall beside it and sat down with his back against the trunk of the cottonwood tree. He didn't want to go up to the house yet. The thought of greeting his parents was not a happy one. When they looked at him he feared they would see only the absence of his brother.

Jim hadn't written to tell them about his wife and child. There had been no time between the rushed marriage ceremony and his deployment to Sicily. Afterwards, caught up in the horrors of the battlefield, he had fought day after day with the expectation of dying. It didn't seem right to tell his folks about Joan and the baby when there was little prospect of them ever meeting their daughter-in-law and grandson. Better to tell them in person – if he survived the war. Now he would have to face up to the fact that he was a husband and father. At some point in the not too distant future he would return to Joan and Jimmy: his wife, a virtual stranger, and the son he had seen for a matter of minutes. He would have also to face up to telling his parents that he wasn't staying at Hollowtree Farm. He was going back to England as soon as he'd sorted things out here.

Why did war make everything so complicated? But it wasn't right to blame it all on the war. Finding out his fiancée was in love with his brother was already enough of a complication.

Running his hand through his hair, he brushed away the sweat that soaked his brow despite the early hour. It was going to be a scorcher today. He sucked on a stalk of grass, drawing the sweetness into his mouth as he and Walt had done through countless summers lying here beside the creek.

What was the point of delaying? Better to get it over and done with. He sprang to his feet and moved towards the farmhouse, visible in the distance. Before going to the house, he walked across to the barn. In the gloom of the interior he gasped. Where once there had been neatly piled bales of hay, sacks of feed and potatoes, bundles of corn and dozens of barrels of apples, now there was a large empty space with a few buckets containing cornmeal and grain. This was where he had discovered his fiancée Alice with his brother. The pain of that memory was gone now, erased by his experiences in Europe and the passage of time. He sat down on an upturned bucket and looked around at the empty space. It made no sense. The barn should be bursting at the seams this time of year. He felt a hollow fear. What was going on? He hadn't wanted to return to Canada at all, but after five years service, almost all of it overseas, and his involvement in the battles in Sicily and Italy, he had been high up the queue for demobilisation. He intended going back to England to settle but first he had to say goodbye to his folks, or maybe persuade them to come with him. Seeing the way the farm had been neglected perhaps that wasn't such a crazy idea after all.

When he emerged from the barn his mother was in the yard, hanging out the washing, her back to him. A rush of affection swept through him. He'd forgotten how much he'd missed her. He glanced at his watch, surprised that she must have been up before dawn to get the washing done already. Unable to sleep perhaps? He waited until she had finished the task before calling her. She was bent over, in the act of picking up the empty basket and she froze for a moment, then turned and ran to him. But how changed she was. Barely fifty, she looked like a woman in her late sixties, her face lined and careworn. Her eyes had lost their sparkle and her mouth was set in what deep grooving suggested was a permanent downward turn.

Jim hesitated, guilt for his part in bringing about this change weighing heavy on him. Then her arms were around him and her head was against his chest and he could hear her sobs. Her body pressed against his, while he stood rigid, uncertain what to do or say.

After a few moments she lifted her head and looked at him. 'Oh, Jim,' was all she said, then again, 'Oh, Jim.' In those two words there was a wealth of emotions: joy, sorrow, recrimination, regret, possibly even fear or dread. She raised her hand and ran it down his cheek. 'Oh Jim,' she said again, this time with a hint of finality.

'Hello, Ma.'

'Why didn't you tell us you were coming? We'd have met you from the station. How did you get here? We thought you were still in Europe. They've been saying how it'll take months to get you all back home. I'd no idea you'd be here so fast.'

'I had pneumonia. They sent me back to Canada on a hospital ship with the wounded.'

'Pneumonia?' His mother's face was concerned. 'How did that happen?'

'The last few months were pretty rough. Rain then snow.'

'You're used to snow, son.' She smiled at him and touched his arm.

'Not sleeping out in the open, underfed and being bombarded all the time.'

Helga's eyes were wide. 'I thought Italy was warm and sunny.'

Jim grunted. 'Actually it's a while since I left there. The army had me escorting wounded men home after I landed in Halifax.'

'So you've been in Canada a while?' She spoke with an accusatory tone.

'Since early April. When the war in Europe ended in May they stuck me behind a desk dealing with transportation. Then out of the blue they demobbed me a few days ago. Guess I was lucky.'

As soon as the words were out he wanted to take them back. Lucky. Yes he had been lucky. Walt had not been lucky. The guilt that had haunted Jim since his brother's death touched him now like a cold hand. If he hadn't joined up, Walt wouldn't have felt he had to follow him. If he hadn't run away from the knowledge that Walt and Alice had betrayed him, Walt would still be alive.

Pushing thoughts of Walt aside, he added. 'Some of the men shipped straight out to the Pacific.'

'Well thank God, you didn't have to.'

'I've been travelling all night. When I got off the train at Kitchener one of the guys gave me a ride into town and I walked from there.'

'You must be exhausted. And hungry. Let's get you some breakfast, son.'

There was the sound of coughing, a rough, rasping rattle

of a noise. Jim's father stood in the doorway. Jim swallowed and taking his mother by the hand, walked towards the house, his heart heavy with dread.

There was no display of emotion from Donald Armstrong. He held out a hand to shake his son's and gave him a nod, while avoiding meeting his eyes. The three of them turned and went inside the house.

Jim ate with a hunger he hadn't known he was feeling. It was a generous breakfast and a delicious contrast to the years of army rations. Home-cured bacon, eggs fresh from their own hens, sausages, fried potatoes and home-baked bread, washed down with hot coffee.

They ate in silence, Helga Armstrong frequently patting Jim's arm, as if to reassure herself that he was still there, while her husband kept his head lowered over his breakfast plate, chewing in silence. But when Jim looked at his father's plate he saw it was barely touched.

Eventually Donald looked up and fixed his eyes on the cooking range as he spoke. 'So you saw him after he died then?'

Jim grunted assent. 'I was at the port when they brought him back.' He felt the blood suffusing his face. His throat felt dry and he gulped another swig of coffee.

'How did he look?' He started coughing.

'Don, no.' Helga got to her feet and started to clear away the plates. 'Don't ask that.'

'I'm entitled to know.'

'He looked…' Jim searched for the right words. 'Peaceful.'

His father snorted in disgust and the snort degenerated into more coughing. 'Cut out the clichés. I was a soldier myself. There's nothing you can tell me that I didn't see at Vimy Ridge–'

Jim was suddenly angry. Angry at his dead brother and angry at the man sitting at the other end of the table. He thought of the last time he had sat at this table, Walt and Alice guarding their secret from him, probably already looking forward to their tryst in the loft of the barn. He'd had no choice but to get out of here then but it was clear his father blamed him for going and for his brother following him to war. But how could his pa have seriously expected him to stay here to face Alice marrying Walt?

He was about to give his father the details he had asked for. He wanted to tell him about Walt's half face, the jagged hole where his right eye had once been, the charred and blackened edges, the burnt vestiges of his once luxuriant sun-bleached hair. Why shouldn't his father be haunted the way he was by that image of Walt? Then he saw the anxious look on his mother's face and instead turned to her and said, 'Like I said, he looked as though he was sleeping. He was at peace.'

Donald Armstrong scraped back his chair and went to move away from the table.

Jim stretched out a hand to stay him. 'Wait, Pa, there's something I need to tell you. Sit down, Ma.'

He swallowed, breathed slowly to steady his nerves then said, 'I got married when I was in England. I have a son. You have a grandson.'

He studied the grain of the table, listening to the sharp intake of breath from his mother.

'Married? A child?' Helga's voice was barely a whisper. 'What about Alice?'

Jim leaned back in his chair, distancing himself, disbelieving what he thought his mother was about to say. 'Alice? What's it to do with Alice?'

'We thought –'

'Thought what?' Jim could feel the anger rising inside him.

'That you and she... after all, you were going to be

married before... We thought now that Walt's gone and her with little Rose to bring up–'

Jim got up so fast that he knocked his chair over behind him. 'Well you did too much thinking. There was never going to be anything between me and Alice once I found out she'd been screwing my brother. My wife is called Joan, since you ask.' He dripped sarcasm. 'And my son is called Jimmy. Not my choice of name but then I wasn't around when Joan had to pick one for him. Maybe if I had been I'd have suggested calling him Walt.' He jerked a hand behind him and pulled the chair up from the floor, shoving it back into place at the table. 'I'm back here to say goodbye to you. I told you when I left before that it was for ever. I couldn't help them repatriating me but I'm going back as soon as I've sorted things out with the army. Joan is British and wants to stay there and I like it just fine over there. Now I'm going to get some air.'

Turning round he saw Alice standing in the doorway. How long had she been there? How much had she heard? Was she a party to the cosy scenario his parents had imagined? Was she harbouring the hope that he, the man she had unceremoniously ditched for his brother, would marry her on his return from Europe? He didn't wait to find out but pushed past her, out into the yard, gulping in lungfuls of air, and began to run towards the pool by the creek.

BY THE CREEK

OBLIVIOUS TO HELGA calling her name, Alice turned away from the farmhouse kitchen and went towards the little cabin beyond the barn that Walt had constructed as a temporary home for them when she'd told him she hated sharing the house with his parents. She sat down on the battered wooden bench outside and tried to pull herself together after the shock of seeing Jim and overhearing the words of her mother-in-law.

Alice was used to people talking about her. When Jim went away after finding out about her and Walt, she sensed everyone in the town of Hollowtree whispering behind her back. She'd tried not to heed the fact that they appeared to be labelling her a scarlet woman, a Jezebel, who had committed the unforgivable sin of abandoning the man she had been engaged to marry, in favour of his brother. The fact that Jim had up and left town to join the army as soon as he found out, had made matters worse. What if he were to die? It would be Alice's fault. But he hadn't died. Walt had. And that was her fault too.

The malicious gossiping of the townspeople was one

thing, hearing what her mother-in-law had just said and seeing the look of horror on Jim's face, when he turned round and saw her standing by the kitchen door, was another. Alice felt humiliated. Diminished. How could Helga Armstrong have seriously harboured the hope that she would marry Jim? That Jim could ever replace Walt for her? That he could step into Walt's shoes as Rose's father?

When she had fallen in love with Walt, Alice had been a woman possessed. A creature strange to herself, hungry for the arms of her lover, heedless of reputation, of Jim's feelings, of the carefully laid wedding plans, of the shock of family and friends. Mindful only of the need to be with Walt. She squeezed her eyes tightly shut, remembering. It had been a kind of madness – and completely out of character. As soon as that first kiss with Walt had happened, she had felt as though she was breaking the surface from deep underwater, lungs bursting, gulping down air, suddenly and completely free.

Jim's only sin had been respecting her too much. Placing her above him, as though she were some kind of deity to be worshipped but not touched. Walt hadn't cared two hoots for conventions, for reputation, for respecting her. He wanted her and he wasn't going to wait for her. His hunger had shocked her, frightened her and then infected her too. In those first passion-crazed days, Alice hadn't stopped to think, to measure the consequences, to weigh them, to balance them, to acknowledge what she was giving up as well as what she was gaining. All she had wanted was Walt. His skin against her skin, his hands tangling her hair, his stubble burning her face as he kissed her with a hunger that she was afraid might consume them both.

Alice hadn't weighed what it would feel like when she wasn't in his arms: when she was facing her parents and his, when she was seeing the hurt in Jim's eyes, when she was being talked about in corners and discussed in the post office or over cups of coffee in the ice cream shop in town. In those moments she wondered whether she had lost more than she had gained. Until Walt would come upon her and touch her, his hot breath on her neck, his hands seeking a passage through her clothing, his mouth pressed hungrily upon hers.

But since the telegram had arrived to tell them that Walt had died in August of 1942, along with nine hundred of his countrymen in the failed raid on the French port of Dieppe, Alice had been hollowed out. Her loneliness and loss were so painful that some days she ran down to the creek out of hearing of her in-laws and screamed until her lungs were bursting. The photograph they had had taken in Toronto on their honeymoon was worn round the edges and stained by her tears. Holding her new-born daughter in her arms she hunted for Walt in the baby's features and wept for the fact that her husband would never see his child.

How could Helga even imagine she would contemplate marrying anyone, let alone Jim? She wished she could get away from here. Take Rose and go and live in the anonymity of the city. Not Toronto. Too many memories of the brief honeymoon they'd spent there. Ottawa perhaps. Maybe she'd find work in a library there.

She got up from the bench and opened the cabin door. Rose was still sleeping. Alice thought of cooking breakfast for them both but didn't feel hungry. The child had been late to bed last night. When she woke and found her mother gone, she'd wander over to the house and Helga would give her breakfast. Alice closed the door and set off, walking slowly to the creek, where she knew she'd find Jim.

SUNSHINE HAD TURNED the pool into a plate of polished silver. It dappled Jim's legs under the canopy of the tree and bathed his feet in light. The warmth made him drowsy, heavy-eyed. He had slept little on the train. But his head was in turmoil, resisting sleep.

Why had he come home? When he'd left in 1940 he'd told himself it was forever. He wished he were back in England.

He looked up as Alice sat down a few feet away from him, her legs tucked beneath her on the ground. Jim said nothing.

'I had no idea,' she said. 'Helga said nothing to me before. That was as much of a surprise to me as it must have been to you. It's been hard on both of them. Losing Walt, then living in fear they would lose you too. I've become very close to them. And there's Rose, of course.'

Jim closed his eyes.

They were silent for a few moments, then Alice said, 'Did he really look peaceful? Did you really see him?'

'The dead always look peaceful. If you'd seen as many as I have, you'd know it doesn't make a lot of difference how they die. Once they're dead they all look at peace. Maybe they are.'

Alice gave a little sob. Jim squeezed his lips together. 'Look, I'm sorry, Alice, but I don't want to think about the war anymore.'

'I'm glad you were there when they brought his body back from France. I'm glad you were with him. Did you see his grave? Where is he?'

'In a cemetery called Brookwood, close to where we were garrisoned. He's in the Canadian section.'

'The Canadian section,' she repeated. 'Is it a pretty place?'

Jim looked up, uncertain how to answer. 'I suppose so. There's grass and trees.'

'Grass and trees. He'd have liked that. I wish I had a photograph of his grave.'

'I'll ask... I'll ask my wife. Maybe she can borrow a camera and get a photograph or ask someone in the garrison to get one for her. I'll write.'

'You would? Thank you, Jim.'

Alice pulled her skirt down over her knees where it had started to ride up. Jim looked at her again, for the first time noticing how pretty she still was. There was a sadness in her eyes that hadn't been there before but she was still the blonde, porcelain-skinned beauty he had once believed himself to be in love with. He told himself she was a pale creature, dull compared to Joan. But as he watched her he felt his stomach clench as though he had been punched. His breath caught in his throat at the memory of kissing her. He closed his eyes and summoned an image of Joan, dark hair swinging around her face, eyes laughing, then narrowing in suspicion. Joan was like a cat, always watchful, cautious, mistrustful, projecting confidence to mask her insecurities – but with an inner fire. Jim swallowed. It had been so long since he had known the touch of a woman. He leaned back and looked into the leafy canopy above him.

'Why didn't you tell your folks you'd got married?'

He shrugged. 'Seemed better to wait 'til I could do it face-to-face.' He jerked his back away from the trunk of the tree and said. 'I didn't think I'd make it through the war alive, so there didn't seem any point. Didn't want Ma and Pa knowing they had a grandson if there was no chance they'd ever get to meet him.'

'Was it terrible? The fighting?'

He looked at her and decided she lacked the imagination for more than platitudes. 'Sometimes. But there was no time to dwell on it. We just got on with the job. And to be honest, I'd rather not talk about it.'

She nodded, smoothing her hand over her skirt. 'I'm glad you have a wife, Jim. You deserve to be happy. What's she like, this Joan?'

'I haven't seen her in two years. Or my son.'

Alice wiped a hand across her eyes. 'At least you got to see him and will see him again soon. Poor Walt never saw Rose. She never had a chance to know her daddy.'

Jim looked down. 'There's a lot of children can say that. It doesn't make it easier, I know, but that's war.'

After a few minutes silence, Alice said, 'I had no idea Ma…Mrs Armstrong was holding out for you and me to… to…' Her words trailed away. She looked up at him, her face anxious. 'You must understand, Jim, what she said has nothing to do with me. I'll never marry again. So even if you weren't married already I wouldn't…'

'I know,' he said at last. 'Let's forget about it.'

'Your mother has been good to me. Told me to call her Ma right after we got wed. I didn't expect that. Not after what happened. Then when Walt went to England, I offered to move back to my parents' place, but your folks wouldn't hear of it. What with my daddy's drinking, it was never good at home, and then when Walt and I – well Daddy disowned me. Called me names. Your Ma was awful good to me. She was mad at Walt but never anything but kind to me.' Alice unbent her legs and rearranged them on the opposite side, tugging at the hem of her skirt again.

'You still haven't told me about her,' she said at last. 'What's she like, this Joan?'

'She's dark-haired. Wears it like this.' He moved his hands to just above his shoulders. 'With a big roll in the front.'

'She pretty?'

'I guess so. I like her well enough.' He couldn't help smiling.

'How did you meet her?'

'In a bar.'

Alice looked shocked.

'It's different over there. The pubs are lively places. Piano music. Noisy. Friendly. Women as well as men. Old and young. Not like the miserable hotel beverage rooms here.'

'So she was drinking in there?'

He nodded.

She smiled. 'Imagine!'

'With her cousin. My friend started dating her cousin and that's how Joan and I got together. I suppose you could say we were thrown together.'

'You don't sound too enthusiastic.'

Jim smiled again. 'I wasn't at first. She was engaged to marry another guy.' He paused then added, 'But he was killed. Out in the African desert.'

'I see.' Alice looked away, then turning back to face him again, said, 'So you're going back there? You'll live over in England?'

'That's the plan. I can't imagine Joan living here. She's a town girl. Likes the movies. The flicks they call it over there. She loves adventure pictures. Errol Flynn. Sword fights. That sort of thing.'

'There's nowhere to watch films in Hollowtree. She'd have to take a train all the way to Kitchener.'

'It wouldn't be fair to expect her to live here,' he said. 'She's close to her family. They've helped her bring our boy up while I was overseas.' Jim felt a sudden longing for Joan to be here with him now, to take form and make concrete the image of her he had been trying to conjure in his head over the two years since he'd seen her. It was as if he had ceased to believe she existed and would only be sure of her when she was in front of him. In his arms. He closed his eyes. When he opened them again Alice was watching him.

'I just wanted to clear that up with you. Wanted you to know that I had nothing to do with what Ma said. She needs to get used to the idea of you being married. But there's something else you need to know.'

Jim felt his skin prickle. He had a feeling he knew what was coming.

'You must have noticed things look different round here?'

'There's only one field planted if that's what you mean? I was going to talk to Pa about that. I suppose it's been too much for him. But why hasn't he hired help in? Fallow fields don't pay bills.'

'He's not well, Jim. You've heard him coughing. We've been really worried but he won't see the doctor. He's not been the same since you and Walt went away. Then when we got the news about Walt it just about broke him. It was bad for me but I have Rose to keep me going. It was as if he lost the will to live. Couldn't see the point any more.'

Jim got up and moved a step towards her.

Alice rushed forward and flung her arms around him. 'I'm so glad you made it through, Jim. I'm sorry for hurting you and I'm glad that you've found happiness. Now why don't you come and meet your niece.' She smiled but the smile somehow didn't make it as far as her sad eyes.

Jim nodded and walked beside her back up the meadow towards the farm buildings.

SAVE THE FARM

ROSE WAS in the farmhouse kitchen helping her grandmother bake scones. Helga Armstrong looked up when Jim and Alice entered the room, then bent over to remove the first batch from the oven. Jim breathed in the warm smell of the scones and felt a rush of nostalgia that caught in his throat and took him by surprise. His mouth filled with the remembered taste of his mother's scones, warm from the oven and dripping with butter.

'Come and meet your Uncle Jim, Rose,' said Alice, stretching her hands out to her daughter.

Jim's throat constricted as he looked at the child. The spitting image of her father. Her dense crown of blonde hair had the same thickness as Walt's, but was cut in a long bob and tied back with a ribbon. Her eyes were of the brightest cornflower blue, just as Walt's had been, and she had the same skinny legs that were slightly bowed. A pair of bony knees completed the picture and he remembered Walt as a small boy wearing shorts and following him about every-where. The little girl ran to her mother and studied her new uncle surreptitiously from behind Alice's skirt.

Jim hesitated for a moment then bent down and scooped Rose up, swinging her around the kitchen as she squealed in delight.

'Mind you don't make the child sick,' said Helga. 'She's just had her breakfast.'

Jim put Rose down and Alice took her daughter's hand and led her from the kitchen. 'We'll leave you folks some time to catch up with each other,' she said.

The little girl gave Jim a shy smile as they walked out the door.

Jim looked at his mother but she kept her eyes fixed on the pile of floury dough on the table top, refusing to meet his gaze. In the corner, Donald Armstrong was sleeping in his armchair, a rug over his knees. His breath was wheezing, rasping, strained.

'How long since he's been sleeping during the day time?' Jim asked.

'Long enough.'

'What do you mean, Ma? Pa has never been one to sit around.'

'I suppose he reckons there isn't anything worth getting out of that chair for,' she said at last, wiping her hands on the front of her apron. 'I think he's just waiting for the good Lord to take him.'

'Don't say that.' He laid a hand on her arm. 'And the farm? There's only one field planted.'

'And that one only thanks to Jed Harris and Fred Summers, who came by and seeded it. I think they were hoping it would inspire your pa to do the other ones, but he barely even noticed.'

'And the livestock?'

'Not much left now. Just a couple of cows, a few pigs and a dozen hens. I see to them.'

Jim sat at the table, his head in his hands. 'You can't live on that.'

'No, son, we can't live on that. Fellow from the bank came to see your pa last week, but he had to go away again as he got no sense out of him. He's buried his head in the sand. No. Worse. He knows but he just doesn't care.'

'Have you tried talking to him?'

She threw him a look. 'What do you think, son? Of course I have. He just said things could wait until you came back.'

Jim shook his head and turned to look at the sleeping man. 'I told you, Ma, I won't be staying. I'll do what I can until my discharge papers are sorted and I can pay for the passage back to England. But after that I don't know. Maybe you should sell the place?'

She jerked her head back. 'Sell the place? We'll never sell the place. You and Walt were born here and your pa and I will die here.' She gave a little cry and wiped her eye with the corner of her apron, leaving a trail of flour over her nose.

Jim leaned forward and dusted it off, then took his mother in his arms as she began to sob.

'He's bad, Jim. Won't see the doc, but I know he's bad. Coughing all the time. No appetite. Thin as a twig. Sleeps most of the day. Yesterday he coughed so much there was blood all over the front of his shirt.'

Jim opened his mouth in shock. 'Coughing blood? As bad as that? Why won't he see the doc?'

'He's afraid. Scared they'll try and send him away to the hospital. Says he'll never leave the farm again unless it's to be carried off in a coffin. Way he's going I don't think that will be long.'

Jim shivered, dismayed, struggling to accept that the hale and hearty man he had left five years ago was now reduced to this. He didn't want to believe what his mother was saying. 'Don't talk like that, Ma.'

'You heard him coughing this morning. It's like that all the time. He barely eats. Sleeps all day and then he's awake coughing all night long. I'm exhausted with it, son.' She pulled a chair out from the table and sank into it.

'Why don't you go talk to the doc and get him to come over here?'

'Don't think I haven't thought of that. But Don said he'd never forgive me. Said he doesn't want some quack filling him full of chemicals.'

'Dr Peters isn't a quack.'

'Dr Peters is dead. Killed over in France in '44. It's Doctor Robinson now and your Pa won't have anything to do with him as he never served.'

Jim absorbed the information. He'd seen too many men killed in the war to be surprised by Dr Peters dying. He was more surprised that he himself had made it through. 'But Pa didn't think anyone should serve. He was dead against me and Walt joining up.'

'He was. But when Walt died he wanted everyone to go out there and fight. When he saw folk doing ordinary jobs he'd get mean about them. Why should they be safe here with Walt dead and you risking your life?'

'War's over now, Ma. We have to get on with life and forget these things.'

'Some things can't ever be forgotten. You should know that.'

Jim studied the worn wood of the kitchen tabletop. 'We have to do something. We can't just watch him die.'

'If you were to stay here things might be different, Jim. He might listen to you. If you got the farm back on the right track he might find the will to live again. A hope for the future. You might be able to persuade him to get medical help.'

'I can't come back, Ma.'

'Can't or won't?'

Jim looked up and met her eyes.

'I'm sorry about what I said this morning, Jim. I should never have said it – but I always harboured the hope. That you coming back would heal the wounds and you could help raise Rose and make your peace with Alice. I love Alice like she's my own daughter.' Her face was set in a frown. 'And you should have told us about your wife and child. Why in heaven's name didn't you, son?'

'It didn't seem the right thing to put in a letter. We got married in a hurry. I was being shipped out to Sicily. No time even to get the CO's permission. I had to plead with the chaplain to marry us without it. We never even had a honeymoon. I was confined to barracks straight after the ceremony then boarding a troop-ship three days later.'

'That seems hasty. Why did you leave it to the last minute? Weren't you sure about marrying her?'

'No. I was sure. I wanted us to be married before I left for the Mediterranean so that if anything happened to me she'd get a widow's pension. I didn't want her and… I mean I didn't want her to be left short.'

Helga looked at him with narrowed eyes. 'You're not telling me everything, son. I can read you like a book. So you went off to Sicily right after the wedding and then you were fighting in Italy. You never wrote to say you went back to England.'

He looked away. 'I didn't.'

'So how did you manage to father a child if you were in Italy and she was in England? You telling me you and she jumped the gun?'

He looked down at the table again. 'I only found out about Jimmy the day before I went to Sicily. I'd no idea. It was just one night. We weren't going out together. It was an accident. In fact she was meant to be marrying another guy.'

He looked up and saw the revulsion on his mother's face. 'It wasn't how you think, Ma.'

'No? You're telling me I'm wrong to think my son has got himself hitched to the kind of woman who jumps into bed with a man when her fiancé's not looking. A loose woman. A cheap slut. Is that the sort of girl you've gone and got yourself married to? And that's why you're walking out on us here? Leaving your daddy to die while the farm goes to wrack and ruin. I'm ashamed of you, Jim. What kind of man have you turned into? Not the one I thought I'd brought up. Not the one your father has always been proud of.' She got up from the table. 'You disgust me.'

Jim scraped back his chair and was on his feet. He grabbed her by the arm, angry, and pushed her back into her seat.

'You sit down and listen to what I have to say, Ma, before you rush to judging me. I don't hear you calling Alice a slut for jumping into bed with Walt when she was engaged to me.'

'That was different.'

'How different?'

'Alice is not that kind of girl. You know that as well as I do. She's a good girl. She just couldn't help herself.'

'You don't even know Joan. She's not a slut. Even less so than Alice. You've no idea what it's like to be in the midst of a war. Never knowing if you'll live or die. People behave differently when they think they may not see the night out, let alone the year. We had to share a bedroom in a London hotel because she was doing a favour to her best friend. She didn't even want to sleep with me. It was colder than the Arctic circle. No fire. Not enough bedding. Pitch black with the blackout. She climbed in with me to keep warm. We went to sleep. That was all it was meant to be but then it just happened. Neither of us planned it. We were half asleep. I wanted to see her again but she wouldn't because she was engaged to the other fellow. She didn't love him but she's that kind of woman. Loyal. She'd told him she would marry him and she intended to keep her word. Then he was killed. I heard about it just before I went off to battle so I called round to give her my condolences and there she was with Jimmy. With my son.'

'She saw you coming all right.' Helga's tone was bitter. 'How do you even know he's your son? She could have been sleeping with other soldiers. It could have been the man she was engaged to.'

'She didn't sleep with any other men. Didn't even sleep with the chap she was going to marry. She was a virgin until that night. I don't know why I'm telling you all this as it's none of your damn business and it doesn't even matter as you'll never have to meet her – or your grandson.' He thumped the table and ran his hands through his hair.

'Calm down, son.' It was his father's voice. How long had he been awake and listening? 'Your ma's only–.' His words were consumed by a coughing fit. When it finished he spoke again. 'Give her time. She'll come round.' More coughing.

Helga moved across the kitchen and knelt in front of her husband. 'You need a bowl?' she asked.

'Need quiet. No arguments.' He waved her away with his hand and gestured to Jim to come and sit beside him.

'I'm dying. Nothing to be done about it. But I won't die in a hospital. I'll die here with my family around me. You too, Jim.'

Jim was about to speak but his father raised a hand to quiet him. 'I just want one thing.' He began to cough again and this time Helga ran for a metal bowl and put it under his chin.

Jim saw the brightness of blood as his father coughed into

the receptacle. When the fit stopped Donald spoke again, the words rasping out between coughs.

'Get the farm back on its feet. Bring your wife and child here. If they settle, that's good. If they don't, just give it 'til I'm gone.' He lifted his hand to silence Jim who was about to speak. 'I want to see my grandson before I die. Grant me that, won't you?' He leaned back in his chair and closed his eyes, squinting in pain. Bending his head over the tin bowl he began coughing again.

Jim looked at his mother and she shook her head.

Kneeling, he put a hand on his father's back to support him as he coughed. The old man's bones stood out under his shirt, sharp-edged against Jim's fingers. His father was hardly an old man. Fifty-five wasn't old in anyone's book, but Donald Armstrong looked like a man in his eighties. Jim squeezed his lips together, breathed in a long breath and said, 'I'll write to Joan and talk to the army about getting her and the baby over here.'

He took his father's hand and pressed it in his, but Donald was sleeping again.

His mother nodded her thanks.

Jim shook his head. 'I just hope he can hang on 'til they get here. It could be months.'

THE TELEGRAM

Nine months later, Aldershot, England June 1946

The telegram from the Canadian Wives Bureau lay on the table between them. Joan lifted her eyes and stared up at the ceiling.

'I've waited so long, but now it's finally happening I'm terrified.'

Her cousin leaned forward and put her hand over Joan's. 'That's understandable. When you want something so much and it's such a big change. A new country. A new life.'

Joan ran her fingers over the woollen bobble on top of the knitted tea-cosy, then lifted her hands to cover her face. She gave another shuddering sigh.

Ethel picked up the teapot and refilled Joan's cup, then her own. 'Think about Jimmy. He needs his dad.'

'He needs his nana, his grandpa, you, Aunty Vi. He doesn't know his dad.' Joan's voice was sardonic, a hint of anger underneath. 'How can I take him to a foreign country to live with complete strangers? He's only three.'

Ethel sipped her tea. 'It's not for ever is it? And Jimmy's young enough to adapt quickly. He'll have forgotten us all before you're even on board ship.' She hesitated then said, 'Don't you want to be with Jim?'

Joan's head jerked up and she splashed her tea into the saucer. 'Of course I want to be with him.' She bit her lip. 'But me going over to Canada was never part of the plan. He told me he'd left for good and he'd find a job in England.'

'We've been through that, Joan. You know why he's doing it. It's not his fault his dad's dying. And anyway it's just 'til he can sort things out so they can sell the place.'

Joan nodded. 'I know, I know.'

'Besides, things are tough here and no sign of it getting better. I read in the paper yesterday we'll be paying off our debts to the Yankees for years to come. We may have won the war but it doesn't feel like it. Just think, Joanie. No more rationing. You'll be eating proper food again. And it has to be good for Jimmy being on a farm. Heaven for a kid, if you ask me!'

Joan smiled. You're right but it doesn't stop me being scared about it. It's been so long since I've seen Jim. People change in three years.' Her fingers played with the woollen tea-cosy again. 'If it weren't for me having Jimmy, he'd never have married me.'

'Stop that right now, Joan. He came to find you, didn't he? And he'd tried to see you before, but you shut the door in his face.'

'He came because you went and fetched him. If you hadn't dragged him over here so he found out about the baby, he'd have gone off to Sicily when his unit was posted and I'd never have heard from him again.'

'I didn't drag him here. He wanted to see you. You kept shutting him out. I had to step in. He had a right to know he was a father. He loves you.' Ethel leaned back in her chair and closed her eyes. 'Why are you trying to mess things up for yourself, Joan? Why can't you just be happy? A new life with the man you love is there waiting for you. All you have to do is get on a boat.'

Joan said nothing, feeling guilty, knowing Ethel would give anything to be in Joan's position. Ethel's fiancé, Jim's best friend, Greg, had died from a brain haemorrhage five years earlier.

'You do love Jim, don't you?'

Joan squeezed her lips together then said, 'More than anything. Oh God, Ethel. I love him so much.' She looked at her cousin, eyes brimming with tears. 'That's why I'm scared. I don't want to make him unhappy. I don't want him to look at me and see responsibility and duty. I want him to want me, not be lumbered with me. He's back in Canada. The war's over. He'll be getting back to his old life.'

Ethel groaned. 'I don't know what to do with you, Joanie. Jim joined up to get *away* from his old life. He fell in love with you. He has a son and wants to be with you both. He writes to you regularly saying that. Don't you think if it was up to him he'd be here right now? You know perfectly well they had to repatriate the men before the wives. It's not as if you're unusual. There are thousands of other women in the same boat.' She smiled. 'In a couple of days, you will be, literally!'

'I know. I keep telling myself it's not for long. But what if he doesn't mean it? If I get there and he tells me he's changed his mind and he wants us to stop there for good? That would kill me, Ethel.'

'Come on. He's not going to do that to you. How many times did he sit in the Stag and tell us all he was never going back to Canada? But he wouldn't be human if he didn't want to help his folks when his dad is dying. And you wouldn't think much of him if he didn't.'

The logic of Ethel's words was clear, but Joan couldn't help the crippling self-doubt. It had been she who had set in motion the relationship with Jim Armstrong. She'd initiated their first kiss, flirted, toyed with him – at first because it had been an amusing distraction, and then because she had fallen head over heels for him.

The night their son was conceived she had climbed, uninvited, into Jim's bed, despite his making it clear he wanted nothing to do with her because she was engaged to marry someone else. The morning after, she had been overwhelmed with guilt about what she had done and made it clear to Jim that she wanted nothing more to do with him. The hurt in his eyes had been plain.

Joan looked up at her cousin. 'You're right. I pushed him away after what happened between us in that London hotel, but I did it to protect myself from getting hurt. Now I have a fear that it's all going to go wrong. I don't want to let him down.'

Ethel reached across the table and took Joan's hands in hers. She smiled. 'Stop it right away. Stop trying to predict the future. That's enough of that!' She squeezed her hands tightly. 'Listen to me. You love Jim. He loves you. You both love Jimmy. The horrible, miserable years of the war are over. You all have a chance for a new beginning. It will work if you want it to work. Do you want it to work?'

Joan's voice was barely a whisper as she said that yes, she did.

Ethel swigged down the rest of her tea and jumped to her feet. 'Come on then, girl. You have packing to do. I'll give you a hand.'

The instructions in the telegram were blunt and business-like. Joan had just forty-eight hours before she had to be on a train to London. There was no information about the sailing. Just a rail warrant. She would be met from the train and transported onwards from there. Not even an indication of the port of departure let alone the name of the ship. The war had ended just over a year ago but security was just as tight. With so many women and children to transport to Canada, not to mention the repatriation of the troops themselves, the wait had been long and frustrating. She had already gone through a lot. To get on the list to travel to Canada she had had to attend a medical examination, where she had been poked about in a manner she'd found humiliating.

'They want to check we 'aint got the clap,' another war bride had told her as they'd sat in the waiting room. 'Makes me bloody laugh. If we've got the clap it's them as give it us!'

WHEN THE TRAIN pulled into Waterloo, Joan's stomach clenched and she gulped. This was it. She felt for Jimmy's hand and looked over at Ethel, eyes brimming with tears. Her mother had been too upset to accompany them, preferring to say goodbye on the platform in Aldershot. Before they'd left for the station her mum had told Joan she'd sewn some money into the lining of her suitcase – 'Enough to get you home of it doesn't work out.'

From the train, Joan was ushered with Jimmy to a group of wives and children gathering outside the station, ready to board a double-decker bus. The small boy stood beside her, his face bemused and tired – this was his first trip on a train and his first time away from Aldershot. Joan flung her arms around Ethel and clung to her, both women conscious that it could be months, even years until they met again. Falling in love with a man from the other side of the ocean carried its costs. She thought of her mother's anguished weeping and how her stepfather and Ethel had to pull them apart to prevent Joan missing the train.

She was not alone. All around them, families were going through emotional partings. She fumbled in her coat pocket for a handkerchief and wiped her nose. Once the last few stragglers had appeared and been counted by the Canadian soldiers organising them, they were told to get onto the bus. The luggage had already been loaded from the train into a van.

'Where are you taking us?' Joan asked the soldier who was marking them off on his clipboard.

'Can't tell you that, ma'am.'

'But my cousin wants to see me off on the ship.'

'Not possible.'

'Well, can you tell us the name of the ship and the port where it's sailing from? Then I can come along under my own steam.' Ethel gave him a winning smile.

'Sorry, ma'am. That's classified.'

'But the war's over! More than a year!' Joan gasped, as she realised she was already to be separated from her beloved cousin.

'I don't make the rules, ma'am. Now hurry on board or we'll have to leave without you.'

Joan turned to Ethel. 'Come and visit me, won't you? We can both save up for your fare. Promise me.' She clutched at Ethel's sleeve. 'And write. You will write, won't you?'

Ethel's eyes were sad, no doubt thinking that it should have been her too getting on that bus. Life was so unfair.

'Of course I'll write.'

'And you will visit?'

'We'll see. You'll probably all be back here anyway before I get a chance.' Ethel made a little choked sound. 'And... I don't know if I could face it. You know why. And then there's Mum – all on her own. But we'll see.' She blinked back tears and tugged at Joan's lapels, pulling them into alignment.

'Look at you. All skew-whiff. What'll you do without me, cousin?'

Joan flung her arms round Ethel's neck and sobbed. Then remembering Jimmy, standing beside them, she told the little boy to give his aunty a kiss. The realisation that the adventure on a train was something more serious seemed to dawn on the child. He began to cry and sat down on the pavement, banging his heels in anger, born of bewilderment.

'I want to go home,' he wailed.

Joan pulled him to his feet, impatient, anxious and wanting to go home herself. She pulled a rare lollypop out of her pocket as a bribe and coaxed him onto the bus.

The windows were steamy with the breath of so many weeping women and crying babies. Joan wiped off the condensation and waved to Ethel as the bus drew away. She continued to stare out of the window long after her cousin had disappeared from view.

They crossed the river and passed through Trafalgar Square, heading north to Oxford Street and along to Marble Arch. The bus drove past countless bomb-damaged buildings, rubble still piled up awaiting clearance. The city looked drab, battered, ruined. It should be a time of hope but as Joan looked through that steamy window she thought that London and Britain seemed beaten down and tired. Perhaps she was doing the right thing going to Canada. What would it be like to be in a place where bombs had never fallen? Not that it was a place untouched by war. She'd read somewhere that more than sixty thousand Canadians had lost their lives in the war, almost six thousand in the battles for Italy, in which her husband had served.

Joan thought of the last time she had been to London, back in late 1941. She had spent a miserable day alone after Jim had gone off on his own rather than spend time with her.

She hadn't blamed him – she knew his friend Greg had tricked him into coming to London without telling him that she and Ethel would be there. Jim had been set up. But it had left her with no choice but to absent herself and leave Ethel and Greg to spend time together. Joan would die rather than be a wallflower.

She bent forward and stroked Jimmy's blond hair as he sat quietly on her knee, sucking his lollypop and staring out of the window at the passing sights. That had been a miserable day, but one that had ended with Jimmy's creation and brought her to this journey today. She breathed in the familiar scent of her son's hair. He was a tiny version of his father. Her heart swelled with love.

'Are we nearly there, Mummy?' The little boy twisted round to look at her.

'Why do kids always ask that? No matter where you're going or how long it takes.' The woman next to her addressed her for the first time. She was blonde with heavily rolled curls framing her face, huge eyes and cherry red lipstick.

Joan smiled. 'He's been such a good boy so far. Haven't you, Jimmy?' She dropped a kiss on the top of his head then wriggled around in her seat and offered a hand to the woman. 'I'm Joan. Joan Armstrong.'

'Sandra Watson.' The woman was holding a sleeping baby in her arms.

'How old?'

'Eight months. Her father and I only had five nights together before he got shipped home. When I found out I was expecting I was hoping to get an early passage so I could have the baby in Canada but they wouldn't let me travel until after she was born. Barry, he's my husband, has never seen her. How old's your boy?'

'He's nearly four. And my husband only saw him for a few hours when he was a tiny baby. Got sent off to Sicily, then fought his way up through the Italian mainland. He's been back in Canada over a year now.'

Sandra nodded. 'It's hard, isn't it? Not seeing them for so long. It's not natural, is it?'

'No – and it's a bit scary.'

'You're dead right about that. I keep thinking he might have gone off me!' The woman giggled and nudged Joan in the ribs. The expression on her face indicated that she thought that a highly improbable outcome. Joan wasn't so certain in her own case.

'Where are you heading? Where's your husband from?'

'All the way. Vancouver Island. They told me it's a long journey once we get ashore as it's on the other side of the country.'

'On the west coast?'

'No idea. I'll find out soon enough.'

Didn't you look on a map?' Joan was incredulous.

'Wouldn't know where to start. I 'aven't a clue about maps and suchlike. And what difference would knowing where it is make?' She laughed. 'Can't do anything about it, can I? What about you?'

'Ontario.'

'So where's that?'

'Eastern Canada, so not as far as you have to go.' She smiled apologetically. 'I went to the library and looked it up. Daft, I know.'

'Blimey, girl! You a teacher or something?'

Joan bristled. She hated the idea of being thought posh. 'No. I worked in a fish and chip shop before the war. I just hate not knowing what I'm letting myself in for.'

'A chippy? I'd never have guessed. You look too refined.

So what does your old man do for a living now he's back on civvie street?'

'He's a farmer.'

'Get you! Mine works in a garage. A grease monkey they call 'em. But he can rub those greasy hands all over me any time.' She giggled, adding in a conspiratorial whisper, 'I can't wait. Don't know about you, but when you've 'ad it, it's jolly hard doing without it.'

Joan blushed. She wasn't ready to admit to her new friend that she'd 'had it' on only one occasion and that hadn't been enough to make her miss it.

The bus jerked and made a sharp turn right, just before they reached Marble Arch. A few minutes later they pulled up outside a large house.

'Everybody off!'

Sandra gave her shoulders a little shake and grinned, as they stood together on the pavement. 'This looks very posh. Living the high life, are we? Can't wait!'

The crowd of women and children made their way up the stone steps. Once inside the imposing building, any delusions that they were entering palatial surroundings were banished. The plaster walls were cracked, the paint was flaking off and there was a strong smell of Jeyes Fluid. Joan rolled her eyes at Sandra. 'You were tempting fate, you were.'

Her new friend laughed and said, 'Oh, it's my fault, is it?'

They were shown into one of a series of dormitories, crammed with camp beds and bunk beds. They had been told to bring only essentials with them as hand luggage, just enough for overnight, and to wear trousers if they had any, in readiness for boarding their ship tomorrow. The rest of their luggage was being transported straight to their ship.

'Women without small children take the top bunks please,' a woman in Canadian army uniform called out.

Joan looked around in dismay. She hadn't expected to

stay overnight in London. There'd been no mention of that in the telegram. All she wanted now was to be on that ship. The room was packed. Children were fractious and mothers were trying to calm them. She held Jimmy's hand tightly and looked around her. The little boy was sucking his thumb and his eyes were heavy. She prayed he wouldn't start crying.

'Bit of a dump, isn't it? Let's hope we're not stuck 'ere too long.' Sandra, still holding her baby, headed through the door back into the hallway. 'I'm going to have a look round. I'll need to feed the baby soon and I don't fancy doing it in there.' She nodded her head back towards the dormitory. 'You coming?'

It took only a few minutes for them to establish that the building contained more sleeping accommodation, a huge dining room, with wooden trestle tables, and a room with toilets and long rows of washbasins, all of which were in use by harassed mothers. Back in the hallway a queue for the single pay telephone snaked into the dining room.

A bell rang to summon them to their evening meal. Joan had no appetite for the mince and potato stew, followed by jam tart and custard, instead focusing on helping Jimmy as he mopped up his portion with gusto.

A woman from the Canadian Wives Bureau came into the room and banged a gavel on a table for attention.

'Tomorrow morning you will be leaving here at six o'clock. It is your responsibility to have yourselves and your children ready to depart by five forty-five. We will not wait for stragglers. If you are not ready to board the bus we will depart without you and you will need to make your own way home and will go to the back of the queue for a future sailing. Is that clear?'

There was a murmur of assent around the room. Sandra looked across at Joan and winked. 'Miserable old cow.'

'When you are on the buses you will each be issued with a

travel permit. This must be handed over when you arrive in Canada. You will be taken to your port of departure where your vessel will be waiting for you.'

The realisation dawned that it was to be their last night in Britain.

VOYAGE TO CANADA

EARLY NEXT MORNING, the women and children emerging from the anonymous hostel were bleary-eyed. Mothers dragged tired children by the arms and pushed them onto the waiting buses. Babies were crying and nursing mothers were ushered to the back of the bus where the windows had been covered with sheets, in case a passing motorist or pedestrian might see the mothers breast feeding. But there was no one around at this early hour, just the odd milk float trundling by with its rattling cargo.

Joan took a seat near the front of the bus, letting Jimmy have the window seat. He immediately knelt up, nose pressed against the pane.

'He'll have to sit on your knee, ma'am. It's a full house today.' The speaker was a Canadian WAAF, her smile far too bright and cheerful for such an ungodly hour.

Joan lifted her son onto her lap as Sandra dropped into the seat next to her.

'Ooh good. Did you save it for me? Ta, love,' she said.

Joan accepted the unmerited gratitude with a nod.

'I just chatted up one of the lads and managed to worm

out of him where we're going.' Sandra lowered her voice and breathed into Joan's ear. 'Sarfampton,' she said. 'Good job it's not Liverpool or we'd 'ave bin all day getting there. Gettin' excitin' now. We'll be on board ship and maybe on our way by tonight.'

THE SHIP TOWERED over the war brides gathered on the quay. The stark realisation that they were about to leave behind everything they had ever known resulted in an adrenaline-charged mixture of high excitement and sudden fear. Joan lingered at the end of the queue, watching as others pushed ahead eager to get installed on board. Two women standing near her were crying. They clung to each other, each rein-forcing the other's fears, their tears becoming more frantic as the queue shortened.

'You need to get on board, ladies,' a Canadian ATS woman said. 'We can't wait for ever.' She looked at Joan. 'You know these two?' Joan shook her head. 'Well, get yourself up the ramp, before the berths are all taken.' She leaned down and whispered something to Jimmy then produced a boiled sweet, which he accepted with glee.

'I can't,' one of the young women wailed. 'I just can't do it. I don't want to go.'

A Red Cross helper approached. 'No one's forcing you, dear. It's a free country. That's what we fought the war for. Don't you want to give Canada a chance?'

'I'm scared of the sea. We might sink.'

'Not much chance of running into a U-Boat these days, duckie,' a passing sailor said.

But the girl was immune to reason. 'I'm not getting on that. I just can't do it.'

Joan understood her fear. She wasn't keen on spending the next week tossing about on the Atlantic. Not to mention the unknowns that lay on the other side of it, but when she'd married Jim it was for better or worse so she led her little boy up the gangplank and onto the ship. On deck, she looked back at the quayside and saw the Red Cross woman leading the two reluctant brides away. Joan couldn't decide whether they were brave or lily-livered. Perhaps it took guts to refuse to go. She wondered about the husbands who would be waiting for them. Would they be devastated or relieved? How many of these marriages would stand the test of time? Would her own? She squeezed her lips tight and then smiled encouragement at Jimmy and went down into the bowels of the ship.

The first thing that struck her was the smell. The ship stank of disinfectant. Joan gagged. How was she going to put up with this for days?

Any hopes that they might be sailing in pre-war luxury conditions were abandoned when the women saw the sleeping accommodation. The cabins had been knocked through to create large and very public dormitories as bad as the hostel in London. Each one was to house thirty women. Joan hesitated on the threshold of one and then heard Sandra's voice.

'Over 'ere, Joan. I've bagged you a bed.'

It was a three-tier bunk, with Sandra on the bottom berth beside her baby in a bassinet. Joan was sandwiched in the middle with Jimmy allocated the top bunk. Joan took one look at it and decided she and Jimmy could bunk in together. She didn't want to risk him trying gymnastics and falling out of the berth.

Once the sleeping accommodation was sorted they were shown around the ship. To Sandra's delight there was a shop on board selling rare delights that were only pre-war memories.

'Look 'ere, Joan. You seen what they've got? Ooh... chocolates. I can't remember what a choccie tastes like. I'll soon find out though. Gosh, look!' She elbowed Joan in the ribs. 'Face powder. Revlon, doncha know. When did you last see that, eh?'

Joan decided to pass on the chocolate but bought a carton of cigarettes and a packet of Lux Flakes. Her joy was short lived when she discovered that the only water available on board for washing was sea water. Trying to work up a lather in salt water would be an impossible task.

There were more surprises in store when they filed into the dining room for their first meal on board. This time it wasn't only Sandra squealing with glee. 'White bread!' Joan said. 'Oh my giddy aunt. I'd forgotten that such a thing existed. No more of that horrible, grey, dried-out bread that tastes like baked gravel.'

They sat at the tables and were served with a welcome drink – glasses with ice cubes bobbing inside and a mist on the glass, and a brown liquid inside.

'What's this then?' Sandra asked the steward.

'That's Coca Cola, ma'am. You never tried that before?'

Sandra curled her lip then took an experimental sip. 'Ooh it's bloody lovely. It's the most delicious thing I've ever tasted in all my born days.' She downed the glass and gave a loud burp, then began to giggle.

Joan took a sip and had to agree the taste was unusual but very enjoyable.

'I'll 'ave another of them if you're offering, mate.' Sandra thrust her glass at the passing steward.

'Coming right up, ma'am.'

So excited were the women by the fluffy white bread rolls and the delicious cold Coca Colas that nobody noticed the ship had started moving until there was a sudden jerk.

'We're off then,' said Joan. 'No going back now.'

'Going back? No chance. I can't wait!' said Sandra, as she

tucked into the huge meal in front of them. 'I don't remember the last time I had grub like this. And so much of it. Don't even care what Canada's like. It's going to be all right with me if it has no rationing. I don't know about you, but I'm going to eat like a horse.'

Joan, while enjoying the roast meal in front of them, felt her appetite couldn't do the portions justice. After a few mouthfuls she felt full. 'All the years of rationing must have shrunk my stomach. I can't manage any more.' She laid down her knife and fork.

'Wimp!' said Sandra. 'What about pudding?' There's ice cream and sponge pudding. I'll have yours if you can't manage it.'

'You're welcome. All this food makes me feel guilty with everyone at home still putting up with rationing.'

That night Joan was vindicated in her more moderate approach to the food on offer. The combination of too much rich food and the churning of the sea beneath them caused sickness among most of the war brides, Sandra included. Joan lay, unable to sleep, listening to the groaning around her and the patter of footsteps towards the latrines. It was going to be a long voyage.

Many of the women suffered with seasickness for the entire crossing, including Sandra, who only emerged from lying on her bunk in misery the day before they reached Halifax. Joan was secretly glad. She appeared to be immune to the seasickness and found that, apart from the over-crowded sleeping arrangements, the voyage was congenial enough. Every night before going to sleep they were advised to adjust their watches by half an hour and all the ship's clocks were put back every night. During the long days Joan walked the decks with Jimmy and often carried Sandra's baby so that the child could get some air and her mother could have a break. Those of the wives able to rise from their beds were offered classes about life in Canada. Joan went along but found it hard to pay attention. She'd find out soon enough anyway.

JOAN and a newly recovered Sandra stood at the guardrail as the ship docked in Halifax. The afternoon was hot; sunlight bathed the white-painted buildings, making them appear like freshly bleached sheets. It looked a cheerful place. On the quayside a brass band was playing *Here Comes the Bride* to greet the new arrivals.

'Doesn't look too bad,' said Sandra. 'A bit of change from all those bombed out buildings back home. I've had enough of rubble and rationing.'

'The Germans never really bothered with Aldershot. Just a couple of stray bombs.'

'Blimey, girl, you were lucky! All those nights I spent sleeping in the bloody underground.' She stroked her baby's head. 'Looks nice here. Not at all what I expected Canada to be like.'

'We've not even seen it yet. There's thousands of miles of it, said Joan. Not wanting to sound critical, she added, 'But so far so good.'

After being processed for entry into Canada on board, the British wives were escorted from the ship, posses of Canadian soldiers carrying their luggage to the train which was waiting right opposite the boat where it docked at Pier 21. Joan was taken aback by the size of the great locomotive, which dwarfed those she was used to at home. Home. She would have to stop thinking of England as that. This was home now – at least for the foreseeable future. She swallowed the lump in her throat and squeezed Jimmy's hand. Like all little boys, the sight of the train made everything else pale into nothingness for him. He was already jumping up and down in excitement at the prospect of riding in it.

Red Cross ladies were patrolling the platform, proffering advice to the newcomers and plying them with women's magazines for the journey ahead.

'Will we get to Vancouver before bedtime?' Sandra asked one of the helpers.

'Oh, I expect so. But it'll be a bedtime next week,' the woman replied, grinning. 'Canada is a big country and you're going all the way across it ma'am. You'll be on a train for days.'

'Blimey, O'Reilly,' said Sandra. 'Days on a bleedin' train. I'll be 'alf-dead by the time I get there, what with the baby and all to manage. I 'ope my fella appreciates what I've 'ad to go through to get 'ere, with the bloody seasickness 'n'all.'

Joan turned and looked enviously back to the quayside, where a small group of women were in the arms of their husbands – their destination in or near Halifax. Journey's end. The brass band broke into a rendition of *You are my Sunshine*.

The prospect of a long train journey was daunting but at least she didn't have the mammoth trek across a whole continent that lay ahead of Sandra. The two women settled into the carriage. A couple of Dutch women, whom they had met on the ship, smiled a wordless greeting and slid into the seats opposite. Joan ascertained that they were travelling as far as Quebec and were married to a pair of brothers. When the train finally pulled out of the port her stomach felt hollow, her nerve endings singing. Every moment that passed was bringing her closer to the time of reckoning, her reunion with Jim.

Three years was such a long time. What had he seen in his two years of fighting? His letters had all been brief and unenlightening, describing the advance up the boot of Italy, but offering no information on how that advance had been undertaken. Joan was not naïve. She knew he must have witnessed some terrible things. Being at war had to change a man. But his letters to her were anodyne. He wrote about the heat, the miserable rations, and how much he missed her. Most of the letters were given over to questions about her and Jimmy. Letters were anyway hit and miss. Often he had moved on before her reply reached him, then when the post caught up with him he would write to tell her of his joy at receiving a bundle all at once. For her part, she wrote about Jimmy, recording his progress, each small development from first tooth to first step and first word. As to the latter, she lied and told him it was Dadda. But Joan had written nothing of what was in her heart, of her fears and feelings, of her doubts and longings. How could she? She barely knew her husband and felt unable to bridge the gap between being strangers and then all too briefly lovers. She could count on her fingers the number of times they had met. Theirs had not been the lightning bolt of love that Ethel and Greg had experienced. At least not on Jim's part.

Jimmy had found a friend in a little girl in the same carriage and was happily running up and down the coach, then kneeling beside her on a seat with their noses pressed against the window, watching the scenery rush by. Sandra had fallen asleep and Joan thumbed through the pamphlet she had been given on the ship, *"Welcome to War Brides"*. To her surprise there was a section on life on a Canadian farm. *"A Canadian farm home is not luxurious. You have only one chance in five of having electric light"*.

Her heart sank. What had she let herself in for? She read on about the even greater chance of the absence of plumbing and the prevalence of what was delicately described as *"outside facilities"* and suddenly the little house in Aldershot assumed stately proportions.

REUNITED

THE TRAIN JOURNEY from Halifax to Montreal took more than a day. There, they changed trains for Toronto, where Joan said goodbye to a tearful Sandra. Despite their brief acquaintance they had formed a strong attachment. Both were embarking on a life-changing venture, without knowing what was in store. Sandra's cheerful optimism had buoyed Joan up and she was glad she had not shared the journey with someone who was uncertain about whether she'd done the right thing.

Joan gripped Jimmy's hand and followed the Red Cross lady who led the large contingent of women heading for Southern Ontario. Each of them was accompanied by a soldier, who carried their baggage from one train to the next.

Neither Joan nor Jimmy could sleep when they got on board, Jimmy, because he was excited by the prospect of getting to meet his father, and Joan, because she had convinced herself that after travelling so far, and for so long now, they must almost be at their destination. The train stopped frequently, dropping off women at every station. For the past two hours she had been sitting with her lipstick on, her coat buttoned up and her handbag in her lap, ready to go. Every station that wasn't hers was a disappointment. Exhausted after the days of travelling, Joan was relieved when at last her name was called out.

She was one of half a dozen war brides told to leave the train when they pulled into Kitchener. It was dark. A small crowd was waiting on the platform to meet them. One family had turned out en masse and were carrying a banner made out of a bed-sheet, hand-painted with the words, *Welcome Nancy!*

Joan looked around, suddenly nervous, unable to spot Jim. All the other women appeared to have found their loved ones – although one looked disappointed to be met not by her husband but by his parents. Better than not being met at all. She shivered and looked around at all the happy reunions. It was chilly after the humid heat of the day and panic rose inside her. What if he'd got the wrong day? What if he'd changed his mind and wasn't going to turn up at all? What if this was the wrong stop? Her heart was pounding inside her ribs and she struggled to breathe.

Then she saw him. It took her a moment to realise that it was Jim as she had never seen him out of uniform. Unlike many of the Canadian husbands, who seemed to have a flamboyant dress sense, he was not wearing a loud checked jacket or garishly coloured trousers. Instead of the favoured gangster-style fedoras, Jim had on a cap and was wearing a rather drab-looking jacket over a pair of plain well-pressed trousers. He looked uncomfortable in the formal clothes as though unused to wearing them. She felt a surge of joy as he turned his smile on her and moved forward to greet her. The scar across his left cheek had faded and his skin was tanned, his blonde hair longer than she remembered and bleached by the sun. The smile illuminated his face and he stretched out his arms. Joan ran into them and he lifted her up, swinging her off her feet.

Relief suffused her. He did want her. He did love her. He had missed her. When he put her down and bent to kiss her, she clung to him, breathing in the smell of him, clutching his jacket, as if he might disappear if she let him go. She started to speak but words were inadequate so she kissed him again. And again. She could go on kissing him for ever. Suddenly she remembered Jimmy and she broke off the kiss. The little boy was standing watching them, shy and uncertain. She called to him.

Jim squatted down beside the child and held a hand out solemnly to shake his son's. As Jimmy hesitated, Jim gathered him into his chest, bending to kiss the crown of his head. He looked up at Joan and she could see in the faint light from the lamps on the platform that his eyes were moist.

'How do you do, Jimmy? Looks like you're already almost a man. I hope you took care of your mother on the journey?'

Jimmy twisted his head away, turning to Joan for reassurance.

'This is your daddy, Jimmy. Say hello.'

The child's hello was barely a whisper.

'He's been really excited about meeting you but he's bushed,' said Joan.

'Bushed?' Jim sounded shocked.

'Tired,' she said.

'Means something different here.'

She smiled. 'You going to enlighten me? Or do we have to play your favourite questions game again?'

He pulled her into his arms. 'I've missed you, Mrs Armstrong.'

'Well?' she said.

'Here, it means mental problems from being on your own

too long. It's what people get if they're stuck up north in the woods all winter – they go crazy.'

Joan laughed. 'Bloody Canadians. Why can't you speak proper English?'

'Just be thankful I'm not a Yank.'

She put her head on one side and considered for a moment. 'I could put up with that. They've got loads of money. I could have as many pairs of nylons as I wanted and live in a great big house.' She winked at him. 'Have you got a great big house?'

Jim didn't answer. He bent to pick up her bags. 'Let's get your stuff in the truck. We've a an hour's drive ahead of us.'

They left the small city and drove through moonlit roads that were little more than farm tracks. The truck bounced along and Joan braced herself and Jimmy, who was asleep on her lap, against the frequent bumps and potholes. Beside her, Jim was silent, his eyes on the road ahead. Joan felt nervous again. He was a virtual stranger to her and here in Canada he was at an advantage. Joan didn't like not knowing what was ahead of her. She liked to know where everything was, what to expect, no surprises.

After a while he spoke, his eyes still staring into the darkness. 'There's lots I want to do on the farm. Things were neglected while I was away. Pa let the place go but I'm making things better. Bit by bit. It'll take time but I want to make a home that's fit for you and our boy. I just hope you can be patient until then, Joan.'

'I read all about it. They gave us a book on the ship. It said lots of farms are quite basic. No plumbing. Is that what you're trying to tell me?'

He glanced at her sideways. 'There's that.'

She laughed. 'You're pulling my leg aren't you? *Your* farm isn't like that, is it? Primitive?'

'There's a pump in the yard. We heat the water on

the stove.'

She groaned. 'And what about what they called "the facilities"?'

'Outside.'

'Our house at home has an outside toilet. The whole street does. I can cope with that.' She tried to sound confident.

Jim grunted. 'It's not quite the same. You have to walk a bit further than a couple of feet across the back yard. It's a good forty feet away. In winter that can feel like a mile.'

'Well, if you're planning to fix it up I can manage for a while if you're quick about it. And we'll be going back to England before too long, won't we?'

He said nothing and she turned to look at him, seeing his frown of concentration was now accompanied by tightly pursed lips. Joan swallowed, suddenly afraid.

Jim took his eyes off the road for a moment and looked at her for the first time since they'd left the station. 'I want us to try and make a go of living here. We can have a good life. I have big plans for the farm and want to be able to hand it on to Jimmy just as Pa is handing it on to me.'

She took a sharp intake of breath. 'Why didn't you tell me this before? Why did you wait until I got here? Did you think I wouldn't come otherwise?'

'No. It's not like that. I meant what I said before, but things have changed. I realise now how much the farm means to me. It's in my blood. Farming is what I was always meant to do. I love it – the work, the place itself, the way of life. If I was in England I'd probably have to work in a factory or something and I couldn't stand that. I've worried about it night after night and how you might take it, and I've tried to think of an alternative, but I don't think there is one.'

He swept his hair back out of his eyes and exhaled slowly. 'Look, Joan, I'm certain this is the right thing for *all* of us. I promised my father I'd put things right and he seems a little better than he was when I first got back. But he still may not last long if it's what I think it is. The cancer isn't going to go away, but just having me around and seeing the farm getting back to rights has made such a difference to him. It's as if he wants to hang on to what life he has left, whereas before it felt like he was wishing for death to come sooner. And then there's Ma. She's never known anywhere else but the farm. It'll be tough for her when Pa's gone. I can't just abandon her.'

Tears prickled in Joan's eyes. It was like a punch in the stomach, listening to him talking like that. She felt betrayed. He could have been honest. Told her the truth in his letters. She would have come anyway. Wouldn't she? But she knew she probably wouldn't. Did he know that too? She remembered the two women who'd refused to get on the ship at Southampton.

'You tricked me. What am I supposed to say to my mum? To Ethel? How the bloody hell do you think they're going to take it?'

'I'm sorry.'

'Sorry? You're sorry? Sorry isn't good enough.' She was angry and the tears were brimming.

'Give it time. You'll love it as much as I do. I know you will. It's beautiful here. There's hills all around and a creek which widens into a pool where you can swim. Jimmy's going to love it. What kid wouldn't?'

Joan bit her lip and forced back the tears. Maybe he was right and it would take time to adjust. And what choice did she have? She had to give it a chance. She'd married him for better or worse.

'Electricity?' she said at last.

'Electricity?'

'Is there any? That book they gave us said the chance of

51

having electric light was only one in five.'

Jim reached a hand out and squeezed her knee though the thin skirt of her dress. 'Like I say, I have plans. Getting a generator is one of them. There's all kinds of grants available to veterans for housing and farm improvements. The government's handing out money right left and centre. Just you wait, Joan, I'll make Hollowtree Farm like a palace.' He looked sideways at her again in the gloom of the cab. 'I can get a loan to pay for the generator. It'll take a bit of time to rig everything up, but I can do it. Gasoline's dirt cheap now and we won't have to drive around in this old thing. I'm getting us a new car. It's all going to be fine.

WHEN THEY REACHED Hollowtree Farm the place was in darkness.

Jim fumbled around in the gloom as they entered the kitchen and lit a lamp.

'You hungry?' he asked. He was speaking in a stage whisper. He lifted a linen teacloth covering a plate where some cold ham and bread were laid out.

Joan shook her head. She had a sleeping Jimmy in her arms. 'Need to get him settled.' She looked around. As well as a scrubbed wooden table there was a pair of armchairs either side of an iron stove, each covered with a crocheted throw. A sideboard stood on one side and a series of cupboards and a sink on the other.

Jim indicated the sink. Still keeping his voice low he said, 'I put that in when I heard you were coming. It's cold water but at least it's inside the house. Before that we had to bring it in from the well every morning. Took me a week to lay the piping.' He turned on the tap and grinned at her as the water gushed forth. 'Ma wasn't sure about it at first. She's used to the old ways of doing things. I'm still trying to convince her about the generator. She's scared the place will blow up. I'm going to install a water heater too so you won't have to boil water on the stove all the time.'

Joan bit her lip and told herself things could have been worse. The lady who talked to them on the ship about life in Canada had said some places didn't even have a well and people had to get water from a lake or river – melting it from snow in winter.

'So where do we take a bath?' She tried to keep her voice low as it was clear he was worried about waking his parents.

Jim pointed to a large tin bath that was hanging on the wall by the door. 'I'm going to put a proper bath and a toilet in.'

She closed her eyes and tried not to think about the prospect of taking a bath in here in the middle of a Canadian winter. 'You mean we have to bath here in the kitchen?'

He smiled. 'Not quite as bad as that.' He opened one of the two doors to reveal a small room, empty apart from rows of shelves packed with jars and bottles and a table in the corner on which was placed a large ewer and washing bowl. 'I built this onto the side of the house before I went to England. Plan was that it would be the bathroom, but we never got round to it. Ma's rather taken it over for her canned vegetables. We've always put the tin bath in here. But soon–'

She interrupted him. 'Soon you're going to fit it out with hot and cold running water and a proper bath.' She rolled her eyes.

'The kit's already delivered. It's all piled up in the barn. Once I've got the winter wheat in I'll be starting work on it.' He pulled the door shut again.

'Where's Jimmy's room?' she asked. 'I want to get him down before he wakes up.'

Jim looked sheepish. 'He's in with us. It's the room I used to share with my brother. It's a bit cramped but it won't be for long. I'll show you but we'll need to be very quiet as Pa's a light sleeper.' He put down the oil lamp and took the sleeping child from her arms.

Her heart sinking, Joan picked up the lamp and followed him as he opened the other door to reveal a narrow staircase. At the top was a tiny landing with two doors, one shut and the other opening onto a twin-bedded room. From behind the closed door came the sound of laboured breathing, as though the sleeper was struggling for every rasping breath.

She pulled back the covers of one of the beds and Jim put Jimmy down, fully-clothed, pulled off his shoes and drew the covers over him.

Jim looked at her as they stood in the narrow space between the two beds. Suddenly awkward, she whispered, 'Can we go downstairs for a while?'

He nodded and they returned to the kitchen.

'Will he be all right? He won't wake up?' said Jim.

Joan nodded. 'He barely slept on the train. He's been so excited since we arrived in Canada. He's fallen in love with trains.' She realised she was gabbling.

'Come with me.' Jim took her hand and led her outside the building.

Moonlight washed the farmyard in a soft light. Joan started to walk across the yard towards the big wooden barn.

'Not that way,' he said. They walked hand in hand to a little grassy hollow just below the house. It was only a short distance away, but the sloping ground meant that the house was out of sight. They settled down on the grass.

'You going to kiss me properly now, Jim Armstrong? I've waited three years for this.' She turned to him as his arms went around her and his mouth met hers. She gave a little groan and gripped him tightly, rolling onto her back.

When they surfaced from the kiss, she tugged at the front of his shirt, her fingers feeling in the dark for the buttons.

'Aren't we going to wait until we're in bed?' he said.

'Call that thing up there a bed?'

'You didn't seem to mind being squashed in a single bed with me when we were in London.'

'I don't think I want to be reminded of that night. It wasn't the romantic setting a girl dreams of. This time I'd like to have space to make love to my husband.'

He started to laugh. 'But outside? On the grass?'

'Where's your sense of adventure, Jim Armstrong? What could be more romantic than being here under the stars, by the light of the moon? It's just like a scene from a film I saw a few weeks ago. Now what was it called?'

'Shut up,' he said, and his mouth found hers again.

Kissing him, all her doubts and fears disappeared. She could face anything as long as she had Jim with her.

He whispered in her ear, 'I've dreamt of this for so long.'

As he entered her they were blinded by light from a torch and a strangled cry of surprise from above them caused their love-making to come to an abrupt end.

'What are you doing out here, like a pair of animals? This is a good Christian home and I brought you up to show some respect, Jim Armstrong.'

Joan scrambled onto her knees, trying to readjust her clothing. She was embarrassed – more than that – humiliated.

'What the hell do you think you're doing, Ma! Switch that torch off. You're blinding us.' Joan had never heard Jim angry before.

Mrs Armstrong's voice was cold. 'What kind of woman are you? And you've a child up there who's crying his eyes out.'

Joan leapt to her feet and began to race up the slope. Behind her she could hear the argument between Jim and his mother continuing.

NIGHTMARES

JIM STRUGGLED to control his anger. Why the hell was his mother behaving this way? She was no longer the warm-hearted, mild-mannered woman he had known all his life until he had left for war. Grabbing her by the arm he shook her, furious at how she had treated Joan.

Helga jerked her arm away. 'I've every right,' she said. 'This is my home. I expect you to behave with respect and decency, not cavort about having sexual relations in a field like the animals.'

'It's the middle of the night. We wanted some privacy. Hell, Ma, I haven't set eyes on my wife for three years. It's you should be showing some respect and living some of your so-called Christian values. How do you think Joan's going to be feeling right now?'

'I don't care how she's feeling. A decent woman wouldn't take off her clothes in a field and do what you were doing like a pair of yard dogs, where any folk could come across you. That woman needs to respect how we do things here. It's my home.'

Jim grabbed at his mother again. 'When you were trying

to persuade me to move back here against my better judgement you weren't saying it was *your* home – you were trying to convince me it was *mine*. I've dragged Joan across the Atlantic, away from her family and friends. She's given up everything to be with me and you've treated her like a slut. I'd agreed we'd live in England after the war and it was you who persuaded me to move back here. I'm ashamed of you, Ma.' He kicked out at a tree stump.

Slumping down onto the grass, he held his head in his hands. What had he done? Why had he ever thought this would work?

There was silence for a moment then his mother sat down beside him and laid a hand on his arm. Jim shrugged it off.

'I'm sorry, son,' she said at last. 'I was shocked. I didn't expect to find you like that. I only came looking as the child was crying. I tried to comfort the boy but he was frightened and was calling for his ma.' She paused and looked at him, her face in shadow. 'I was wrong. I'm sorry. Things get the better of me easily these days, with your father being so ill. And with Walter gone and poor Alice on her own. I can't seem to think straight about anything any more.'

Jim sighed. All very well for her to apologise to him but how on earth was she going to build bridges with Joan? Eventually he said, 'I need you to be supportive of Joan. Not undermine her. Can you do that?'

There was an uncomfortable silence. Then she said, 'I just don't like the look of her. Brassy. That's what I'd call her.'

Jim closed his eyes.

'But if that's what you want I'll try my best.'

'It's not just for me. It's for your grandson's sake.'

She reached for Jim's hand and held it as they sat there in the glow of the moonlight. 'The boy looks like you.'

'You think so?'

'He has your eyes. He's the image of you when you were his age only with darker hair.'

After a few moments she spoke again, her voice quiet and a little hesitant. 'You still having trouble sleeping, son?'

He shrugged.

'Maybe now she's with you, it'll help.'

Jim was about to point out that being squashed together in a single bed with Jimmy sharing their room was hardly the recipe for a good night's sleep, but he swallowed the words and said nothing.

'When your father came back after the first war he couldn't sleep either. Every night, tossing and turning, crying out from terrible dreams – just like you do.'

'You've heard me?' Jim was stunned. She'd never mentioned it before.

'Night after night. I wanted to wake you up from whatever you were dreaming about, but your father told me not to. Said it would pass. It did with him. But it took years. Have you tried talking to him about it?'

'I don't want to talk to anybody about it. I just want to forget. Same as he did.' He clambered to his feet. 'Come on, let's go back. You need to get some sleep yourself.'

WHEN JIM RETURNED to the bedroom he found his wife sleeping, curled round their son. They must both be exhausted from the lengthy journey. He bent over them and dropped a kiss first on the little boy's head and then on Joan's cheek. It was damp from her tears. His heart ached with the weight of responsibility. A shaft of moonlight caught her face and he stood looking down at her. Brassy, his mother had said, but he thought her beautiful. Her dark hair spread, thick and glossy, across the pillow and his chest tightened as he looked at her. He bent again and brushed her cheek with his lips. She stirred slightly in her sleep but didn't waken.

There was no space for him to squeeze in beside them so he lay down on the other bed and tried to sleep. Every time he closed his eyes, it was the same. Instead of the velvety darkness and quiet oblivion he craved, he was bombarded with images of smoke, flashes of fire and ruined buildings, and his head throbbed with the noise of battle.

Years, his mother had said. If it went on much longer he was afraid he'd lose his mind. There was no one to talk to about what he was going through. No one who would understand. He thought about telling his father, but it wouldn't be right to rake all that over with him. Jim would just have to get on with it and hope that with time it would pass.

Lying there in the dark, he tried to suppress the visions. Almost the whole of December 1943 they'd fought in the fields and the streets of the town of Ortona on the Adriatic coast, at terrible cost. So many of his countrymen had died there, trying to take that Italian town and push the enemy north.

The chill fear of climbing through a deserted building, not knowing if a booby trap, a land mine or a sniper's rifle was on the other side of a door. Smashing bricks out of the internal walls of houses to break into the next one. Mouse-holing they'd called it. It sounded like something done quickly and deftly – tiny holes nibbled in the wainscoting – but in the town of Ortona they had burrowed through the walls of buildings on a grand scale, moving house to house, ready to shoot German soldiers on the other side of the walls before the Gerries could take them out.

Men bleeding to death. Vineyards awash with mud and dead bodies. Rain-soaked wizened grapes withering on unharvested vines. Bloodied stretchers. Climbing over the corpses of men he'd eaten army rations with a few hours earlier. Narrow rubble-filled streets where you couldn't tell who was watching you, waiting to blast your brains out.

Jim squeezed his eyes tightly shut. The smell of mud, cordite and shattered masonry filled his nostrils. The noises were real and present now. The crack of sniper fire. The distant rumble of artillery, then an eerie silence, followed by the scream of aircraft and the boom-boom of explosions. Burying his head in the pillow couldn't shut it out. Mortar fire. Exploding grenades. Torrential rain. Screaming rockets. The terrible wail of the Moaning Minnies as they screeched through the air seeking their targets. Make it go away!

Exhausted, he gave up trying to sleep. Before dawn, he dressed quickly and went outside.

He decided to make a start on planting the second-crop beans. The soil was perfect. Not too dry and not too wet. He'd made up his mind to gradually switch the farm away from wheat production into fruit and vegetables. The orchards had been a minor sideline under his father's management, but, after attending a lecture for returning veterans on new trends in farm management, Jim wanted to increase the acreage given over to apple production. It was a long term vision, as it would take years before the young trees produced a substantial crop. Meanwhile he was concentrating on planting beans, potatoes, corn and cabbages. No point trying to compete with wheat against the prairies of Saskatchewan, Alberta and Manitoba. In this part of Ontario the opportunities were in more intensive farming. His father had been sceptical at first but, unable to take on the responsibility himself, he had eventually accepted the sense of Jim's arguments.

He dragged the sacks of beans from the barn to the field that he had already tilled ready for planting, feeling his way in the pre-dawn gloom. By the time the bags were all lined up ready, the sun was breaking over the horizon, painting a rose-pink tint over the lightening sky. Tearing open the sack, Jim began to walk the strip, planting as he went. It was back-breaking work, but he relished it. Physical effort, repetition and concentration, obliterated his thoughts of war. The soil here was clean, unpolluted by the blood of fallen soldiers, undisturbed by the tracks of tanks and unbroken by mortar craters. The smells were of the rich loamy earth, cut grass drying for hay in the next field, the only sounds his own breathing and the chatter of starlings.

It was no wonder his father had let the farm fall into neglect. There was more work than one man could reason-ably tackle. Before the war there had been three of them as well as the hired seasonal hands. Now there was Jim alone. Hiring in labour was hard now. Back in the pre-war days, with mass unemployment, men jumped at any chance of casual work, but in this post-war period there were not enough men to go around and the economy was growing rapidly. Jim would need to make some radical changes. He pursed his lips thinking about the promises he had made to Joan about a generator and water heater and fitting up a bathroom. The time and money that would take would be better invested towards the mechanisation of the farm. He needed a combine, vats for sorting and drying beans, equip-ment to spray the crops, a motorised tractor: the list went on. Why had he made her those rash promises?

Guilt about the way his mother had spoken to Joan made matters worse. Suddenly the idea of Joan adapting to life as the wife of a Canadian farmer seemed an impossible dream. But what was he to do? He couldn't abandon the farm and his folks now. And he didn't want to leave here. He loved the land. He was determined to make Hollowtree a successful enterprise. If he didn't, what had it all been for? All that death, suffering and sacrifice to make the world a place fit for their children to live in. Jimmy may be a young child but time moved so fast and it wouldn't be long before he'd be old enough to help out. Jim had to make the farm into somewhere worth handing on to him. Joan would have to wait a while until he could afford to remodel the house. If only he could get a decent harvest this year and plant the entire acreage next spring, there'd surely be enough money for him to do some modernisation of the house next summer. Maybe then, once they had some funds behind them, he could think about building a new house, somewhere that would be their own with all modern conveniences, like in the magazines his mother and Alice pored over.

He ran his hands through his sweat-damp hair. Glancing at his watch and seeing it was time for breakfast, with a heavy heart he headed towards the farmhouse.

MEETING THE FAMILY

JOAN CLUTCHED her little boy's hand as they entered the kitchen and tried not to let him sense that she was as terrified as he must be. Helga Armstrong was standing at the range cooker. It had been the delicious aroma of frying bacon that had hastened Joan to get out of bed, dress and come downstairs.

Helga looked up, nodded curtly at Joan and addressed Jimmy. 'Don't be shy, Jimmy, come and sit down. Meet the family. I'll have you something good to eat in no time.'

Jimmy hesitated, turning to his mother for reassurance. Joan stood in the doorway, looking round. A young woman was sitting at the table, and beside her a girl of a similar age to Jimmy. The woman smiled but didn't get up.

'You must be Joan? Welcome to Canada! Come and sit down. I'm Alice, Jim's sister-in-law, and this is my daughter, Rose.'

The woman had a face like a china doll, blonde hair, porcelain pale skin and eyes as blue as Jim's. So this was Alice, the woman her husband had once planned to marry. She reminded Joan of Veronica Lake, with one side of her silky blonde hair falling over her face so that she had to keep pushing it back out of her eyes. Joan felt a little stab of jealousy.

Joan avoided looking at her mother-in-law. Her cheeks burned as she thought about the things Helga had said to her. Deciding to ignore her, she sat down opposite Alice and offered her hand. Alice, surprised, accepted the hand but a little smile flitted across her face as though she was amused by the idea of the handshake.

The little girl was already tucking into a plate of pancakes and showed no curiosity about either her aunt or her cousin. Alice studied Joan unashamedly. Joan gave her a weak smile and wished that Jim would arrive.

Helga placed a plate of pancakes, dripping in maple syrup in front of Jimmy. 'Here you are, sweetheart. Ever tasted maple syrup?'

Jimmy shook his head. His lip was trembling and he looked about to cry.

'Well, you've a treat in store. My own syrup, from sap from our own trees. Pancakes made from eggs from our own hens.' Helga turned back to the stove and began serving up bacon and pancakes to the adults.

Jimmy looked at his mother, evidently nonplussed at the idea of eating something that looked like treacle and came from a tree. Before she could say anything, Alice jumped to her feet and came round the table.

'Here, Jimmy, I'll cut the pancakes up for you and you can see if you like them. Look at Rose. She's nearly finished hers. Ma makes the best maple syrup in the county and her pancakes are almost as famous as her butter pies.' She picked up the boy's cutlery and cut the pancakes into neat squares.

Joan bristled. Who did she think she was? She looked around the room. 'Where's Jim?'

'Out in the fields. I saw him planting beans in the small field beyond the barn as I came across,' said Alice.

Swallowing her annoyance and the dislike for Alice that was already bubbling in her, Joan decided to make an effort to be friendly. Alice was at least more affable than their mother-in-law. Helga still had her back to her and gave no indication of any softening in her hostility.

'Do you live nearby?' Joan was wondering whether it was usual for Jim's brother's widow to drop in on them for breakfast.

'Rose and I live here.' Alice sat down again as Helga handed out plates of bacon and pancakes. 'In a little log cabin behind the barn. My late husband fixed it up for us before he went to England.' She looked down at her plate. 'Ma wanted me to stay on here after... after we found out Walt wasn't coming home.'

This was news to Joan. Why had Jim never mentioned the fact that his sister-in-law – his former fiancée – was living here too? She was saved from replying to Alice by Jim opening the kitchen door and coming in. She looked up at him expectantly, smiling, and hoping he would come over to her and give her a kiss. But he pulled out a chair and said, 'Pa still sleeping?'

His mother plonked a plate in front of him and nodded.

Jim ruffled his son's hair. Jimmy stared at him with curiosity and, as Jim began to eat, the boy picked up his fork and started eating too.

'I wondered where you'd gone when I woke this morning,' said Joan.

Jim leaned his head to one side and gave her a wink. 'Up and about for hours. I'm up at five most mornings but I couldn't sleep last night so I made a start around four-thirty.' He turned to address his mother and Alice. 'Got a good start on the beans in the barn field. Should be done by the end of today. Slow work though, doing it all by hand. We're definitely going to have to apply for a loan for machinery.'

Alice leaned forward. 'You need a hand? Once I've got Rose over to my mum's I can come across and help you plant.'

Jim shook his head. 'No need. I'm making good progress. I've got a rhythm going. Maybe tomorrow you can lend a hand when I start to bring the hay in.'

'Goody!' shouted Rose. 'Can I ride on the hay cart?'

Jim nodded and the girl bounced up and down in her chair. He turned to Jimmy. 'You ever ride on a hay wagon?'

Jimmy's eyes widened. 'Is it like a train?'

Jim and Alice laughed, then Alice said, 'It's pulled by a horse. You like horses, Jimmy?'

As the farm-related conversation continued, with Helga also participating, Joan felt like an outsider, sidelined and inconsequential. Even Jim appeared to ignore her, Jimmy had been absorbed into their tight knit unit, and she was left outside looking in.

The meal was rapidly consumed by all, except Jimmy who was a habitually slow eater and Joan, whose nerves made her queasy and allowed her to manage only a few mouthfuls, delicious though the pancakes were. She was anyway still adjusting to living without rationing, and the generosity of the helping was too much for her.

Jim got up to return to the fields and Mrs Armstrong announced that she was going to feed the chickens and churn the butter. Alice said goodbye to Joan, telling her she would be gone for an hour while she took Rose into town to spend the day at her grandmother's. 'We can have a proper chat when I get back.'

Before Joan could reply, Alice had gone, taking her daughter with her. Jimmy continued to plough through his pancakes, a blank look on his face, reflecting his contentment with the meal. Joan got up and began to clear the plates away, remembering that in order to wash the dishes she was going to have to boil water on the stove. She looked around for a suitable vessel to use.

'Behind that curtain under the sink.' The words were rasped out amidst a bout of coughing.

Joan jumped. The man standing in front of her had the same thick blond hair that Jim had, only turning to a dull grey around the temples. He must once have been a fine-looking man but his eyes were rheumy, his face looked as if it had not seen a razor for several weeks and his skin had a greyish tinge. Joan noticed a couple of spots of blood on the front of his shirt. He pointed at the sink behind her. 'You'll find a pan under there to boil the water in.'

'I'm pleased to meet you, Mr Armstrong. I'm Joan, Jim's wife, and this is your grandson, Jimmy.'

The man nodded at Joan and gave a military salute to the little boy. 'Call me Don,' he said. 'Not you,' he added to Jimmy. 'You can call me Pop.'

Jimmy looked at his grandfather in awe. 'Pop? Like Popeye?'

The boy was answered by a fit of coughing.

'Have you got a bad cough?' Jimmy asked.

'You could say that.' Don lowered himself into a seat at the table. 'Did I smell bacon and pancakes?'

'Of course. I'm sorry. I'll make you some,' said Joan, trying to remember the last time she'd had fresh eggs to make pancakes.

'No. The smell's enough for me. You can give me some coffee though.'

Joan fetched the coffee from the stove, poured a cup and placed it in front of her father-in-law. By now he and Jimmy were deep in conversation, punctuated by frequent coughing fits, which seemed to fascinate the little boy. She found the metal pan under the sink, filled it from the tap and set it to boil on the cooker. When the dishes were done she poured herself a coffee and topped Don's up. There was no sign of any tea and she told herself she would have to ask Jim about shopping and to clarify who did what. She sat down next to her son and sipped the bitter brew.

'How old's the boy?'

'Four next birthday. November.'

He nodded. 'Helga says you had him before you were wed?'

She blushed and stared into her cup.

'Things happen when a war's on. Time is a scarce commodity.' He held his hand to his mouth as if to hold back the urge to cough again. 'My wife makes me take too many darn pills,' he said, in a *non sequitur*. 'Not that they make any darn difference. They're in a bottle on that shelf. Can you fetch me two of them?'

When he'd taken his medicine, he looked at Joan appraisingly. 'Can't fault my son's taste in women. You're a pretty girl. No wonder he couldn't wait 'til he'd got a ring on your finger.'

Joan blushed again and looked down at her hand. She still didn't have a proper ring on her finger. Not one given her by Jim. They had borrowed Ethel's mum's ring for the hasty wedding in 1943 and then later she'd bought herself a cheap utility ring for the sake of appearance. It left a nasty green stain on her finger from the fake gold – copper she imagined. She'd been nursing the hope that Jim would have remembered and bought one to give her when she arrived here. She bit her lip. Don't get upset. Keep calm. Deep breaths. 'We were married at short notice. Jim was about to sail for the Mediterranean.'

The man nodded, then said. 'Pay no attention to Helga.

She'll get used to you. The important thing is that Jim loves you. That's all that matters.'

Joan felt her lip trembling again and turned her head away. Her voice brittle, she said, 'I've never been on a farm before. It'll take a bit of getting used to. I lived in a town.'

'Thank you.'

She looked back, frowning in puzzlement.

'For agreeing to come here. Must have been hard for you.'

She turned to Jimmy. 'Why don't you go outside and see if you can find your grandma. Maybe she'll let you help her feed the chickens.'

The child needed no further encouragement. 'Chickens!' he cried and ran outside.

Donald fixed his eyes on her, a paler, cloudier version of Jim's. 'I mean it. Leaving everything behind. Can't be easy. Helga needs to understand that. Trouble is, she spent most of her youth on a farm about ten miles from here. That's the extent of her experience of the world. Well, she was actually born in Germany but she doesn't care to remember that. Understandably...' His words came out between laboured gasps for air. 'I was in the last war. In Belgium. I've seen a bit more than I'd like to have seen.'

Joan spoke, more from a desire to relieve him from the effort of talking, than to reply. 'Apart from a short spell in a military camp, I've lived in the same place all my life. Saying goodbye to my mother and the rest of my family was the hardest thing I ever had to do. I did it believing it was only for a while but now...'

'He told you it was just 'til I die?' He nodded his head.

Joan looked down, avoiding his eyes. 'I thought...but Jim says he never wants to leave here. No matter what. Says the farm is in his blood.'

'He's right about that. Shame it took him so long to realise it. He told you why he joined up? About finding his brother and Alice together?'

She nodded, not wanting to be reminded of the fact that Jim had once been planning to marry Alice.

'He was angry and hurt and it made him believe he hated everything about this place… But with Walt dying and me on the way out, things looked different when he came back. And then marrying you and having the child. That's also made him see things differently… He wants to put down roots and build a life for you all and what's wrong with that?'

Joan couldn't think of anything to say to the contrary.

'Jim finds it hard to express what he's feeling. Specially after what he went through in Italy…' The coughing fit lasted longer this time and Joan looked at the man anxiously.

'He doesn't talk about it, but I can guess… I felt the same about the other war. You see things no one should ever have to see outside the gates of hell… You think you're in hell itself. Can't imagine that hell could be any worse. You religious?'

Joan shook her head.

'I couldn't believe in God any more after what I saw. One thing Helga and I have never seen eye to eye on.'

'Jim hasn't talked to me about Italy. Not even in any of his letters.'

'I doubt he ever will talk about it. Bottle it up inside – that's what he'll do. But we hear him at night, Helga and I. Nightmares… Cries out in his sleep. You'll have to get used to that. Maybe sleeping with you will help.' He leaned back in his chair and breathed rapidly in little gasping breaths.

Joan was about to comment about the sleeping arrangements but held back.

As if reading her mind, he said, 'I'm working on Helga that we exchange beds with you. I'd be a darned sight more comfortable with my bad chest if I were in a bed on my own.'

He bent over as he coughed into his handkerchief. 'But she's not keen on the idea, after thirty years of sharing the marriage bed. In fact I reckon the best thing would be if we rigged up a bed down here for me... Getting up and down the stairs is difficult and before long I won't be able to manage it at all... The little fellow could share a room with Helga then. What do you think?'

Joan wanted to jump up and hug him but she settled for placing her hand over his. 'Thank you, Don.'

'No. Thank you for letting my son come home.'

ACCLIMATISING

ALICE PUT her bicycle away and after glancing towards the house, turned and hurried down to the field behind the barn where she knew Jim would be working. He looked up as she approached, wiping the sweat from his eyes, then carried on with the task.

Alice took a sack of beans and dragged it to the opposite end of the row he was planting. 'I'll meet you in the middle.'

Without looking at her, he said, 'You not got any chores to be getting on with in the house? I told you I'd get by on my own today.'

'Thought I'd let Ma and Joan have some time together. Looks like there's some defrosting needs to happen there.'

Jim grunted but said nothing.

'I got the distinct impression that Ma isn't too thrilled about her. Got off on the wrong foot, did they?'

'What's Ma been saying to you?' Jim stopped and stretched his back, his hands over his shoulders, head back.

'Nothing particular. I just asked her if she'd met Joan last night and she told me she had. That was it. No further comment. But she barely uttered a word to her over breakfast. Seems real strange as Ma is such a warm and friendly person. She's always been so welcoming to me. Did something happen between them?'

Jim continued to place the beans in the drills and said nothing.

'Do you think it's because of all the makeup she wears? Maybe she doesn't approve.' She paused, waiting for a reaction from Jim but when there was none she continued, 'I think Joan's real pretty. I love the shade of lipstick she was wearing when she came down this morning. Such a vivid red. I must ask her what it's called.'

'You've never worn lipstick in your life, Alice.'

'No. But there's always a first time.'

By now they had met in the middle of the row. Jim dragged his sack to the bottom of the next row, out of range for talking.

After a few minutes working, they were in hearing distance of each other again.

'Your boy's a cute kid. It'll be nice for Rose to have someone to play with. She's always been a tomboy and it's been lonely for her here sometimes. Before long Jimmy will be ready for school and they can walk there together.'

Silence.

'Hey, what's wrong, Jim? Cat got your tongue?'

Jim pulled himself up to full height and faced her. 'I'm trying to get the job done. I didn't ask for company and I'm not in the mood for conversation.'

Alice hesitated, trying to decide whether to go or stay. She weighed the few beans still in her hand, tempted to fling them down and flounce off, but decided against it. 'Sorry. I was only trying to help.'

'You can help if you want but if you're staying, no more questions, eh?'

'All right.' She bent down and took another handful of beans from the sack and returned to the task in hand.

DON ARMSTRONG MOVED to his chair by the stove, pulled the crocheted rug over his knees and closed his eyes. Joan decided to leave him to sleep, and go and look around the place to seek out Jimmy. There had been no sign of either her mother-in-law or Alice. So much for Alice promising to return for a chat after dropping her daughter in town. And Mrs Armstrong had been icy to the point of rudeness at breakfast. But Joan liked her father-in-law. Liked him a lot.

The first thing she had to do was find the toilet. She'd seen there was a chamber pot in the bedroom, but she hadn't used it and was now desperate to relieve herself.

She looked about her. The sun was warm on her skin as she tottered across the yard in shoes unsuited to walking around a farm, anxious to avoid stepping in anything unpleasant. But everywhere looked clean. Not even any puddles to avoid: there had evidently been no rain for a while. The hens were scratching about on a stretch of grass near the barn, clucking happily. A couple of horses grazed in the meadow beyond. The barn, a tall red painted wooden structure, towered over the house. The cabin where Alice mentioned she lived must be at the far side, away from the house, as Joan couldn't see it from the yard. A white picket fence ran on either side of a dirt track, stretching out of sight. In the distance were trees. She turned to look in the opposite direction and saw the ground falling away in a grassy sward towards more trees. That must have been where they had been last night. Beyond the trees she caught a flash of water reflected in the sunshine. In the far distance were low hills. Everywhere looked green and lush. Sunlight probably showed the place in its best light but she had to acknowledge that it was pleasant.

Between the house and the barn, set back behind some latticed fencing she saw a small wooden hut like a sentry box. The biffy they called it. Jim was right – it was quite a walk from the house. No wonder they kept the pots in the bedrooms. She swung open the door. It was dark inside and she shuddered, hoping there weren't any spiders. There was a candle on a shelf beside the lavatory, which was just a hole in a plank of wood. A bundle of neatly cut squares of newspaper hung from a string on a hook in the wall. At least it didn't smell too bad – it didn't smell good either – an odd chemical smell. Peering into the hole, she saw it was too dark to see what lurked beneath. She didn't want to sit down, fearful of what might be lurking in the depths, but unable to hold out, she gritted her teeth and perched on the seat. The wooden door didn't reach to the floor and she felt embarrassed knowing that anyone passing would be able to see her feet under the door. At least everyone was in the same boat.

Her task complete, Joan went across to the barn to look for Jimmy and his grandmother. She stood in the doorway, her eyes adjusting to the gloom. There was a musty smell of straw and grain and the air inside the building was cool.

Jimmy was giggling. His grandmother stood over him, her hands above his, letting him believe it was he who was operating the milk churn and making the cream. The woman demonstrated a patience and good humour with the child that Joan found surprising after the hostility she had shown to her. She leaned against the doorpost, smiling as she watched them, unobserved. Then Helga turned and saw her. Joan flinched as her mother-in-law threw her a look of undisguised hostility. She was tempted to walk away, go back to the house and leave Helga Armstrong to play her game alone. But she was the newcomer and she would have to make an effort, no matter how distasteful that might feel. She would have liked nothing better than to hurl an insult Mrs Armstrong's way, but instead she called over to Jimmy and went towards them.

'Have you had a good time making the cream? Are you going to show me how you do it?'

The little boy grinned. 'It's hard work, but I'm good at it now, aren't I, Gramma?' he boasted. 'Let's show Mummy how.'

'You've done such a good job, my angel, that we're all finished here,' said Helga, her eyes fixed on Jimmy, as if Joan wasn't there. She took Jimmy's hand. 'Now I'll show you those kittens.'

Joan watched as her mother-in-law disappeared into the gloomy interior with a delighted Jimmy. In anger and frustration she went back outside, walked to the top of the grassy slope, sat down and fumbled in her pocket for a cigarette. Her eyes burned with angry unshed tears. Damn you, Helga Armstrong. You'll not get the better of me.

A BELL RANG out from where it hung outside the kitchen door, presumably the call for the midday meal. Joan got to her feet, gritted her teeth and made her way towards the house. Maybe she should have offered to help prepare the food, but she would probably have been rebuffed. She ducked into the makeshift bathroom and washed her hands.

In the cool of the kitchen she saw Don was already at the table and with relief she sat down and was rewarded with a smile and a pat on the hand. 'You had a good look round, girl? Has Jim given you the tour?'

Helga turned from the stove and placed a pot on the table. 'Jim's got work to do. He's got no time to be wasting giving tours of the place. She'll find out what's what soon enough.'

She reached for a loaf of bread and a crock of butter. 'That is if she puts on some suitable clothes and a decent pair of shoes.' For the first time since her outburst the night before she addressed Joan directly. 'You won't get far in those things once the weather changes. Hope you've got something sensible in all that luggage of yours.'

Joan didn't know what to say, but Don spoke for her. 'Leave the girl be, Helga. She's only just arrived. Needs to get her bearings and it might be Christian to help her do that. Why don't...'

Coughing defeated his attempt to finish the sentence. At that moment Alice and Jim entered the room. Joan looked up at them. Alice had a dirty streak across her forehead and both had soil on their hands.

'Get yourselves in there and wash up before you sit down,' said Helga. 'Looks like you both should have worked up a good appetite.' She opened the other door and called up the stairs to summon Jimmy, then untied her apron and took her place at the table.

Jimmy clattered into the room like a little dervish. 'Mummy, Gramma let me play with the kittens.'

'Then you'd better go in there and wash your hands too. Daddy will show you.' Joan pointed at the door to the 'bathroom'. To her annoyance she could hear Alice's laughter from inside.

When the three returned to the kitchen and took up their places around the table, Mrs Armstrong said grace. Joan had already picked up her knife and fork and had to put them down quickly, unused to grace being said at mealtimes. She squirmed in her seat. Nothing she did was right. They ate in silence for a few minutes and Joan looked over at Alice, trying not to feel irritated that the woman had evidently spent the morning out in the fields helping Jim. She wished now she had gone to seek him out herself rather than worrying she'd be in the way. Apart from Don it felt as though the entire family was united in a quest to make her feel out of place. She tried unsuccessfully to catch Jim's eye.

Jim put down his knife and fork. 'That was real good, Ma.'

Immediately, Alice lifted the lid off the pan and spooned some more stew onto Jim's plate, replacing the lid afterwards. Joan stiffened, fighting to repress her anger and jealousy. How dare she? Acting as though Jim were hers. Just as she had done at breakfast with Jimmy. Did she and Mrs Amstrong have some kind of pact to make her feel as unwelcome as possible? She felt her skin prickle and knew her face was flushed red with anger. What should she do? What should she say?

Alice leaned forward and said, 'Now I promised we'd have a chat, didn't I? Why don't you come into town with me when I go to fetch Rose? I can show you around the place and we'll have a chance to get to know each other.'

Joan wanted to say no, to put Alice down, to rebuff her as she had felt rebuffed herself, but that would be a fatal mistake. Wrong footed again. Relieved to have thought of an excuse, she said, 'I'd have loved to come with you but I can't leave Jimmy.'

'Jimmy will be fine with Ma,' said Jim.

Jimmy began to bounce up and down. "Yesssss! Can I play with the kittens again, Gramma?'

'Of course you can, angel.' Helga stroked the little boy's hair.

Joan was seething. 'No, Jimmy. I think you and I will have a walk around the farm this afternoon.'

Jimmy groaned. 'I want to play with the kittens. Please, Mummy.'

Jim looked up. 'Let the kid play with the kittens. He's got long enough to get to know the lay of the farm. You go with Alice. She can show you around town.'

Alice grinned at her with what Joan took to be satisfaction. She determined not to let her see how she was feeling.

Joan got to her feet, looked at Alice and said, 'Come on then. Show me this town.'

'You ride a bike? There's a spare one in the barn.'

'Not if I can help it. I prefer to walk.'

'Town's five miles away. I have a seat on my bicycle for Rose. You can get one fitted in town today for Jimmy. It'll save you a lot of time. At least while the weather's clear. Once the snow comes we'll have to go on the wagon or in the truck. Unless you fancy trying snowshoes.'

Joan felt sick with the realisation that there was no ten-minute bus ride to a town where she could find everything she needed. From the sound of it, trips to the town of Hollowtree were going to be on strict rations. A wave of homesickness swept over her.

'I'll go and change,' she said.

Five minutes later she returned wearing trousers and flat shoes and tried to ignore the glances exchanged between the two other women.

Since her pregnancy with Jimmy had forced her to leave the ATS, Joan had done little physical activity. A short walk to the shops or pushing the pram around the park was about the sum of it. Now pedalling along an unsurfaced track with frequent slopes brought the sweat to her brow. Alice cycled quickly, the road being as familiar to her as her own skin. Joan wondered if she was speeding along just to show her up and determined not to say anything or stop to get her breath back. It was a warm afternoon and her underarms were soaked and she could feel the hair plastered to the back of her neck. She cursed silently.

When they finally reached the town Alice led her to a café in the main street and treated her to a strawberry milk shake. Joan had to admit to herself it was one of the most delicious concoctions she had drunk since she'd first tasted coca cola on the ship. They sat at a table by the window, looking out onto the street.

'I've just remembered. I have something for you.' Joan fumbled in her shoulder bag and pulled out a photograph. 'Jim asked me to get this for you. It's your husband's grave.' She handed it to Alice.

Alice studied the picture. 'There's no proper headstone. Only a bit of wood.'

'There are so many graves. All over Europe. They're working their way through them all. That's only temporary.'

'Did you take this?'

Joan shook her head. 'My cousin Ethel's fiancé is buried in the same cemetery. She took the pictures. I bought a Box Brownie for her as her present last Christmas.'

Alice handed the picture back.

'No, keep it. I got it for you. Jim said you wanted to see where your husband was.'

'I did. Thank you. But I don't want to keep it. You can give it to Ma – or to Donald.'

Joan frowned. She'd paid for the photograph to be developed and expected Alice would be more grateful that she'd made the effort.

Alice twisted her wedding band around her finger. She looked up and said, 'What did you expect me to do? Put a picture of my husband's grave in a frame and hang it on the wall?'

Embarrassed, Joan put the picture back in her bag. Why had Jim asked her to do it? She'd have been better forgetting the request. He clearly had as he hadn't even mentioned it. Now Alice had another reason to dislike her. No. She had another reason to dislike Alice.

Joan looked out of the window, turning her attention to the town as Alice slurped her milkshake in silence.

It was a small town. Probably no more than a few hundred inhabitants. Across the street from them was a grain store and next to it a general store which was doing a brisk trade in everything from haberdashery to farming tools. A lean-to was attached to the side of it, where it appeared that repairs to cars and trucks took place. Joan studied the passers by. Most of the men were dressed in overalls, although one or two were flashy dressers, sporting jackets that clashed with their trousers. Like a bunch of spivs, she thought. The women, in contrast, were dressed drably. If that was what farmers' wives looked like she wanted none of it. A horse-drawn open buggy pulled up outside the store and a couple dressed in black got down and went inside.

'Did you see them?' she said to Alice. 'They were wearing fancy dress. Is there something going on?'

Alice frowned. 'Really?'

'Yes. They were both in black and she had skirts that swept the floor and a old-fashioned bonnet on her head. He was wearing a big wide straw hat and a suit with a stiff white collar. They looked like they'd just stepped out of a cowboy film set in the last century.'

Alice laughed. 'Mennonites. There's a lot round here. It's their religion. They keep the old ways. Very industrious, god-fearing people. They all dress like that. And they don't believe in war. Keep themselves to themselves but they're good people and very good farmers.' She swirled her straw around in her milkshake. 'Did you and Ma have a fight last night?'

Joan felt herself blushing. 'What makes you ask that?' Defensive.

'She's such a sweetie and yet she seems in a strange mood today. Hardly spoken all day.'

'It must have been a shock, finding out that Jim had got married and had a child,' Joan said.

'She's had nearly a year to get used to that. And she seems to have taken to little Jimmy. They're already best of friends.'

Joan stared out of the window, wishing herself thousands of miles away. Longing to be sitting in the back kitchen at Aunty Vi's, sharing a cuppa with Ethel. 'Then I have no idea. Do you?'

'Well, I did wonder as I'm sure I heard shouting last night. Something woke me up but when I got out of bed it was all quiet. Did something happen?'

Joan squeezed her lips together, struggling to suppress her fury. 'Not that I know of. We arrived very late last night and I didn't hear anything. Maybe you had a dream.'

Alice said nothing and they lapsed into an uncomfortable silence.

After a few minutes, she leaned forward and put a hand on Joan's wrist. Joan instinctively wanted to pull her hand away, but forced herself to do nothing.

'I do hope we can be friends. It's been lonely for me since my husband went away. Well, until Jim came back.' She laughed. 'But you know Jim. Doesn't say a lot, does he? At least not any more. Not since the war.'

Joan looked at her, curious now. 'No, I don't know actually. Until last night I hadn't seen my husband for three years.'

Alice looked at her with a soulful expression. Joan noticed again how flawless her complexion was. I bet she's never had a spot in her life, she thought.

'He had a bad time in Italy. All our boys did. It was brutal.'

'Did he tell you that?'

'Not exactly. He finds it hard to speak about it. But Ma hears him at night. Those walls are paper thin. He cries out in his sleep. Odd words. She says he sounds terrified.'

Joan felt herself bristle again. 'I don't feel comfortable talking about Jim when he isn't here.' She wanted to add - *or talking about him at all with you when he is none of your business.*

Alice was oblivious to Joan's tone of voice and said, 'It will take you a while to adjust to our ways here and I want you to know, Joan, that anything I can do to help you, just ask.'

Joan reached into her pocket and pulled out a pack of cigarettes, offering one to Alice, who declined with a look of ill-disguised horror.

'If you don't mind me making one teensy-weensy suggestion… it might be a good idea to go a bit easy on the cosmetics and the cigarettes. At least out in public.'

Joan took her cigarette from her lips, too amazed to speak.

Alice went on. 'It's just that people round here tend to take rather a dim view of women who smoke and wear lots of lipstick.'

Joan put her head on one side, waiting.

'They think it's unladylike.'

'Unladylike?' Joan repeated.

Alice gave a little laugh. 'You probably think we're very unsophisticated and you wouldn't be wrong. And of course it's up to you, and once people get to know you …but if you want to fit in quickly. Well. That's my advice.' She gave another little laugh. 'And I don't even charge for it.' She slid out of the banquette. 'Time we got a move on. I want to pick Rose up before my dad gets home. I like to keep out of his way as much as I can. But first we need to call in to the store and see about getting that seat for the back of your bicycle.'

Joan was speechless, unsure what to do or say next.

Alice went to collect Rose while Joan waited for the seat to be fitted to the bicycle. When it was done and Alice returned to find her, she led her along the main street, pointing out the various landmarks. Hollowtree was so small it made Joan's home town of Aldershot seem like London in comparison. Besides the two or three stores, the café, the town hall, a shabby looking hotel with a beverage room, which Alice told her, with curled lip, was a beer saloon for men only, there was a small stone building which housed the library where Alice said she worked part-time.

'It's a great little town,' said Alice. 'We even have our own newspaper, The Hollowtree News.' She pointed to a tall brick-built building behind the main street.

They walked on. 'That's the flour mill. And that there's the fire station. There's a tannery on the other side of town, and a lumber mill. We're very proud of the library though. It was built around forty years ago. There's a public park with a pond opposite it. The kids like to go boating there.'

'Where's the pictures?'

'Pictures?'

'The picture house. Cinema. Movie theatre. Whatever you call it.'

Alice shook her head. 'There isn't one. Nearest is in Kitchener. That's a good hour's drive away.'

'I know where it is,' said Joan, her heart sinking. She lived for going to the pictures. No more Errol Flynn. No more Joan Crawford. What kind of place was this and how on earth was she going to make a life here?

JIM'S STRUGGLES

THE FULL MOON hung in the sky like a pale gold coin. Jim gazed at it and thought how strange it was that he had looked up at that same moon from England and Italy. No matter what the surroundings, what terrible events were happening, the moon waxed and waned in the same indifferent way. He imagined Italian *contadini*, rebuilding their war-shattered homes, staring up at it across the world and dreaming of a time when life would be normal again. One evening, when he was stationed in the English seaside town of Eastbourne, he'd sat with his back against the sea wall, on the shingle of the beach under a full moon with the woman he had fallen in love with over two short and memorable months. Gwen. The moon they had looked up at then was something to be feared, a beacon for German bombers, lighting their path across the English Channel and illuminating their targets with precision. But there had been no bombs that night and he and Gwen had talked until after midnight when they snuck back to the house to make love until the small hours. He shivered at the memory and imagined holding her in his arms again, feeling the softness of her mouth on his.

He'd not allowed himself to think about Gwen since the war. After he'd left Eastbourne and before he sailed for Sicily, he'd committed to Joan and told himself he wouldn't think of Gwen any more.

Now he was unsure.

When he was fighting alongside men who died in the bitter and bloody combat that had characterised the Italian campaign, all the time he'd willed himself to get through it for Joan and Jimmy. But now he was no longer certain he loved Joan.

He'd always known it was a different kind of love from the one he had felt for Gwen. That had been a brief intense passion: stolen moments that they'd both known couldn't last, while until now he'd believed his love for Joan would be a lasting one. A mutual attraction of opposites. He'd been intrigued by her – uncertain where he stood, as though at any moment she might pull the rug from under him, and the very uncertainty had fuelled the attraction.

But now the doubts had come. Here in rural Canada Joan stood out like an alien being. She was a city girl, and found the countryside a hostile and foreign land. Her well-coiffed hair, bright red lipstick and English accent attracted Jim and repelled him at the same time. He couldn't deny that he found her attractive but he was constantly aware of the disapproval of his mother and the curiosity of Alice and others at her ways. It made him feel conspicuous, the likely subject of gossip and speculation and he didn't like that. In some strange way he felt ashamed of Joan and the fact that she didn't fit in – and he was ashamed of himself for feeling like that. There was something ridiculous about the way she tottered across the farmyard in high heels and nylons. He'd commented to her that more practical clothing might be more comfortable but she had looked askance and said something about keeping up standards and not letting herself go.

Ever since she'd arrived here at Hollowtree Farm, he'd felt guilty. He'd dragged her here to Canada, breaking his promise that they'd live in England, pulling her away from her family and her home. His mother had made no attempt to conceal her hostility and Joan must feel isolated and alone. And yet he couldn't bring himself to change that.

She'd been here a week and they still hadn't managed to make love. The presence of Jimmy, sleeping beside them in the other bed, the sound of his father snoring and struggling to breathe, and the awareness that his mother was lying on the other side of the thin bedroom wall possibly listening, had inhibited them both. As each day passed, the impasse between them seemed harder to breach and their isolation more permanent.

A soft breeze caressed his face and he smelled the scent of newly-mown hay. How could he ever have imagined giving the farm up? It was the only thing that helped him forget what he had witnessed in the war. No, not forget, that was impossible, but it helped keep it at bay, in the past. The nightmares that disturbed his sleep and the images that were etched on his brain every time he closed his eyes, became faded, hazy, distant when he crumbled a handful of rich loam in his hands or caught the sweet smell of fresh manure. If he were to live in England, the memory of war would be everpresent – especially in Aldershot, where Joan came from. As a garrison town, the place was full of soldiers and he would be constantly reminded of what he had seen and – worse – what he had done.

His reveries were broken by the touch of a hand on the back of his neck. Joan slipped to the ground beside him and placed her hand on his thigh. 'I wondered where you'd disappeared to,' she said. 'I woke up and you were gone.'

The night was warm and she was wearing only a thin nylon nightdress, flimsy. Like a lot of her clothes, it was inappropriate to life on a farm. His mother – and probably Alice – would have worn a long cotton gown, cool in the hot humid nights, then warmer as the air chilled, replacing it with heavy flannel as fall turned to winter. But Joan dressed as if she were in a Hollywood movie, in garments designed to enhance, to seduce. Her leg was exposed above her knee, firm but pale, washed in moonlight. With a gasp he reached for her and pulled her into his arms. As soon as their mouths met, Jim was lost. All the frustrations of the past days, weeks, years, evaporated as he kissed her, drowning himself in her. This time there was no interruption from an angry Helga.

Afterwards they lay side-be-side and hand-in-hand on the grass, looking up at the moon.

'I'm sorry,' he said, at last. 'You didn't get a great welcome when you got here.'

She squeezed his hand. 'I think you just made up for that.'

'It's been hard for my mother, you know… getting used to the way things have changed.' He hesitated a moment then decided not to tell her about Helga's hope that he would have married Alice. 'I didn't tell her about you and Jimmy until I got back here last year. It was a shock. And what with my brother dying and Pa being so sick, things have been rough for her and I guess she's taking it out on you. Give her time and she'll come round.'

Joan said nothing.

'And she already dotes on Jimmy.'

'She doesn't like me.'

'She doesn't know you. When she does, she'll love you. How could she not?'

'Because I'm not very loveable.'

'Stop fishing for compliments, Joan!' He laughed and rolled onto his side so he could see her face.

'I'm not. It's true.'

'Well, I love you.'

She considered his words for a moment then said, 'You want me. To have sex with me. But you don't love me.'

Jim propped himself on one elbow and looked down at her, frowning. 'That's crazy. Of course I love you. Why are you saying this, Joan?'

'Because I made all the running with you. You'd never have asked me out otherwise.'

Jim groaned and rolled over on to his back again. 'How many times, Joan? You were engaged to another guy. That's why I didn't chase after you. Hell, it would have been very different if you'd been available.'

She reached over and picked up her pack of cigarettes where she'd dropped them beside her when she arrived, took one out, lit it and exhaled slowly.

'I wish you wouldn't smoke,' he said, then immediately regretted saying it. She turned towards him and blew a smoke ring that sat over his head like a halo. 'It's just that round here, ladies don't usually smoke.'

'Ladies? Well that's okay, as I'm no lady. Your mother and your old girlfriend made that quite clear.' She scrambled to her feet and started to walk back towards the farmhouse.

Jim jumped up and caught her wrist, drawing her back to him. 'Don't let's quarrel. I'm sorry. It was my fault for spoiling things.' He held her close against him, feeling the swell of her buttocks through the flimsy fabric of her nightgown. 'How can you doubt how I feel about you?' He tilted her head back and bent to kiss her again, his hands moving under the nightdress as he pulled her back down onto the grass.

A FEW DAYS later Joan went into town to meet another English woman. She was eager for the meeting with the only other war bride in Hollowtree. Mary Hinton's contact details had been given to her by the Red Cross. At last, a chance to develop a friendship, to share experiences, compare notes. Even though she'd had little in common with Sandra, her travelling companion, these past days Joan would have given anything to have still had Sandra to talk to. All she wanted was someone who would understand what she was going through. So she vested this Mary Hinton with all her hopes as she pedalled into town to meet her in the café.

As soon as Joan entered the room and saw Mrs Hinton sitting in one of the booths, she knew a friendship was unlikely to develop between them. The woman looked several years older than her and had a stern demeanour. She was wearing the drabbest clothes Joan had ever seen and didn't offer up so much as a smile when Joan approached. But determined to look for the best in the woman, she smiled brightly and sat down opposite.

'I'm having tea. What about you?'

'Nothing for me.'

Already feeling deflated, Joan ordered a cup of tea for herself.

The conversation was one-sided. Joan described the circumstances of her own recent arrival and asked Mary Hinton about her story.

'I came to Canada ahead of my husband, while the war was still on.'

Joan was surprised. 'Gosh, that must have been hard.'

The woman shrugged. 'Depends what you're leaving behind. I was glad to get away from the bombing.'

'But it must have been difficult for you, being apart from your husband and in a strange country? Were you staying with his family?'

'Yes.'

Joan sipped her tea and wondered what she would have to do to get the woman to open up. 'Do you and your husband still live with his parents?'

'I do. He's dead.'

Joan gasped. 'Your husband's dead? I'm so sorry.'

Mrs Hinton shrugged again, as though losing a husband was akin to misplacing an umbrella. 'Killed in Germany just before V.E. Day.'

'That's terrible, Mrs Hinton. 'What a tragedy. Are you going back to England?'

'Nothing for me back there. I've no family.'

'I see. So you've decided to stay on with your late husband's family?'

'Yes.'

Joan took another slurp of tea and wondered how much longer she would have stay, to avoid looking rude. 'Do you like Hollowtree? Is there much to do here?'

'I like it well enough. My husband's father is a minister in the chapel next to the printing works. I work to support his ministry.'

'It must be good to feel useful, to be able to muck in with your in-laws and help out like that.'

'The Lord giveth and he taketh away. I am proud to be able to serve him. You a church-going woman?'

Joan said she wasn't.'

'Never too late to find a home in the Lord.' She shuffled in a carrier bag and pulled out a pamphlet. 'Take this. Read it.'

She leaned towards Joan and quoted, *'All we like sheep have gone astray; we have turned every one to his own way; and the Lord has laid on him the iniquity of us all.'*

Joan shuffled uncomfortably in her seat.

'Services are listed on the back.'

The woman got up from the table and put her bag over her arm. 'Hope to see you at service then.'

As her thin, badly dressed, lisle-stockinged figure left the café, Joan knew there was no chance of that happening.

Her hopes of finding a friend and confidante dashed, she paid the bill and headed for home.

A FEW DAYS LATER, the Armstrong family were gathered around the kitchen table for the evening meal. Jim had spent the afternoon clearing weeds ready to plant potatoes for the winter. He'd tried to encourage Joan to spend some time with his mother, or to go with Alice into Hollowtree, but she insisted she wanted to be with him. She'd sat atop the fence for a while, then, after studying what he'd been doing, she'd jumped down and knelt beside him, pulling weeds. Jim had found it distracting. Instead of knuckling down to the task in hand, she would weed for a while then, bored, would try to draw him into conversation. Jim was irritated. He had lots to do and needed to get on with it. Eventually Joan had given up and wandered off to look for Jimmy, irritated that Jim was unwilling to play along. For the rest of the afternoon he had brooded. Why couldn't she settle down and at least have a go at adapting to the life of a farmer's wife? She seemed to have no conception of the importance of running the farm, of getting it back from the brink of ruin. He knew she was missing her family but dammit all, why couldn't she make more effort?

Now at the table he looked at her but she avoided his eyes. Her face and neck were red from the sun, but she looked listless, playing with her food rather than eating. She was painfully thin from the years of rationing and Jim hoped she would benefit from all the farm produce and home cooking that his mother served up, but she had yet to show much appetite. As he ate his own supper he wished she could find her spark again. The previous night when they'd made love out in the meadow, she was the old Joan, but his rebuff today had sent her back into a picture of misery.

At least Jimmy was adapting well to life in Ontario. Spoilt by his grandmother, already shyly making friends with Rose and clearly hero-worshipping his newly acquired father, he was lively, tanned and healthy.

Jim's reveries were interrupted by Alice.

'You'll never guess who I met in town this afternoon when I was picking Rose up?' Alice looked around the table at the faces turned towards her in anticipation.

'Well, spit it out then, girl.' Helga helped herself to another piece of meat loaf.

'Tip Howardson. Back at last from the war. And quite the hero.'

Jim put down his fork and glanced at Joan, who appeared not to be listening.

Alice looked over at Joan and added. 'Sorry, Joan. Local gossip. Tip was at school with us. In the same class as Walt and me. In the same regiment as Jim and Walt but no one had heard from him in years. Not even his folks.'

Joan's voice was shaky. 'Will you excuse me. I feel a bit unwell. I'm going to lie down. I'm sorry.'

Helga raised one eyebrow and and rolled her eyes at Alice.

Jim looked at Joan in surprise, then said, 'You all right?'

'I'll be fine. Don't worry. I think I caught too much sun this afternoon.'

When Joan had left the room, Jim turned his attention back to Alice. 'What did that lying son of a bitch have to say for himself?'

'Jim Armstrong. There'll be no talk like that at my table.' Helga's tone was angry. 'I don't care what you think of Tip, I won't stand for that kind of language. And especially not in front of the children.'

Jimmy and Rose were tucking into the meatloaf, oblivious to what was being said.

Alice passed Jim a bowl of carrots. 'I had quite a talk with him. He wanted to offer his condolences about Walt. Said he'd left the regiment before Walt was killed. Told me he was sent on a special secret mission undercover behind enemy lines.'

Jim almost choked on his food.

'He was working in France with the resistance. He was picked out specially and no one in the regiment knew about his mission. Nearly got killed several times.' She paused and added in an undertone so that Jimmy and Rose wouldn't hear, 'He didn't say so in so many words but I got the distinct impression he was caught by the Nazis and tortured. He's lucky to be alive.'

'Don't listen to a word that bas... that man says. He's a liar and a lowlife.' Jim pushed his plate away, his appetite gone.

'What's got into you, son? Tip's always always been a lazy devil, and not much help to his father on the farm, but he's from a good family and I won't have you speaking about him that way.' Helga was frowning. 'That man has served his country. One of the first to volunteer and the Howardsons have always been good neighbours.'

Don banged his fist on the table. 'If Jim is speaking ill of him there has to be a reason. What you got against the man? Tell us or hold your peace.'

Jim hesitated, reluctant to revisit what had been a painful time for him, then said, 'He caused the death of my best friend. He picked a fight with me. Took a bottle to my face. How do you think I got this scar? It wasn't from the Germans.' He closed his eyes for a moment. 'My pal, Greg Hooper, came to my defence and Howardson laid him out with one almighty punch to the head. I was in the infirmary for a week but Greg fell down and never got up again.'

Helga gasped. 'Tip killed him?'

Jim told them that Greg had sustained a brain haemorrhage, due to a congenital defect. 'After Greg's death, Howardson was court-martialed and dishonourably discharged. As well as causing the brawl he was mixed up in other stuff. Everyone hated Howardson. Everyone. All sorts of stories came out. He was running a black market racket and there was talk that he'd got a girl pregnant. They shipped him back to Canada.'

'When was this?'

'Back in 1941. Aldershot camp.'

'So where's he been all this time?' Alice sounded disbelieving.

'Must have scuttled away somewhere where no one knew him – but it certainly wasn't behind the lines fighting with the French Resistance.'

'Why would he lie? Invent stuff like that?'

'Because he doesn't want anyone here to know what kind of snake he is.'

Alice looked dubious. 'He seemed to have a very convincing story. I can't believe he'd just make all that up.'

'So you're saying *I'm* making it up?' Jim narrowed his eyes as he looked at Alice, struggling to accept she preferred to believe Tip.

'I'm sure there has to be some explanation.'

Jim scraped back his chair and got up from the table. 'Greg, the man who died, was engaged to marry Joan's cousin, Ethel. I didn't realise Joan knew Tip's name.' He jerked his head towards the door to the stairs. 'But it looks like she did.' He left the room to follow his wife upstairs.

In the bedroom he found her lying curled up on the bed. 'You know who Tip Howardson is then? I didn't realise you and Ethel knew the name of the man who was responsible for Greg's death. I'm sorry, Joan.'

She swivelled round and sat up, looking at him in horror. 'I didn't know.'

Jim swallowed, a bitter taste in his mouth. 'So why did you leave the table?'

'I told you. I think I have a touch of sunstroke. I was sitting on the fence watching you working most of the afternoon.'

'You need to wear a hat in this weather.' He stroked her hair, feeling the dampness of it, then bent over her and kissed her tenderly on the forehead. She leaned against him and he cradled her, stroking her hair and dropping little kisses on her head. 'My poor Joan. My lovely English rose. We're going to have to take more care of you.'

She leaned against him, as he continued to soothe her. After a minute or two she said, 'So the man who killed Greg lives near here? Why didn't you tell me that before?'

'Because until tonight I had no idea he was here. No one's seen him since he was dishonourably discharged after what happened to Greg. Like everyone in town I presumed he'd slunk away somewhere where no one would know him. Over the border probably. I certainly didn't expect him to show his face round here again.'

'But they told Ethel Greg died because he had an abnormally thin skull. That he could have died any time.'

'That was true. The doc told me it could have happened playing a ball game. He was unlucky. But it was Howardson who knocked him out. It was Howardson who got Greg confined to barracks the night of his engagement party. It was Howardson who caused Greg and I to spend a night in the local police station when we were trying to break up a fight in the town. The man is a complete bastard. All sorts of other things came out at the court martial. And to think the son of a bitch tried to convince Alice he's some kind of bloody war hero.'

Joan turned her head and said, 'We've talked enough about him. I hope I never get to run into him or I don't know what I might do to him for ruining our Ethel's life.'

Jim bent over her and kissed her slowly.

'Now I'm feeling better, Doctor Armstrong, so how about I get that son of ours to bed and you can take me skinny-dipping in that pool you were telling me about?'

'You got a date.' He pulled her into another kiss.

SWIMMING

JOAN LOVED TO SWIM. In Aldershot she'd been a regular visitor to the bathing pool that opened about ten years before the war. She and Ethel would often spend whole Sundays there, lying on the lawns that surrounded the water, bringing a picnic and swimming lazily around the large V-shaped pool or diving off the spring board, avoiding the small boys who dive-bombed off the high board.

Before the war, Pete, the boy she became engaged to, and Ethel's brother John, would join them and now she thought back fondly to those sunny afternoons sitting on the rim of the circular fountain in the middle of the pool, flirting and chatting with Pete. Poor Pete. Killed in the African desert with the Eighth Army, fighting Rommel. She wondered what she'd be doing now if he hadn't died. How would he have reacted to the discovery that she'd had a child with a Canadian soldier? But she knew the answer. He'd have been hurt but he'd have forgiven her and married her anyway. He'd have treated Jimmy as though he were his own. Joan could do no wrong where Pete had been concerned. He would have crawled on his hands and knees all the way back from El Alamein if she'd asked him.

But even that would never have made her love him. Not after she'd laid eyes on Jim.

The following day, lying alone beside the natural pool in the creek that ran along the edge of Hollowtree farm, Joan was overwhelmed by sadness and nostalgia. They had won the war but they had lost a whole world, a whole way of life and so many fine men. Pete would have been a good husband. He'd have provided for her and Jimmy – he'd been a shift supervisor in a local factory. Maybe they'd have had more children. She tried to picture her life as it might have been, but the more she did, the more she realised that regardless of being uprooted from home, cold-shouldered by Jim's mother and in unfamiliar and somewhat primitive surroundings, she wouldn't swap. A mere touch from Jim sent shivers all over her and she ached for him so much that it hurt. She wished she could be sure he felt that way about her.

Lying by the pool, thinking about how she and and Jim had made love there the previous night, she began to feel drowsy from the heat of the sun and was starting to drift off, when water hit her face and upper body, sending shockwaves through her, so cold, it burned. Blinded, she wiped water from her eyes and scrambled to her feet, heart pounding.

Peals of laughter erupted. Alice. Holding a metal bucket in her hands.

'Sorry. Couldn't resist. It's a family tradition. Consider yourself initiated.'

She sat down on the ground beside Joan and began to peel off her clothes. Underneath, she was wearing a swimsuit that showed off every curve and made Joan embarrassed by her own baggy pre-war costume. Alice got to her feet and walked to the edge of the pool, jumping with an exaggerated splash into the water.

When she surfaced she called to Joan. 'Come and join me! Water's lovely. Or can't you swim?'

Furious, but determined not to let Alice get the better of her, Joan ran to the edge of the pool and executed a perfect dive into the water. 'Like a fish,' she said. Then she climbed out, grabbed her discarded clothes, flung a towel around herself and headed back to the house.

It wasn't quite three o'clock and Joan decided to go into town – a chance to explore it alone without following Alice's agenda. She wheeled her bicycle out of the barn, then leant it against the picket fence and went back to the kitchen. Helga was baking at the table, with Jimmy perched on a chair beside her watching the process in fascination.

'We're going into town, Jimmy. Come on.'

Jimmy groaned. 'I want to stay with Gramma. She says I can put the jam in the tarts.'

'You can do that another time. You're coming with Mummy this afternoon.'

'Let the boy be,' said Helga. 'He's no bother.'

'I didn't say he was. I happen to want to spend some time with my son.' She narrowed her eyes at her mother-in-law and held her hand out for Jimmy's.

Sensing his mother was in no mood for argument, Jimmy put his hand in hers and let her lead him out of the house.

Pedalling along with Jimmy safe in his newly fitted seat behind her, Joan felt liberated. The afternoon was warm but not oppressive – there was a slight breeze and the air was fresh. She'd had enough of being bullied and sidelined. Alice was always superficially friendly but Joan decided she was sly and resentful under the cheery exterior. The bucket of water, presented as a friendly joke and a family ritual, was a mean trick and Joan rejoiced that no one could get the better of her in a swimming pool. It was no fancy lido, like the bathing pool in Aldershot, but the experience of swimming in the wild outdoors, especially swimming naked with Jim the night before, was superior. As for Helga – if she thought she could appropriate Jimmy for her own and alienate him from his mother she'd have another think coming. She felt Jimmy's little hands around her waist, his fingers clutching onto her and his head against her back. She began to sing *Don't Sit Under the Apple Tree* and was gratified to hear Jimmy giggling and humming along with her. Life here wasn't so bad after all.

Without the need to keep up with Alice, she could pedal along at her own pace and this time was able to enjoy the scenery between the farm and the small town that bore the same name. For the most part it was farmland and she realised that a lot of it was probably part of Hollowtree Farm. It dawned on her the enormity of the task Jim had to get the place under control again, with no help. She couldn't help worrying about him. In their narrow bed at night he often thrashed around in his sleep in the grip of terrifying nightmares. They happened almost every night and Joan was uncertain how to react to them. She had tried broaching the subject only for Jim to close down, revert to silence and absent himself. Whatever it was he didn't want to confront it or talk about it. Instead, she held him in her arms, her hand over his heart while he slept, waiting for the beats to calm.

In the town, Joan left her bicycle against the railings by the public library and, holding Jimmy's hand, led him into the little park opposite. There was a large lake, fed by the river that passed through the town. Two small canoes were on the water, two boys inside them, paddling back and forth.

'Mummy, Mummy. Look at that!' Jimmy rushed down to

the water's edge, watching in fascination as the boys raced each other across the width of the pond. Joan wondered why they were not in school then remembered that it was the summer holidays.

One of the boys steered his canoe towards the bank where they were standing.

'You want a ride?' The kid, who looked about thirteen and had an unruly shock of red hair, was addressing Jimmy.

The little boy jumped up and down in delight. 'Yes, please!' He turned to Joan. 'Please, Mummy! Do let me!'

Joan reached for her son's hand. 'No, Jimmy. Those are big boys. When you're a big boy you can have a ride in a canoe.'

'I *am* a big boy. Daddy says I'm a big boy. Not fair.'

Cursing her stupidity for bringing him to the lake, she took him by the hand and dragged him back towards the bicycle. By now Jimmy was wailing. She squatted down beside him and tried to dry his eyes with a handkerchief. 'When you're a little bit older, Jimmy. You're too small right now.'

Jimmy jerked his head away. Thrusting his lower lip out, he said, 'I hate you. You're mean. I like Daddy and Gramma and Aunty Alice better.'

Shocked and cut to the core, Joan got to her feet, picked her son up and wedged him, howling, into the bicycle seat. She pedalled away from the town, her eyes blinded by tears of hurt and anger. After a mile or so, Jimmy's wailing had subsided into sobs and she slowed down. Wiping her arm across her own eyes she pulled over to the side of the road.

'I'm only doing it because I love you, Jimmy. I couldn't bear it if anything happened to you.'

The only response from behind her was more muffled sobbing.

'Tell you what, when we get back I'll take you for a swim

in the pool on the farm. I can hold you up in the water and show you how to swim.'

'Don't want to swim. Want boat.' More sobs.

Stifling her irritation she said, 'Little boys aren't allowed to go in a canoe until they know how to swim.'

'Who says?'

'It's the law. If Mummy let you get in a canoe without knowing how to swim the policeman would put me in jail.' She hated lying but anything to stop him blubbing. She didn't want to return to the farm with a crying child for Helga to tut over and Alice to offer child-rearing advice.

Handing Jimmy a sweetie, she said, 'How about it, pal? Shall Mummy give you a swimming lesson?'

'All right,' he said, sucking on the candy, pacified.

WHEN THEY RETURNED to the farm, Helga flung her arms around her grandson as though she had been fearing for his life.

Joan moved across to the door leading upstairs then, hand on the knob, turned back to face her mother-in-law. 'Mrs Armstrong, we need to talk.'

Alice who was sitting at the table, helping her daughter with her reading, looked up.

Helga was bent over the boy, smoothing down his ruffled hair. 'Talk away. No one's stopping you.'

'In private.' Joan was determined not to give way.

Sighing deeply, Helga pulled off her apron and headed for the door. 'We can talk outside then.'

Joan followed her out of the house. Helga crossed the farmyard and stood leaning against the pasture fence, her elbows supporting her. 'Well?'

'I think we got off on the wrong foot, but it's time to make our peace.' Joan swallowed and felt herself shaking.

Helga looked at her steadily but said nothing.

Joan played with her right earring, twisting it around as she tried to conquer her nerves. 'We both love Jim,' she said at last. 'At least we have that much in common.' She paused trying to read something in the woman's face, but Helga remained inscrutable. 'Jimmy too. That's clear.'

Helga's eyes stared back at her, blank.

'It's not easy for me. Coming here to a strange country to a completely different life from the one I'm used to. But I did it because I love your son. I did it in spite of the fact that he promised when we married that we would live in England. I've left my family behind. My mum was devastated. Can you imagine how that feels?'

'Can I *imagine*? I don't need to imagine. My younger son is lying dead in a grave somewhere in England. At least you're alive. At least *your* mother can read your letters. So don't you talk to me about what it's like to be parted from your family. Don't you dare.' She pushed herself off the fence and walked back to the house, leaving a stupefied Joan.

Joan leaned against the fencing, shaking. What more could she do? Why was the woman so hostile? Should she speak to Jim? Did he know? Did he care? Her eyes brimmed with tears and she bit her lip but the woman was not going to get the better of her. A wave of longing to be home in Aldershot swept over her and she gave an involuntary sob.

She felt a hand on her back and turned. It was Don. He took a pipe out of his pocket and lit it, drawing on it in between coughing.

'Don't say a word. I know I shouldn't smoke but I've few enough pleasures and if it knocks a few more hours off my time so be it.' He took the pipe from his mouth and nursed it as if the act of holding it was as pleasurable as smoking it.

Joan took out her handkerchief and blew her nose, hoping he hadn't seen that she was on the verge of tears. She pulled her cigarettes out of her pocket and took one out. Don lit it for her and she drew on the tobacco, feeling its calming effect.

'Don't mind her. She'll come round in the end.'

Unable to take it any more she said, 'I don't know what I've done for her to hate me so much.'

'She doesn't hate you. She's testing you. Has it in her head that you're going to break Jim's heart so she's trying to push you. If you leave him to go back to England it'll be sooner rather than later.'

Joan gasped. 'What?'

'Twisted logic, I know. She doesn't think you're cut out to be a farmer's wife and the sooner you realise that the better. I don't happen to agree with her. What do you think?'

Joan looked at him in astonishment. 'I can't believe what you're telling me. She's trying to drive me away? She wants me to go back to England?'

Don started to cough. Joan watched him anxiously as she waited for him to reply.

'She doesn't *want* you to' he said at last. 'She thinks you're going to, and reckons it'll be as well to get it over and done with.'

'Why should I leave him? I love him!'

'I know that and you know that. But Helga thinks she knows better. She knows what it's like to have a husband back from a war. When I fought in the last war she was left here with two small children. The war years were hard for her. You know she was born in Germany? Her family moved here when she was a girl. People round here didn't take too well to anything or anyone German. She's worked hard to lose her accent but even though folk knew she was married to me and I was fighting against the Hun it still didn't sit well with some people. Things were tough for her and then when

I got back it was hard coping with me. She knows you and Jim are going through that now.'

'What do you mean? What are we supposed to be going through?' She tried to keep the irritation from her voice. Don was the only person, apart from Jim, she felt was on her side.

'War does terrible things to a man. Shell shock, we used to call it. It was a long time after I got back before I had a decent night's sleep, before I stopped having nightmares, feeling guilty for being alive when so many others weren't. Jim's going through something similar.'

Joan knew he was right. In the early hours of the morning she'd been woken when Jim, in his sleep, began thrashing his legs up and down in the bed and rolling from side to side.

'Battle fatigue, they call it now. And survivor guilt. That's what Jim's going through. I spent years feeling angry, wanting to lash out at anyone I reckoned was in my way or might get in it.'

'But Jim isn't like that.' Joan wanted to defend him.

'It's like balancing on a knife edge. Slightest thing can tip you over. To tell you the truth, Joan, he's been better since you've been around. Maybe that's worrying Helga too. She's scared he's going to slide downhill once you're gone.'

Joan's mouth was open. 'I can't believe what you're saying. She's scared if I leave he'll be in a bad way, so she's trying to get me to leave?'

'I told you it was twisted logic. She just wants to get it over with. So he can get on with his life. And then…'

'And then what?'

'Nothing.'

'Come on, Don, you were going to tell me something else.'

He stuffed the now dead pipe between his lips and looked into the distance. Speaking out of the side of his mouth, he said, 'She'd harboured the hope that he'd eventually marry

Alice. You know they were to be married until my younger son stole her from under his nose.'

Joan felt cold, despite the warmth of the afternoon. 'I knew they'd been engaged. I knew she'd ditched him for his brother.'

'Jim made it clear the moment he got back from the war that he was married to you and that was how it was going to stay.'

Joan shivered, suddenly afraid.

'I shouldn't have told you. Me and my big mouth.'

'I'm glad you did,' she said. 'It explains a lot. Thank you.'

Don turned to look at her. His rheumy eyes were sincere. 'My son loves you. Who can blame him? And to be honest, Alice and Walt were much better suited. Jim and Alice – nah. No matter what Helga might think. I know my son.'

Joan put her hand on his. 'Thanks for being so kind to me, Don.'

He lifted her hand and squeezed it in his, then turned away as a long overdue fit of coughing took over.

LAND GIRL

EVERY MORNING, Jim rose before five. The custom of the inhabitants of Hollowtree Farm was to retire early as well. For Joan this was a revelation and not a pleasant one. She thought with nostalgia of her old life in Aldershot. In the days when she'd served in the fish and chip shop her hours were semi nocturnal – the busiest part of the day being when the pubs closed. Afterwards, her time in the ATS had brought army discipline into her life. It had felt like torture but compared with the hours kept on a Canadian farm it had been cushy. In the army, everyone had seized any available opportunity to go to the pictures or the pub. Here, not only was there no cinema within miles, women weren't even allowed in pubs. Not that you could call the hotel beverage room a pub. She'd peered through the grimy windows to see a dreary space, devoid of any decoration or furniture apart from a few wooden chairs, more like a bus depot waiting room than a place to share a convivial drink with friends. Jim had explained that until 1927 alcohol was under prohibition in Ontario and since its limited legalisation its sale was strictly controlled through hotels' beverage rooms, which were made deliberately unwelcoming institutions. No wonder the Canadians had made the most of the pubs of Aldershot.

By now the corn had grown so high it reached over Joan's head. She walked along the rows between the tall maize plants, lost in the lines of vegetation, only the sky above her. The corn stalks were brown, the leaves shrivelled and dried in the sun, the weight of the plump ripened cobs weighing them down. Joan liked to walk through the fields, invisible to anyone, alone. Lonely. It was hard not to give way to the overwhelming homesickness that often beset her. How different her life would be if she had Ethel or her mother close by. Someone to turn to, someone to raise her spirits when she felt low. That was what her husband was meant to do, but Jim was preoccupied, working hard to turn the farm around and to run crying to him would only make things harder for him when all she wanted to do was offer support.

She sat on the ground, hidden away between the tall stalks and reached into her pocket, pulling out an envelope and her cigarettes. The letter was postmarked Vancouver and must be from Sandra, her friend from the voyage. Joan lit a cigarette and began to read it, her heart sinking. Sandra was going back to England. All her opportunistic banter on the journey, her confidence in her ability to adapt to life in Canada, had dissipated. After three weeks she had found her husband in the back seat of a motorcar he had been supposed to be mending. The car's owner, an attractive blonde, had been in there with him, under him in fact. Sandra had forgiven him, only to find lipstick on the collar of his overalls a few weeks later. Her patience having run out, she was going back to Britain. "I've had it up to here with his lies," she wrote. "Can't wait to get home. First stop, the eel and pie shop for a nice supper. London here I come!"

Joan stuffed the letter back into her pocket and lay back

on the ground, looking up at the blue sky above. It was hard not to envy Sandra. The thought of the long voyage home wasn't appealing – and so much worse for Sandra, facing that long train journey across Canada, this time alone with no kind Red Cross ladies to guide her and no soldiers to carry her luggage. But to go home. To be back in England, back with her family, back in familiar surroundings. Listening to Workers' Playtime on the BBC, going to the flicks on a Saturday while her mum babysat for Jimmy, going for a port and lemon in the Stag with Ethel afterwards. Yes, Joan envied Sandra all that. But it would be without Jim. That made it unthinkable. She hadn't caught him having it off in the back of a car with another woman and was never going to. She was certain of that.

With Helga continuing to cold shoulder her, Joan lacked any tasks to do around the house and the farm. The farm-house was cramped and her mother-in-law made it clear that the kitchen was her domain, so Joan was bored, lonely and increasingly depressed. Every offer of help was either ignored or rebuffed. She had never felt so useless. Her only pleasure was time spent with Jimmy and the brief time she was able to spend with Jim. In their cramped bedroom, in the confines of a narrow bed, with the presence of a sleeping child in the room and the knowledge that her in-laws were on the other side of a thin partition wall, love making was mostly non-existent, as she felt inhibited and tense. Jim for his part was tired, this being the most demanding time of year for a farmer, particularly one struggling to keep the farm going with no help. Joan constantly offered to help him, but he brushed away the offer, telling her that by the time he had shown her what to do he could have done the job himself. She didn't believe him, but was unwilling to confront him and risk alienating him as well his mother, so low had her self-confidence plummeted.

She spent as much time as she could with Jimmy, conscious of the fact that she would be losing him to school before too long. But she had to battle with Helga for Jimmy's attention. His grandmother lured him into her kitchen with the prospect of licking the spoon and scraping the bowl when she made cakes, into the barn, where she let him help her churning butter and collecting eggs, or into town, which she always visited using a horse and cart. Joan had yet to be asked to accompany her on these occasional trips. Rose was another distraction for the boy, sharing her toys with him and showing off her skills at horse riding. Alice had offered to teach to him to ride – a promise that had Jimmy jumping up and down in delight and one which made Joan despair of ever seeing her son at all. And then there was Jim. The little boy was in raptures whenever his father let him ride on the hay wagon or watch him working.

Remembering her own promise to teach him to swim, Joan told Jimmy they would have their first lesson the following afternoon – only for the child to complain that he had a tummy ache. Days passed and, with all the competing pleasures awaiting the small boy, somehow they never got round to it.

Alice and Rose returned from the town one afternoon carrying a puppy nestled in a straw basket. They brought it into the kitchen when the family gathered for supper, and formally presented the dog to Jim.

'I know how much you must miss Swee' Pea,' said Alice. 'When I saw this little creature I just knew she was made for you, Jim.'

Before Jim could say anything, Jimmy had jumped down from the table and was crouching down beside the little dog, squealing in joy. 'Daddy, Daddy! We've got a doggie! Look, look! Oh please can we keep it?'

Jim laughed. 'Course we can. I've had a mind to get

another dog ever since I came home. The place isn't the same without a dog. Thank you, Alice, for thinking of me.' He squatted down beside his son and picked the puppy up and looked at it closely. 'A fine beast,' he declared, putting the animal down again. 'Now we need to find a name.'

'Let's call him Popeye, Daddy. Popeye the Sailor Man!'

Jim grinned and shook his head. 'He's a she, Jimmy.'

'And I thought I was Popeye,' said Don.

'No, just Pop. And you don't like spinach.'

'Do you like it, Jimmy?' His grandfather leaned forward in his chair.

'Ugh. No! I hate spinach.'

'But that's what made Popeye strong.'

'Popeye's not real.' Jimmy folded his hands over his chest in defiance.

'So what shall we call her?' Jim picked up the puppy again and handed her to his son.

'She can be Olive Oyl.'

His grandmother shook her head. 'I'm not calling a dog Olive Oyl. Even if she does eat all her spinach. Olive will have to do for me.'

Dogs don't eat spinach.'

'What do they eat then?'

'Meat.'

'In that case shall we give him your dinner or are you going to eat it all up?' Helga Armstrong picked Jimmy's plate up from the table and waved it over the puppy's head.

Jimmy looked ruefully at the dog then scrambled back into his seat.

'I can't thank you enough, Alice.' Jim flashed a grin at Alice as he sat back down at the table. Joan watched as Alice simpered and felt a sudden urge to slap her self-satisfied face.

Seeing the way the whole family had been overjoyed at the arrival of Olive the dog made Joan feel more isolated. She had never had a dog. They made her nervous. Damn Alice. How could she compete?

THE NEW TRACTOR HAD ARRIVED. Its advent was timely – the corn was ready for harvesting. Jim rigged it up to the corn picker as Joan, Jimmy and his father watched.

'I still reckon you'd be better off using the horse.' Don's grin showed he didn't really mean the words.

'The tractor can do much more than a horse. This will have paid back every penny we've spent on it by this time next year.'

Joan watched, fascinated, as the tractor took off, Jim riding on top and the corn picker rigged behind it. He progressed steadily down the first row of corn, the picker threshing the tall dried stems and moving them up a conveyor belt into a husker which separated the ears of corn from the brown stems. Chaff and dust flew out behind and the engine roared, the smell of gasoline heavy in the air. Jim moved back down the next row as the pile of ripe corn cobs grew higher in the trailer behind.

When he reached the bottom he called out to Jimmy. 'Want to ride up top with your daddy?'

Jimmy ran towards the tractor, the new puppy running along behind him.

'Wait!' Joan screeched. 'I don't think he should be up there with you. He's too young. It's dangerous.'

"Don't coddle him.' Jim was laughing at her. 'He's a farm boy. Needs to get used to be being around machinery. I'll make sure he's safe.'

Joan felt wretched and looked at Don, who nodded in agreement with his son. Jim stopped the tractor, climbed down and hoisted Jimmy up to the platform, then took up his place again, this time with his son on his knee.

'He's right,' said Don. 'Kids grow up fast on a farm. It's a mother's instinct to protect her child but the lad has to toughen up. And he's keen to learn.'

'He's only three!' Joan wailed.

She looked up as the tractor passed and knew she had lost the battle as a delighted Jimmy waved to her. 'Look after Olive, Mummy!'

His laughter rang out over the thrum of the tractor and the hum of the conveyor belt. It was hard to take a stand against his undoubted happiness. The child was loving every minute of his life on the farm. Compared to this, Aldershot had little to offer. All the more important that she found a role for herself and a way to come to terms with this very different way of life. She lit a cigarette and walked away. The dog could look out for itself.

She headed for the creek and followed it down to the pool where she sat under the tree. She felt something wet and rough against her ankle and saw that Olive Oyl was happily licking her skin. Joan jerked her leg away. 'Go away,' she said. 'I don't want you. I don't like dogs.'

The dog sensed her rejection and backed off, curling into a ball and settling a few feet away from her.

Joan finished her cigarette and thought through her dilemma. After throwing the problem round her head and working her way through several more cigarettes, she made two decisions. First of all, she would quit the smoking. Down to her last pack from the carton she had bought on the ship, it wasn't right to expect Jim to fund her habit when he didn't smoke himself and clearly disliked it. She was also sick of the silent disapproval she sensed from Helga every time she lit up. Part of her wanted to continue in defiance, but it was not helping her cause. Like it or not, unlike the situation back in England where virtually everyone she knew smoked, here in Hollowtree it was seen as something only done by men. Her second decision was to persuade Jim to let her help him on the farm. Why not learn to drive the tractor, to operate the corn picker? She could start by getting out and doing some of the weeding that was needed. There was a new machine on order that would take on that task, but in the meantime there was no reason she couldn't get out there with a hoe and get rid of the worst of the weeds. Tomorrow she would go into town and buy some stout boots. A pair of farm overalls too. The clothing she had brought with her consisted mainly of a few flimsy dresses, a couple of blouses and one pair of trousers. With rationing there had been little opportunity to replenish her wardrobe – she had used her coupons on fabric to make maternity clothes when pregnant with Jimmy. And of course there were the years when she had been in uniform. But she'd always prided herself in looking her best. It was hard to see how she'd manage that now in attire more suited to a land girl.

Jim wouldn't like it. He'd made it clear that he didn't think she was cut out to work in the fields. He'd never explained why – whether he didn't like to think of his wife labouring beside him, or whether he believed her too frail or incapable. But her mind was made up. She couldn't go on watching him day after day, flogging himself to death doing the work of three or more men. And she was worried about his restlessness at night. In his sleep he thrashed about, kicking the sheets off the bed, sometimes emitting strange noises, covering his head in his hands as though protecting himself from an explosion or gunfire. Sometimes he shouted out loud. It wasn't always possible to make out the words, but it sounded as though he was giving orders.

Joan wished he would talk to her about the war and what he had gone through in Italy, but he was obdurate. It's over. No point in dwelling on what's in the past, he would say. All she knew was that he had been in the midst of hard fighting, sometimes hand to hand combat, and had seen action on the Adriatic coast, in the Liri Valley below Monte Cassino, across the Apennines and eventually in the drenched fields and dykes of the Po Valley. He had been promoted to Lance Corporal when he left Britain for Italy in 1943, after three years service, and left Italy as a Corporal. This rise through the ranks had given him no apparent pride or satisfaction. Joan suspected that he saw it as having been achieved at too high a price.

Looking up, she saw the shadows were lengthening and as she drew up her legs and got to her feet, the puppy sprang into life and ran around her ankles yapping happily. She bent down and ran her hands over the dog's back, feeling the soft springy fur of her coat.

'What do you want, you silly dog?' she said at last. 'Are you asking me to be friends?'

The little dog wagged her tail and ran around Joan in excited circles. Joan stretched out her hand and the puppy sniffed it then brushed against her leg. 'All right, Olive, you win. Friends it is.'

SLEEPING ARRANGEMENTS

THE BARN DOOR BANGED. Helga looked up then her face fell when she saw the anger on Jim's face. She stopped churning the butter and told Jimmy to go and play outside in the sunshine while she talked to his father.

'It's got to stop.' Jim stood in front of his mother, his arms folded. 'What the hell are you playing at, Ma? Trying to ruin my marriage?'

'I don't know what you're talking about.' She pursed her lips and looked defiant.

'You know damn well what I'm talking about. You've been behaving like a bully to Joan. Pushing her to the limits.'

Helga stood square to him, her hands on her hips. 'She's been complaining then?'

'No, she hasn't. She's not said a word. But I can see how unhappy she is. I thought it was homesickness but Pa told me this morning what your stupid game is. He reckons you want her to go back to England. Says you think it'll happen sooner or later anyway so you're trying to make it sooner.'

His mother said nothing for a while. Then she sat down on a hay bale. 'You'll thank me for it in the end, son. I promise you. She's not the one for you. She's a foreigner and a city girl.'

'And what on earth are you?'

'I've lived here for forty years now. I'm a Canadian.'

'How would you have felt forty years ago if someone had treated you the way you've treated my wife? You call her foreign. You couldn't even speak English when you first got here.'

'That means I know what it's like to be an outsider. Don't you get that, Jim? People used to spit at me in the street back in the first war because I was German. I know how hard it is. And that woman hasn't the backbone to stand up to it.'

Jim was boiling with rage. 'She's stood up to you, hasn't she? And she's English. We fought on the same side.'

'Look, soon as we get the first flurries of snow she's going to want out of here. Once she's had to fight her way through snowdrifts to get to the biffy. When she's had her first experience of a whole winter below freezing. Isn't it better that she realises that now?'

'Who the hell are you to decide what's right for my family?'

'Language, Jim.'

He leaned over her and yelled. 'I don't give a damn about language. She's my wife. She's the mother of my son and she isn't going anywhere.'

Helga was unmoved. 'You barely know her. That's the trouble with these wartime marriages. They're five minute wonders. The decisions you make in the heat of a war, when everyone thinks they might die tomorrow – that's no basis for a marriage. And in her case, she has the morals of an alley cat.'

Jim jerked her towards him by the arm. 'We've already been though this, Ma. I told you then and I'll tell you again, Joan is my wife and if I had to marry her all over again I'd do so. Your behaviour is not going to drive her away. Not unless we both go. In fact that may not be such a bad idea. Where she goes, I go. And where we both go, Jimmy goes too. Do you really want to drive us all away.'

'Helga's voice was almost a wail. 'But I'm only thinking of you, Jim. I'm trying to protect you.'

He dropped her arm. 'I'm not a five-year-old. I don't need protecting from anyone – except possibly from you. Right now the idea of being on the other side of the world from you has a great appeal.'

The door opened and a shaft of sunlight crossed the interior of the barn. Don Armstrong stood silhouetted in the space then moved into the gloomy interior. 'I told you I'd deal with her, Jim. Now both of you shut it before words are said that can't be unsaid.'

'But–' Helga was red in the face.

'No one's going anywhere. I've not waited five years for my only surviving son to come home for you to drive him away, Helga.'

'I'm not trying to drive–'

'I said, shut it. Now I happen to have got fond of that girl and I can tell you now she's not the sort to be called a quitter.' He reached in his pocket and pulled out his handkerchief, covering his mouth as the coughing started.

Taking advantage of his coughing, Helga started to speak again, but this time Jim intervened. 'Pa's right. Joan isn't a quitter. But I warn you, Ma, I won't stand by while you make her life a misery. I'm ready to walk right off this farm and take my wife and son with me.'

She stood between them, looking from one to the other, but realising that she was defeated. Father and son were a united front.

Don went to her and put an arm round her shoulders.

'You'll get used to her in time. She's a good girl. Has a bit of spark. I like that.'

Helga looked down at her feet.

'I'm not done yet,' he said. 'Those two and the boy shouldn't be crammed into that room in two narrow beds. You and I need to change places with them, Helga. It's not right for them to be starting married life like that. A husband and wife need to have privacy and a chance to be close to each other at night. There's many a time you and I had our battles when we were first wed, but by the time morning came we'd always put things to rights and not usually by talking. They should have our bed.'

Helga brushed her husband's arm away. 'We've slept in that bed for thirty years, Don, and I'm not ready to give it up. They can lay me out in my shroud on it before I'll give way.' She folded her arms. 'They could move into the place Walt built and Alice and Rose can move into the house. That's the best solution.'

Don shook his head. 'Alice'll never agree to that and you well know it. What's more, we've no right to ask it of her. She and Walt built that place together. It's hers not ours.'

'It's on our land.'

Jim looked at his mother and shook his head. 'Pa's right. We can't expect Alice to do that. The only solution is for me to build us a bed. I'll move one of the single beds downstairs to the kitchen and Jimmy can sleep down there.'

After more discussion it was decided that the child sleeping alone downstairs was not practical. Instead Helga offered to let the boy come in with her and Don. 'At least until next spring when you can build an extension.'

There was still the matter of Jim constructing a new bed. Yet another task to add to the many he was undertaking without help on the farm. 'I guess it will have to wait until the snow comes. I can work on it then in here.'

'Agreed?'

'Agreed.'

None of them were aware that Alice had been standing just outside the doorway which Don had left ajar.

JOAN WAS in the kitchen washing the dishes from the midday meal.

'How are you and Jim getting along?' asked Alice.

Joan looked up in surprise, frowning. 'Why do you ask?'

'It can't be much fun being stuck in a room with twin beds and a four-year-old for company.' Alice smiled. 'Least, I can't imagine Walt putting up with that.' She gave Joan a wink. 'He built that cabin behind the barn as soon as we decided to get married. Said he couldn't bear the idea of making love with his ma and pa on the other side of the partition wall. Maybe it doesn't bother you and Jim?'

Joan dried her hands.

'Walt was so romantic.' Alice picked up the framed photograph of him that sat on the sideboard. 'We couldn't keep our hands off each other. I don't know how you two stand it. But maybe that side of things doesn't interest you and Jim. Always a bit of a cold fish, dear Jim.'

Joan seethed. Was there to be no end to it? She wanted to thump her sister-in-law. Which was worse? The silent freeze-out from Helga or the sly digs from Alice? She was heartily sick of the pair of them. 'Not that it's any of your business, but Don is planning to talk to Mrs Armstrong about swapping bedrooms. He may even switch to sleeping down here. Says he's finding the stairs hard.'

Alice shook her head. 'Well, that's never going to happen. Not if Helga has anything to do with it. The only way she'll give up her bed is in exchange for her coffin and that's not going to be any time soon.'

Joan turned away and started to put away the clean dishes she had stacked on the table.

'I guess you're going to have to wait till Jim gets round to doing something about it. Good luck to that though. Where Jim's concerned it's always farm work first.'

Alice looked at the clock on the kitchen wall. 'It's time for me to go fetch Rose from my mother's. Anything I can get you in town?'

Joan was about to say no, when on an impulse she asked, 'Do you have a sewing machine, Alice?'

Alice raised her eyebrows. 'Doing some dress-making?'

'A few alterations.'

'I don't, but my mother does. She'd be happy to lend it. I'll pick it up for you when I'm in town.' Bestowing a radiant smile on Joan, Alice left the house.

As soon as she was gone, Joan went upstairs and pushed the twin beds together. She'd join the sheets up in a seam down the middle tomorrow with the sewing machine. They'd just have to put up with a tangle tonight. Why hadn't she thought of this before?

AN UNPLEASANT ENCOUNTER

ALICE HAD BEEN as good as her word and brought the old Singer machine for Joan. While Helga was busy collecting the eggs Joan set it up on the kitchen table.

She had forgotten that Don was sleeping in the chair in the corner, until he moved across the room to see what she was doing.

'Oh, Don, I'm so sorry. I've woken you up.'

'I sleep too damn much anyway. Well, during the day. Just wish I could sleep better at night.' He began to cough.

Joan placed a hand on his arm. 'Why won't you see the doctor? He could give you something to help you sleep and maybe ease your coughing.'

'I know I've got cancer. There's no cure for that. All that gas I breathed in in the trenches. Made my lungs rotten.'

'It might not be cancer.'

He shook his head.

'Please, Don. Even if you won't do it for yourself. Do it for Mrs Armstrong, and for Jim. Do it for me too. We all care for you and it's terrible seeing you suffer like this when the doc might be able to help you.'

'He'll want to put me in the hospital and cut me open. I'm not having that. Had my fill of hospitals after my time in France.'

'Not necessarily. And you can always say no then. Don't cut yourself off from help when that might not even happen.'

He looked at her, then smiled. I'll have a think about it.'

Joan jumped up from the table and flung her arms round him.

'I haven't said I will yet.' But he grinned at her, winked and went back to his chair by the stove.

It took no time at all to sew the bed sheets together and she had finished her handiwork before Helga returned.

If Helga was curious about the appearance of the sewing machine she didn't show it.

'Jim says you want to make yourself useful?'

Joan looked up. 'Yes, of course. What can I do?' She had asked so many times before but always been met with a shrug and been told that everything was under control. *We have a routine, Alice and I - no point in messing with that.*

'There's potatoes to peel and onions to chop. Think you can manage that?'

Resisting the urge for sarcasm, Joan nodded and set about the task, relieved that at last she had been allowed to do something, no matter how minor.

'When you've done that you can give me a hand with the washing.'

The rest of the morning was spent boiling water, washing clothes and linen in a big copper pot, rinsing, wringing and then Joan was left to hang it all on the washing line. Doing the laundry was hardly a task to fill her with joy but achieving some form of acceptance was better than being completely ignored. Helga had little or nothing to say, but Joan took that to mean that she was satisfied with the work she had done.

The meal over, Joan made her escape to the town to change her library book. Afterwards, she decided to treat herself to a milkshake.

The café was deserted when Joan walked in, apart from a lone man sitting up at the counter with his back to the room, so she barely registered his presence. She sat at her usual spot in the window where she liked to watch the world go by. Not that there was much of a world to see: farmers calling at the grain depot or sitting on the steps outside the shabby hotel, chewing the fat; women standing around in the general store, swapping news about forthcoming weddings, births and funerals; old men snoozing on the bench in front of the library; the occasional small party of Mennonites, looking as smart as newly minted coins in their strange garb.

Joan was always alone on these visits now. She avoided coming into town with Alice and knew no one else in the neighbourhood, apart from Mary Hinton and she had no desire to renew her acquaintance with the stern-faced widow.

This morning it looked as though the weather was about to change after a summer of sunshine and heat since she'd been in Ontario. While the heat had frequently, if briefly, been mitigated by showers, today the sky was pregnant with heavy grey clouds. Over breakfast that morning Jim had seemed anxious, worried that, by the time his turn with the rented combine harvester came round, the weather would have turned. Joan hadn't realised how critical the vagaries of the weather were to the prosperity of the farm. At harvest time the local school gave the children time off classes to help out with the harvest and farmers banded together to lend each other a hand to bring in the crops. Jim had spent the two previous days on a neighbouring farm and the favour was due to be returned over the coming days.

She took her library book out of her bag. Her trips to the

library were on days when she knew Alice wouldn't be behind the counter. It was bad enough Alice knowing so much of Joan's personal life without her being party to her choice of reading matter. The book she'd taken out today, *Dragonwyk* by Anya Seton, was a consolation prize to herself. She had seen a billboard for the movie starring Gene Tierney and was wretched when she discovered there was no possibility of her seeing it in the absence of a picture house within thirty miles. Back in England she had rarely had time for reading, but here, she had so much time and so little to do. She opened the book and was soon absorbed in the story. So absorbed that she didn't notice the man approach her table until he'd slid onto the banquette seat on the other side.

'Well, well, well,' he said. 'We meet again.'

She looked up and the blood stopped in her veins. She was too stunned to speak. Sitting in front of her was a man she had never expected to set eyes on again – here, in flesh and blood, in Hollowtree. Her heart hammered.

The man grinned at her. 'Married a soldier, did you, Joan? Maybe I know him?'

She closed her book and pulled it into her lap.

'You're a long way from Aldershot. Missing the fish 'n' chips?' he said.

Slipping the book into her bag Joan went to stand up, mindless of her unfinished milkshake.

'We were just getting to know each other when you ran off and left me in that bus shelter,' he said, his hand gripping her arm.

His hold was like a vice and she looked around to see if anyone was watching, Freddo, the cafe owner, was polishing glasses at the far end of the counter while absorbed in studying the newspaper spread out in front of him.

'You almost got me into trouble for that, Joan. Not very nice of you.' The man's voice was low and there was an unmistakable threat in it. He twisted her arm, forcing her back down into her seat.

The intervening years had not been kind to him. Where once he had been quite a good-looking man, his face was now pale and lined and his hair beginning to thin. His teeth were crooked with evident signs of decay.

'I have to go.' She tried to rise.

He squeezed her arm tighter. 'Running out on me again?' As he spoke she felt his other hand brush against her leg under the table. He pushed aside her cotton skirt and moved his palm over her bare thigh. She was about to call out to Freddo, when the man withdrew his hand. 'Unfinished business.'

Then he slid out of the booth and, with a mock salute, left the café.

Joan was shaking. She had never expected to see that man again, much less here in what was now her home town. She breathed slow deep breaths and took a sip of her milkshake, waiting for her heart to stop pounding.

It had been near the beginning of the war – spring or summer 1940. He'd often come into the chip shop, after the pubs closed. At first she'd thought him a friendly chap, even wondered if she might go out with him if he asked her. He'd told her his name was Bill and asked her name and always remembered to use it. She used to give him a big smile and an over-generous portion of chips, throwing in some of the batter scraps for good measure. Then one night she'd walked home alone through the blackout when she left work. Usually Mr Collins who owned the shop walked her to the bus stop but that night his wife was ill and Joan had told him she could manage on her own as she was used to getting about in the dark now. She'd walked about fifty yards before she noticed the sound of footsteps behind her. She stopped walking and heard whoever was following stop too. By the time she'd reached the bus stop she was absolutely petrified, convinced that someone was following her, uncertain whether to wait in the shelter for the bus, which was due in five or ten minutes, or to walk on, hoping that if necessary she would be able to outrun whoever was following her. In the end, she'd ducked into the bus shelter, switched off her dim blackout torch and stood, trembling in the darkness, against the wooden wall of the shelter, praying that whoever it was would walk by.

But he didn't walk by. As soon as he spoke, to say her name, she was overwhelmed with relief, recognising the Canadian accent and a familiar voice. 'Ooh, Bill, you gave me a fright! I didn't know who was coming up behind me. I doubt I'll ever get used to the bloody blackout.'

He didn't reply but pounced on her, pinning her against the wall of the bus shelter, his beery breath in her face. She tried to struggle but he was too strong. Terrified at the way this man she had thought a genial and friendly person had turned into an aggressive thug, she twisted her head away, but the sheer weight of his body against hers left her powerless, like a trapped butterfly. He moved one hand down and forced it between her legs, tugging at her knickers and she felt his fingers probing her in a place she had never been touched before. She wanted to be sick. The weight and power of him. Moving so fast. Pushing her, squashing the breath out of her. Aggressive. Like an animal. Breathing ragged. She tried to wriggle away from those probing fingers. Tears stung her eyes. Sound of a rip, then her knickers were round her ankles. His hands moved up to her shoulders and he pushed her down onto the bench at the back of the shelter. Positioning himself in front of her, he unbuttoned his flies. Just as his hands went to the back of her head to force it down onto him, there was the sound of laughter. Singing. Someone was coming. She heard voices, a group of Canadians. Bill put his hand over her mouth but she kneed him in his now exposed privates. He bent double in pain.

A voice called out. 'What the hell you doing to that woman? Let her go, fella!'

Bill turned his head and Joan jumped to her feet and ran off.

She had run and run until she reached the next bus stop where there was a bus waiting. Her mother wanted her to report the attack to the Canadian military authorities but she baulked at the idea. It would mean identifying him and possibly giving evidence in some form of military tribunal and she couldn't face that. The next day she'd resigned her job at the fish 'n' chip shop and joined the ATS. She'd never seen him again. Until today.

Joan waited for half an hour in the café, terrified that he might be be waiting for her, somewhere outside. Then, fearful of staying in town any longer, she grabbed her bag and rushed out to her bicycle and pedalled at speed the five miles back to the farm.

She flung her bike against the barn wall and went in search of her husband. He wasn't in any of the fields near the house. In the kitchen Helga and Alice were having one of their exclusive chats and fell silent as she came into the room.

'Where's Jim?' she asked.

It was Helga who answered. 'He's taken the lad down to the pool for a swim.'

'A swim? But it looks set to rain.'

'What does that matter? All the same when you're wet. On a farm you have to take what time you get free. Can't do things on a whim like you city folk do.'

Joan turned to go in search of them, but Helga called after her. 'Letters have come for you. Six of them. Must have all ended up on the same ship across – or got held up in Halifax.' She nodded towards a small pile of envelopes on the sideboard.

Unable to contain her joy, Joan leapt on them, all thoughts of the man in the café receding. Three in Ethel's handwriting, two in her mother's and one from Ethel's mum, Aunty Vi. Mum was never much good at writing – Joan imagined her labouring over the pages for hours. Grinning from ear to ear she took the letters and went outside. She walked over to the meadow and sat on top of the slope leading down to the hollow and tore the envelopes open impatiently. She sorted them into date order and read them quickly then read them again, this time savouring every word. A wave of homesickness swept over her as she imagined her family sitting round the table talking about her, reading her letters. She'd been despairing of hearing from home. She'd written to them almost every day – carefully censored letters, painting everything in a positive light, anxious not to worry them with the truth of her loneliness and the behaviour of her mother-in-law and sister-in-law. But she had heard nothing back until now. She flipped the envelopes over and checked the postmarks again. All different dates. It was hard not to wonder whether, rather than being delayed crossing the Atlantic, Helga had had something to do with their simultaneous appearance.

She stuffed them into her pocket and set out to find Jim and Jimmy. She could read them again before she went to bed tonight.

Sitting under the big tree that overlooked the pool she leaned against the trunk, Olive Oyl lay beside her as Joan watched Jim trying to teach his son to swim, hand cupped under the little boy's chin while Jimmy flailed about in an approximation of the breaststroke. She felt bad as she had promised to teach him herself and hadn't got around to it.

The sun had emerged from behind the blanket of clouds to cast some silvery light over the water, before the fast-approaching dusk. The water shimmered and as she listened to the happy cries of her son, she felt blessed. Jimmy made no secret of his hero worship of his father, watching him at every opportunity, shadowing him as he went about his tasks on the farm. Joan acknowledged to herself that the boy had been missing a male role model. Now with the letters from home she felt better, less alone, more able to bear the separation.

Jim's arms were bronzed from the sun. His body glistened in the water, the muscles on his chest standing out in relief. He looked over and smiled and her heart lifted inside her. On an impulse she pulled her dress over her head and plunged into the pool wearing just her slip over her underwear. Jimmy squealed in delight at her splashing entrance to the water and Jim pulled her into his arms and kissed her. All thoughts of telling him about that man from Aldershot faded away.

ALICE AND TIP HAVE COFFEE

ALICE FINISHED her shift at the library to find Tip Howardson waiting outside on the steps for her. Surprised to see him, she gave him a friendly nod. Tip, for his part, grinned at her and doffed his hat. Seeing the parcel of books in her arms, he rushed forward and offered to carry them.

'No need – my bicycle's right here,' she said, placing the books in the saddle bag.

'In that case let me buy you a cup of a coffee.'

Alice remembered what Jim said about Howardson being responsible for his friend's death and hesitated a moment, then, curious, she agreed.

Once they were settled with coffees in front of them, Alice said, 'I mentioned to Jim that I'd run into you last week. He didn't seem too impressed.'

'Well then, it's just as well I'm not interested in impressing him. You on the other hand–'

'Maybe I'm not that easily impressed.'

'I'll just have to try extra hard then.'

Alice smiled. 'Jim said you got into a fight with him and his friend and the friend died.'

'That's true. Did he also tell you that his friend's death had nothing to do with me? He had something wrong with his skull.'

She nodded. 'Didn't stop you being courtmartialed though.'

'Didn't stop Jim being courtmartialed either.'

This was news to Alice. She swirled her teaspoon round her coffee. 'He didn't mention that.'

'I bet he didn't.'

They sat in silence for a few minutes.

'Look, men were getting courtmartialed by the minute back in those days. All bored out of our brains waiting for action. Too much energy. Most of us got off with a caution.'

'You didn't though. Not according to Jim. He said they gave you a dishonourable discharge and sent you back to Canada.'

Tip laughed and shook his head. 'My cover worked then.'

'What do you mean?'

'I told you before – I was recruited for a special mission in France. They had to go to great lengths to make sure no one knew. Going behind enemy lines is a dangerous business. They pretended Tip Howardson was back in Canada and gave me a new identity.'

'Really?' Alice was doubtful. It seemed unlikely.

He fixed his eyes on hers. 'I was flown out at dead of night and parachuted into occupied France where I joined a Resistance cell.'

Alice sipped her coffee, watching him over the top of her cup.

'Just me and some radio equipment. My job was to send back intelligence on the Germans to London.'

'What kind of intelligence.'

'Troop movements mostly. I had a job washing up in a restaurant. That was my cover. The place was very popular with the Germans. I used to listen through the serving hatch to what they were talking about. Most of the time it was about women or food but I picked up some vital information that probably saved a lot of lives.'

'I had no idea you spoke German, Tip.' She was still sceptical.

'Intensive language training. Not enough to speak it fluently but enough to understand the gist of what they were saying. Important thing was to fit in with the French. At least well enough to convince the Germans. My mother is French Canadian so that was no problem.'

'Wasn't it terribly dangerous?'

'Of course it was. We never knew who to trust.'

'We?'

'There were four of us in our network. A woman I was working with was betrayed to the Nazis and they hanged her. From a lamppost.'

Alice gasped in horror.

'That was after they'd tortured her. She didn't give anything away.'

'How terribly brave.'

He nodded.

'But they never caught *you*?'

'They did. Eventually. I escaped though.'

'Thank goodness. You were lucky they didn't torture you, then.'

'Actually they did. For five days and nights until I got away.'

'How dreadful.' Her eyes were wide. 'What did they do to you?'

'I couldn't tell you, Alice. It wouldn't be fair. You wouldn't be able to sleep at night. Put it this way. I didn't sleep at all while they had me in custody and I'll probably have nightmares for the rest of my life.' He rolled up his sleeve to reveal what appeared to be cigarette burns on his arm.

Alice gasped and reached out a hand and placed it over Tip's. 'I'm so sorry, Tip.'

'Enough of me. Let's talk about you now, Alice.'

'Nothing much to tell. You already know about Walt dying. Killed the moment he saw action. Mowed down on the beach at Dieppe. I was pregnant when I got the news. I have a little girl now, Rose. We both live up at the Armstrong's farm. Walt had built us a little log cabin beside the big barn. Just two small rooms but it's real cosy. I eat with the rest of the family but at least in the evenings Rose and I have our own little place just for the two of us. She sleeps in with me and I've made the other room up real nice as a sitting room. I think they'd like me to let Jim and his wife move over there and me and Rose move into the house but that's never going to happen. That little home and a few lousy medals are all I have left of Walt.'

'Jim Armstrong has a wife?' Tip raised one brow.

'Yes. An English war bride. They have a little boy too. He's a sweet child. They've only been here a few weeks. I think she's finding it hard.'

'What's her name?'

'Joan.'

A smile spread across Tip's face. 'Good for Jim. I'll have to give him best wishes when I see him.'

Alice looked up at him. 'You didn't find yourself a wife over there? No pretty French girl hankering after you then?'

Tip shook his head and looked at her sadly. 'It was too dangerous for me to even think about having a relationship. It wouldn't have been right. Maybe if Françoise hadn't been killed by the Germans...who knows?' He turned and gazed out of the window.

Alice put her hand on his again and gave it a small

squeeze. Howardson turned his hand over and captured hers in his. He lifted it to his lips and kissed it. Alice pulled away, alarmed. He leaned forward and clasped both her hands in his.

'I didn't mean to scare you, Alice. It's just that I've felt so alone for so long and I felt a connection with you just now. We've both suffered so much. You always were a lovely girl. So kind. So understanding. You were wasted on Armstrong.'

She jerked away from him. 'Don't speak of my husband like that. Show some respect.'

'Oh God, I'm sorry. I didn't mean *Walt*. Walt was my friend. I meant *Jim*. Dumping that son of a bitch was the best thing you ever did, Alice Ducroix.'

'It's Alice Armstrong.'

He grinned at her and raised both his hands, palms outward in surrender. 'Sorry, Mrs Armstrong.'

Pacified, she leaned back in her seat. 'You going to buy me another coffee, Tip Howardson?'

MISSING

JOAN'S NERVES WERE FRAYED. Giving up smoking was proving harder than expected and she was irascible, snapping at Jimmy when he begged her to take him into the town again to watch the boys paddling in their canoes. She was also finding her new role as volunteer land girl arduous. Hoeing row after row of vegetables to clear away the burgeoning weed growth was backbreaking work.

When she had first appeared, clad in farm overalls and her hair up in a bandanna, Jim had been surprised – and not in a good way, as if her transformation into farm labourer was an implied criticism of his own shortcomings.

'You're wearing pants,' he'd said, frowning.

'Of course. I always do.' She looked affronted.

'No, you don't. You wear dresses. Pretty ones.'

Joan had looked down at her legs. 'Ah! You mean trousers? Slacks?'

'Like I said, pants.' He'd looked at her, hands on hips, still frowning.

Joan had turned around and seeing no one, unbuttoned

the side of her overalls and plucked at the fabric of her knickers underneath. 'These are pants.'

Jim had grinned and moved towards her.

She'd quickly buttoned herself up and skipped sideways, laughing. She winked at him. 'If you need a closer look at what pants are, you'll have to wait until tonight. 'Now show me what needs doing.'

Today, Jim was working on fixing something under the hood of the tractor and had banned Jimmy from the shed while the work was underway. The little boy trailed behind Joan, his keenness to assist soon dissipated, when he realised that the job involved collecting discarded weeds in a wheel barrow. As the barrow was too heavy for him to push, he had to run up and down between the cultivated rows carrying armfuls of weeds, the puppy running behind him. Soon Jimmy became bored and focused his attention on playing with Olive.

Joan at last found a rhythm in the work. It wasn't enjoyable, but at least she seemed to be making steady progress. The sun was cooler now as the season advanced. Jim had warned her that the fall, as they called autumn here, was brief and shifted into winter almost overnight. She would need to think about getting some warmer clothes before long, as he had told her the temperatures were sub zero for months and snow a constant presence from November until March.

Wiping the sweat from her brow, she straightened up and surveyed the results, hands on the small of her back, stretching newly discovered muscles. At this rate she wouldn't be finished in this field for another couple of days. The sooner the new weeding rig arrived, the better. She reached for the flask she'd filled with water that morning. Almost empty. She took a slug, enjoying the feel of the water in her parched throat. It would have to last her until the midday meal, when she could refill it.

Then it dawned on her. Where was Jimmy?

There was no sign of the dog either.

Groaning, she flung down her hoe and headed towards the barn. Jim would be annoyed with her for letting the child out of her sight and into his way.

The barn was cool as she stepped inside. It was also deserted. She came outside, crossed the yard and went into the kitchen.

'Boots off in here!' Helga turned back to the cooking range where she was stirring something in a pot.

Joan stood in the doorway. 'Have you seen Jim? Or Jimmy?'

'Jim's gone into town. Needed a part for the tractor.'

'He took Jimmy?'

Helga put down the spoon. 'No. He said you were looking after Jimmy.'

Joan froze, her heart starting to race. She took a breath. 'He must be with Alice and Rose. I'll look in the meadow.'

'Alice and Rose went to see Mrs Ducroix. Alice's father's out of town so they took a picnic over there.'

Joan spun on her heels and ran down towards the creek. Please God, don't let him have tried to swim on his own. Her heart hammered against her rib cage. The water's too deep. He could have slipped and fallen. Please God, keep him safe.

She skidded to a stop as she reached the pool. Not a ripple. Not a sound. The water was clear and there was no sign of the child. Sweat pouring down her face she ran back to the barn and climbed the ladder to the hayloft. Jimmy knew he wasn't allowed to go up there. She doubted he could even stretch his little legs between the rungs. She peered over the top into the silent gloom. Nothing and no one. Only dust motes caught in a shaft of light where there was a small gap in the roof tiles.

Her feet barely touching the ladder, she clambered down to the ground. Helga was waiting below, her face carved into deep frown lines.

'He must be still in the field. Perhaps he fell asleep and I didn't see him.'

Joan ran, clutching her side against the stitch that burned through her. She screamed her son's name until her lungs were bursting. The only sound was the squealing cries of a pair of brown-headed cowbirds picking at the ground where Joan had been weeding. She staggered on, moving into the next field where Jim had been threshing corn. Stumbling blindly, she crashed through the tall brown stems, running through the heart of the field, calling to Jimmy in an ever more desperate wail.

When she'd raced across every field, she found Helga waiting in the yard, anxiety etched across her face, hands on hip. 'I've searched every building. He's not here.'

'I've been the length and breadth of the farm. No sign.' A thought crossed her mind, 'Where's the dog?'

Her mother-in-law shook her head.

'Did you look in the bedroom?'

Helga rolled her eyes. 'Of course I did. And in Alice's place. The stable too. Even the biffy. He's not on the farm. Nor is that puppy.'

'Then he must have gone into town with Jim.'

'If he did we'll soon find out.' Helga pointed to a cloud of dust in the distance. 'That'll be him now.'

Jim got out of the truck and walked towards them.

Joan rushed to him. 'Is Jimmy with you?' Her voice was strained.

'Isn't he with you?'

Helga interjected. 'She wasn't watching him and he's disappeared.' She glared at Joan.

Joan spun round, her nerves strained to breaking point. 'That's enough. Keep out of this. Your constant carping is not going to help us find him.' She clutched at Jim's arm. 'Could he have gone with you? Got in the back of the truck without you noticing? The dog's gone too.'

Jim swore under his breath and ran towards the vehicle. He jerked back the tarpaulin that covered the open bed of the truck. Nothing. But it was clear to them all that it would have made a perfect hiding place for the child and the small dog. Jim jumped into the cab and fired the engine. Joan climbed up into the passenger seat.

'Stay here,' he said. 'He might be here somewhere.'

'He's not. We've looked everywhere. And I'm not staying a minute longer alone with your mother. I'm certain we'll find him in town.'

Jim's mouth was set in a hard line and he said nothing, but released the handbrake and gunned the car down the track with a screech of tyres.

They drove the five miles into town in silence. Joan twisted her head from side to side as they sped down the road, in the frantic hope that they might come upon Jimmy on the way. She tried to push her worst fears to the back of her mind. An accident. Abduction.

As they entered the town, Jim spoke at last. 'Where's he most likely to go?'

Then it dawned on Joan. 'The park with the lake near the library. He likes watching the kids canoeing.' An icy cold spread through her veins.

Jim looked at her but said nothing and turned the truck in that direction.

They pulled up outside the library and jumped out. As they

entered the park they saw a crowd gathered at the water's edge. Rose, and Alice's mother, Mrs Ducroix, were among them. Olive Oyl was scampering around the edges of the crowd.

'What's going on? Where's Jimmy?' Jim yelled.

'Jimmy fell out of a boat.' Rose was whimpering. 'Mommy's dived in the water to rescue him.'

Joan and Jim pushed through the crowd as Alice, dripping from head to foot, carried Jimmy's limp body from the lake. Jim rushed to her and took the little boy from her arms. He laid his son on the ground, turned the boy's head to one side and began to pump his chest. Joan knelt beside them, clutching her son's hand while frantically offering prayers. Jim worked at the little boy's chest with grim determination, while the dog wailed plaintively. The child expelled a small quantity of water, opened his eyes and began coughing. Jim held his son against his chest, cradling him in his arms. Joan wept in relief and clung to her husband and son. Jimmy began to cry. Joan took him from Jim and sat on the grass, rocking the boy back and forth, kissing the top of his head, her breathing ragged with relief.

She looked up and saw Jim holding the drenched Alice against him. Alice's mother grabbed the cloth on which their picnic had been laid and handed it to her daughter. Alice in turn passed it to Joan. 'He needs it more than I do,' she said.

Seeing there was to be no more drama, the crowd began to disperse. Jim took off his shirt and handed it to Alice. 'Put this on.'

Joan swaddled Jimmy tightly in the tablecloth, still rocking him back and forth in her arms. Jimmy's face bore a bewildered expression and Joan felt a mixture of relief that he was all right, with anger that he had put them through such fear and agony.

'What were you thinking, Jimmy? You know you were

meant to stay with me. How did you get here? What were you doing in a boat? I told you you're too small.'

In response the little boy began to wail. Joan hugged him tightly and looked up at Jim who said, 'Leave him alone, Joan, he's just a kid.'

'What happened?' Jim asked Alice but it was Mrs Ducroix who replied.

'We didn't realise it was your boy. We could see some kids horsing about in the canoes on the other side of the lake. The little chap was standing up in the canoe and I said to Alice – that child's going to fall in if he's not careful. Then next thing he lost his footing and went in head first. Alice dived in quick as a flash.'

Jim reached for Alice's hands and said, 'Thank God you were here and knew what to do. I can't think what might have happened if you hadn't acted so fast.'

'I only realised it was Jimmy when I reached him. Anyone else would have done the same.'

Joan looked up and repeated Jim's thanks. Jim had his hand on Alice's arm and was gazing at her in a way that made Joan wonder if the feelings that had been between the two of them had not entirely faded. She pushed the thought aside, telling herself to be grateful that her worst nightmares about Jimmy had not been realised.

'Let's get everyone home.' Jim ushered them all over to the truck. You too, Mrs Ducroix. We've spoiled the picnic so you must come to the farm for supper. Ma will have plenty of food and she's always happy to see you. I'll drive you home later.'

Joan was about to climb into the cab with Jimmy, when Jim said, 'Better let Alice ride up front with Jimmy, since she's soaked to the skin. You can ride on the tail with Rose and Mrs Ducroix.'

Trying not to feel resentful, Joan sat on the truck bed atop the tarpaulin with her niece, Alice's mother and Alice's bike. She stared out at the passing scenery in misery as the little girl and her grandmother chattered happily to each other.

Jim was angry with her. But not as angry as Joan was with herself. She imagined what might have happened if Alice hadn't acted so quickly. Guilt ate into her at the way she had failed in her duty as a mother. She had been responsible for Jimmy. He wasn't yet four. She'd let him get into danger. He could have died.

As the truck rattled along the bumpy road, Joan castigated herself. Why had she let her promise to teach Jimmy to swim lapse after his stomach ache? If she'd only set aside a little time each day to build on his first lesson from Jim, the little boy could have been swimming by now. Why had she not kept her eye on him when they were out in the fields? She'd allowed her own selfish concerns to distract her from her responsibility as a parent. Her eyes stung as she imagined how things might have been different, if Jim had failed to revive their son's limp little body.

Grateful to Alice, Joan couldn't help wishing that she had been the one to dive in and save her son. Yet again Alice had asserted her claim to the moral high ground. But Alice had a right to it, whereas Joan didn't.

THE WOODS NEAR THE LAKE

ALICE TOLD herself it wasn't actually a date. She was just in need of some adult company and Tip Howardson had been nothing but kind and friendly. And she'd known him for years. He'd been Walt's friend and in their class at school. Like a brother really. Though brothers didn't look at their sisters the way he looked at her.

So what? There was no harm in a little flirtation. She wasn't going to let anything happen, was she? Maybe they'd go for a walk, get a cup of coffee. Talk. That's all.

And so what if she hadn't mentioned it to her mother when she'd dropped Rose off this afternoon? Or told Helga she was meeting Tip? She knew Helga wouldn't like it. No matter how hard she might try to convince her mother-in-law that she and Tip were just old friends and would probably spend most of their time talking about Walt, it would never wash. And she didn't want to risk Helga telling Jim. He'd been very cruel about poor old Tip. She didn't want to risk them getting in a fight again.

Tip was waiting for her on a bench in the park. Alice didn't want to sit there with him. That was the bench she'd sat on with Jim the day he left to join the army and they'd broken off their engagement. Too many bad memories.

'Let's walk round the lake,' she said.

Tip jumped to his feet and handed her a posy of flowers. 'Picked them myself,' he said. 'Hope you like them.'

Alice was annoyed. How was she going to explain the flowers if anyone saw them? But she forced a smile and murmured her thanks.

As they walked, she told him what had happened here at the lake the previous day.

Tip whistled. 'You dived in and saved a kid from drowning? I bet that was a sight to behold.' He turned and looked at her, his eyes ranging down her body as if imagining it in wet clothing. He gave a laugh that made her feel uncomfortable but a bit excited at the same time.

It was nice having a man appreciate her again. It had been so long. More than five years since Walt had left to follow Jim into the army. Don't think about that, Alice.

'It was Jim Armstrong's little boy actually. His wife wasn't paying attention and the little fellow climbed onto Jim's truck and stowed away when Jim drove into town.'

Tip whistled again.

'Poor child's not quite four.'

'Doesn't sound very responsible of the mother.'

'Exactly!' Alice spoke automatically. 'Though it's probably not entirely her fault. She's not used to country life.'

'That doesn't excuse her not watching over her kid.' There was a curl to Tip's lip. 'You said she's English? I think I might know her.'

'Know her? How?'

'She from Aldershot?'

Alice nodded.

'Yes. I remember a girl called Joan.' He snorted in derision. 'Can't be the same one though.'

'Why not?'

'She was a bit of a tart. Put it about. Slept with half the regiment. Not the sort of woman I'd have expected Jim Armstrong to marry.'

'Thick dark hair? In a bob with a big roll at the front? Quite attractive.'

Tip nodded. 'Well, I'll be damned. So she's Jim Armstrong's missus.' He gave another snort. 'Used to work in a fish and chip shop. Always batting her eyes at the guys. Not my type at all. No class.' He took Alice by the arm and swung her round to face him. 'Not like you, Alice.' He pulled her towards him and leaned forward to kiss her.

Alice tried to pull away. This wasn't part of the plan. His mouth moved against her lips and she felt a surge of pleasure. Then his tongue was in her mouth. She'd forgotten what it felt like to be kissed like this, to be wanted. Her body responded and her arms went round him.

Tip drew back, looked around them and took her by the arm, leading her towards the trees. There was hardly anyone in the park this afternoon. They went deeper into the woods, into the dark silence. Out of sight, Tip reached for her again and pushed her onto the ground, knocking the wind out of her. He lay on top of her, the heat of his breath on her neck and she knew there was no turning back. Half afraid, half excited, she decided not to resist. His hands were already pushing the skirt of her dress up and Alice gave a cry of pleasure as his fingers moved between her legs. She adjusted her position and drew him into her.

It was fast and furious and over quickly. Alice was surprised by the aggression with which he took her, as though he was claiming her, taking possession of her. Both frightening and exciting. All those years of pent up frustration had to find an outlet in the end. She certainly felt nothing for Tip and had no intention of repeating the experience, but it had been a release.

Alice sat up. 'I needed that,' she said, laughing.

'We both did.'

He lay on his back beside her and lit a cigarette. 'You've no idea how long I've wanted to do that, Alice.'

'Make love? So it's been a long time for you too? What about the woman in France?'

Howardson laughed, that snorting laugh of his. She realised she didn't like the way he laughed. Come to think of it, there was quite a lot about Tip she didn't like that much. But she'd liked what they'd just done. Maybe not enough for a repeat performance, but it had served its purpose.

He rolled onto his side and looked at her. 'A long time wanting to do that with *you*.'

Alice brushed dry leaves from her skirt and started to get up.

Tip reached out and pulled her down beside him again. 'Not so fast, angel.'

'Look, we shouldn't have done that. I certainly didn't plan on doing it, but I got carried away in the moment.'

'We both did. But I *did* plan. Well, maybe not plan, but I kind of hoped it would happen. I guess I've been hoping it would happen ever since you began to sprout these beauties in high school.' He stretched his hand out and cupped one of her breasts. 'And I'm hoping it's going to happen again, before too long. Maybe right now.'

She took hold of his hand and removed it from her breast. 'No, Tip. I won't deny I enjoyed it, but that's it. It won't happen again.'

Howardson twisted himself onto his knees and took her hands in his. 'We're meant to be together.'

Alice gave a dry laugh. 'It was just sex, Tip. Yes, we both

wanted it. But that's that. Over. Done. Finished. I enjoyed it but I don't want an encore.'

Tip stood up and pulled her to her feet. He held her by the shoulders and looked into her eyes. 'I want to marry you, Alice Ducroix. And the sooner you come round to wanting to marry me too, the better. But I'm a patient man. I'll wait.'

Alice stared at him in horror. 'I told you my name's Armstrong. And I'll never marry again. Walt was the only man for me. I can't love anyone else that way. What he and I had...' She suddenly felt very lonely and tears pricked her eyes. She turned away.

Tip held her against him. 'I'll take whatever you can give. You may not love me now, but give me time. I know you'll care for me in the end. It may be different from how you were with Walt, but a beautiful woman like you shouldn't be alone. Shouldn't have to live with the Armstrongs. You deserve your own home. A place for you and me and that kid of yours. Maybe we'll have some of our own before long. You'll have a man to support you, to care for you and provide for you. I'll treat you like a princess, Alice. If you stay up at Hollowtree Farm you'll always be on the outside in someone else's home. In Jim Armstrong's home. You deserve more than that, angel.'

Alice backed away, shaking her head.

As they walked back to the town, Alice realised she had left the posy of flowers in the woods. Tip didn't appear to have noticed.

When they reached the railing where she'd left her bicycle she put her arms out, resisting his attempt to pull her into another kiss.

'I meant what I said, Alice. I'm going to marry you. You may as well get used to the idea.'

What had she let herself in for? How was she going to make sure he got the message?

ALICE WAS the last to arrive in the kitchen for the evening meal. She sat down, after ruffling Jimmy's hair and giving him a kiss. 'How's my brave boy? Hope you've been good today? No more falling in lakes and joyriding in your daddy's truck?'

Jimmy grinned sheepishly at Alice and carried on eating his supper.

Joan clenched her hands together under the table. She hated the way Alice behaved so proprietorially towards Jimmy and following her rescue of him yesterday this was clearly going to get worse. She should feel grateful but now that Jimmy was safe and unharmed she could only feel resentment. As a strong swimmer, she wished they had arrived a few minutes sooner so she could have dived in and brought her son out herself. She knew she was being petty but couldn't help it. Last night she'd had to endure Alice fussing over the boy and constant hostile looks directed at her across the dinner table from her mother-in-law.

When everyone had finished Helga's creamed peas and boiled ham, Jim leaned forward and addressed Alice. 'I didn't think you worked in the library on Wednesdays?'

'I don't,' she said, her expression defensive.

'I had to go into town to talk to Hal Grundy and saw you.'

Alice said nothing, rising and gathering the empty plates together.

'Looked to me as though it was Tip Howardson you were walking with.'

Joan looked at Jim in surprise. He appeared to be obsessed about this Howardson chap. As the man responsible for the death of Greg Hooper, she held no sympathy for him, but it was odd how Jim seemed to be so bothered about Alice being friendly with him.

'Yes. I did run into him and we had a few words,' said Alice, her face slightly pink.

'I told you, Alice, Howardson's no good. I don't like the idea of you spending any time with him.'

Joan looked between the two of them, disturbed by this sudden protective display towards Alice.

'What right do you have to tell me who I can talk to? It's none of your darned business.'

Helga was tutting at the end of the table. 'Alice is quite right, Jim. If she wants to be pleasant towards the Howardson boy, why shouldn't she? Especially after all that poor fellow's been through.'

Jim slammed his fist on the table. 'I told you. That crap about him being a hero of the French Resistance is just a pack of lies. The bastard was dishonourably discharged. Don't believe anything he tells you. He's a liar and worse. A bloody disgrace to the Canadian army.'

'That's enough. I've told you before I won't have that kind of talk under my roof. You should know better, Jim Armstrong, than to swear in front of the children. I won't tell you again.'

Don leaned forward and with a rasp to his voice, said, 'Your mother's right, Jim. Cut out the bad language.'

Alice put the dishes in the sink and flounced back to the table. 'You have no idea what Tip went through in France. The dishonourable discharge was just a cover his controllers came up with so the enemy would think he'd gone back to Canada. He had a change of identity and was parachuted into France. He lived as a French man and spied on the Germans.' She folded her arms and threw Jim a defiant look, adding, 'He saved countless lives and the Nazis did terrible things when they caught him after someone betrayed him.'

'That's so much bul… nonsense.'

'And why should anyone believe *you*? Especially as you neglected to mention that you were court-martialled too.'

There was a gasp round the table.

Joan, angry, spoke first. 'Jim was completely exonerated. Everyone knew the other guy started the fight.'

'Stay out of this, Joan,' said Jim.

'So why didn't you mention it then, Jim?' Alice got up and took her daughter's hand. 'Didn't want your pa to know you had a less than perfect record? Come on, Rose. I've had enough of this.'

Helga called after her. 'Wait! There's apple pie and cream.'

'Leave her,' said Don.

'I'll take a couple of slices across later.' Helga shook her head and glared at Joan.

Jim scraped back his chair. 'I'm going to get another couple of rows of that corn done before dark.' He threw a look at Joan. 'Try and catch up on all the time I lost yesterday.' The door slammed behind him.

Joan got up to follow him but felt Don's hand on her arm. 'If you've any sense, you'll let him cool off a bit.'

But Joan had had enough. 'He's my husband. I'm the best judge of that.'

She walked towards the corn field, her heart thumping. She'd every right to talk to him, yet she felt nervous at the prospect. Out of her depth.

Jim was climbing onto the tractor. Rather than tackle him now while he was still angry, she decided to wait a while. She sat down, her back against a fence post, her knees bent in front of her, and watched as he manoeuvred the tractor and picker along the row. If he saw her waiting there he gave no indication.

Why were things so difficult between them? Wasn't she trying her best? Joan felt like a caged animal in a zoo, under constant surveillance from the keepers and the public, taken out of her natural element and deprived of a proper role. Why didn't Jim see that?

His face had a frown of concentration as the tractor roared underneath him and the belt of the picker buzzed as it bounced the corn cobs up the chute and into the catcher behind. Joan longed to have a go. Probably not a good idea to ask right now, though.

The sun was dipping behind the distant rolling hills and the sky was streaked with pink like strands of cotton candy. Looking at Jim's face in the half light, she sighed – even now with him angry and shutting her out, the sight of him made her stomach flip over with a tenderness and longing she had never felt for anyone else. But what did he feel for her? She couldn't lose the image of him holding Alice against him, her wet body soaking through his clothes. And tonight his anger at Alice spending time with this Howardson man. Surely this must mean he still had feelings for her?

Joan couldn't help it. Even though when they made love he was unequivocal in his desire for her, she couldn't help feeling there was something he was holding back. She was confident that he wanted her but couldn't feel so certain that he loved her. Not the way she loved him.

As if he sensed what she was thinking, Jim switched off the tractor, swung himself down and walked towards her. He pulled her to her feet, drew her into his arms and kissed her. She gave herself up to the moment, responding to his kiss and letting him take her by the hand and lead her down through the fields to the pool by the creek.

It was dark when their lovemaking finished. They lay side by side in silence. Joan wanted to cry. Instead of making her feel better, it had heightened her sense of isolation. As if their connection was wholly physical and beyond the reach of words.

Jim sat up, elbows on his knees, staring into the middle distance.

Joan tried to think what she could say to break the silence, but then he spoke.

'I know it's hard for you. Living like this. It's not what I wanted. I want us to be together. Just the three of us. Not stuck under one roof with Ma and Pa in a space too small to swing a cat.'

Joan rested her head against his shoulder. 'I'm sorry about losing Jimmy. I know I was meant to be watching him but I was trying so hard to help you and I'd no idea he'd do what he did.'

He turned to look at her. 'I know that, Joan. I know you love the bones of the boy. I know how distraught you were. How could you think I'd blame you?'

'But you seemed so angry. When we went to look for him.'

'I wasn't angry. I was anxious. Bloody terrified in fact. I was starting to imagine all kinds of things. How could I have lived with myself if something bad happened to our boy after bringing him to Canada? It would be my fault.'

Joan reached for his hand. The warmth of it highlighted the chill of the evening and he put his other arm around her shoulder and pulled her closer. Bending his head he kissed the top of her hair.

'Why are you so mad about Alice seeing that Tip fellow?'

'You know why. I told you. He's the biggest bastard I met in my whole time in the army. And that's including the enemy.'

Joan took a breath. Now or never. 'Do you still have feelings for Alice?'

Jim dropped his arm. 'What kind of question is that?' A deep frown was carved across his forehead and his eyes narrowed. He shook his head in complete disbelief. His eyes raked over her and she felt all the ground they had made up, falling away, leaving her stranded again.

'I'm going to put the tractor away' he said. 'Time you got Jimmy to bed.' He started off back up the field in a half run, leaving her to put on her clothes and head back to the house, alone.

IN THE PO VALLEY

ANOTHER SLEEPLESS NIGHT. His mother had suggested that having Joan with him might help his insomnia and nightmares but it didn't appear to be the case. Joan had woken again in the middle of last night, disturbed by his thrashing around in the bed. He had woken angry and been unable to sleep again while she went off immediately and lay beside him, her face as calm and motionless as an alabaster angel on a tomb.

He had no idea what he dreamt about when asleep, but in the wide-awake, sleepless, small hours tonight he was back in the Po Valley in northern Italy. Lying in the dark, he laid his arm over Joan's waist, hoping that the warmth from her body, and the steady rise and fall of her stomach under his hand as she breathed, would anchor him in the peace of the bedroom. Yet as soon as he closed his eyes he could feel cold rain beating down on his face, icy needles stinging, sharp like paper-cuts until his skin felt flayed.

The rain-sodden farmlands of the Po Valley were dissected by rivers, irrigation canals and ditches. The incessant rain had put them in full flood. Raging torrents of wild water. Still the rain deluged downwards. This farming heartland was spattered everywhere with farmhouses and stone outbuildings, all providing the perfect cover to German machine gunners. The Canadians' slow progress through the rain-sodden landscape was constantly halted, blocked and repelled. If it wasn't an enemy artillery burst, it was yet another river to get across, weighed down with kit, the waters rising, pregnant with weeks of rain. 'The Forgotten Front,' they'd called it afterwards. Men fighting and dying for little or no strategic reason, other than to keep the Germans occupied on their southern front while the real action took place in northern Europe.

Jim turned over in bed, needing to have his body close to Joan's, curving into her back. He tried to focus his mind on the steady rhythm of her breathing but all he could hear was the constant drumbeat of rain on roof, on river, or on fields already awash with mud. The Germans, holed up in dry farmhouses before the weather had deteriorated, had the tactical advantage. Meanwhile, the Canadians pressed forward, boots weighted down in mud, clothes drenched, hair plastered to heads, moving forward to be picked off like ducks in a fairground shooting alley by snipers. Stretcher bearers, recovering the bodies of the fallen, were mowed down themselves as they made their way through the battery of bullets between explosions from bazookas and bursting shells.

'We're all dying.' A young private was screaming next to him, panic and hysteria beating bravery into submission under the unending joint attack by the elements and the enemy.

Jim had turned to the lad and slapped him across the face, fearing that he was about to run forward straight into the line of fire to get it over with. Later that day he'd discovered his efforts had been futile when he passed the boy's bloodied corpse on a stretcher. Can't have been more than eighteen. First month in action.

Just when he thought it could get no worse, the snow came. January 1945. Holed up in deserted farmhouses, the sandbags they had heaped at the doors to keep back the floods, now pointless, as the snow piled up in drifts against them. The Germans, hidden behind the latticework of dykes and ditches, were not giving any ground. Driving rain and icy winds sweeping over the flat, low plains from the Alps. Ground frozen underfoot. Cold, cold, cold.

It was no good. Jim swung his legs over the side of the bed, grabbed his clothes from the chair and went downstairs to dress in the kitchen. Olive Oyl looked at him in expectation as he entered the room. The puppy had been curled up in the warmth in front of the kitchen range but, seeing Jim, she bounded across the room and happily followed her master outside into the dark of the pre-dawn.

Striding over the field with Olive bouncing along beside him, Jim felt a wave of nostalgia. How many mornings had he walked the farm, criss-crossing the fields, checking crops for disease, for growth, for readiness to harvest, with his old dog Swee' Pea beside him? When he'd first had Swee' Pea, the dog had been a puppy, a mere scrap of a thing he'd rescued from the creek. Now Swee' Pea was long gone, like Walt, like Pa soon would be. The weight of melancholia descended on Jim. It all seemed so pointless. So many dead. What for? He'd read a piece in the paper last week about how the whole country was buoyed up by post war optimism. Right now it was passing him by.

It would be easier if he had no family to think about. He could throw himself completely into fixing the farm. But there was Joan and Jimmy. The responsibility weighed him down. He loved them both, didn't he? But their presence made everything more complicated. Joan was trying hard to make it all work. Too hard maybe? The girl who had taunted him with her unpredictability in Aldershot, one minute flirting with him, the next freezing him out, the woman with a passion for swashbuckling movies, sipping port and lemon in the pub: here she was now, struggling to fit in. He had caused this. He'd brought her here, asked her to live in his mother's house, expected her to muck in and find her role.

He realised he'd never heard his mother ask her a question, never heard her make a pleasantry, offer a compliment, asked her to share in the daily tasks. He'd left Joan to deal with this alone, to find a way to propitiate his mother. But why should she? How could she? He knew better than anyone how his mother could be when she took against a person. He'd thought after that first night Helga would soften her attitude but, since his showdown with her in the barn, she was only going through the motions, tolerating Joan rather than welcoming her. Joan had never complained – but she wasn't the complaining kind. If it had been left to her he would never have known about her being pregnant with Jimmy. Fear of rejection. Fear that he would have walked away and left her. In her book it was better not to put him to the test. How could she have thought he would have failed that test? But maybe he was failing it now.

It was all so hard. So complicated. He remembered the time he had believed himself happiest. Those precious weeks by the sea in Eastbourne with Gwen. But perhaps it was only perfect because it was temporary. He and Gwen had stepped away from their every day responsibilities and lost themselves in each other. It wasn't fair to compare those idyllic days with his life now with Joan.

Jim looked up at the lightening sky and whistled for Olive. The sky was heavy with clouds and there was a new chill in the air. Fall was on the way. How was Joan going to cope with her first Canadian winter? Shut up in that house all day long with his mother giving her the cold shoulder? What the hell was he going to do about it?

It was not just Joan who weighed upon him. He had two other worries. His father's chest was getting worse. Before long he'd be unable to manage the stairs and would be confined to his bed. But there was no possibility of him agreeing to go to the hospital. Caring for him would mean more work for his mother. Not such a bad thing? It would leave more room for Joan to help out. And at least Joan and his father appeared to have an affinity. One small blessing. He made his mind up: whether Don liked it or not he was summoning the doctor.

His other worry was Alice. He felt some responsibility for her in Walt's absence. He was absolutely certain more than a friendly accidental exchange had taken place between her and Tip Howardson. A casual greeting in the street did not explain the grass stains on the back of her dress.

ALICE AND TIP

STILL BURNING from her confrontation with Jim about Tip Howardson, Alice wasn't prepared to be pushed around by her brother-in-law. What right did Jim have to tell her who she could see? Who she could be friends with? Damn it all, even if she were to sleep with Tip again it was none of Jim's concern. She was a grown woman. A widow. A mother. She wasn't going to let him throw his weight around.

Jim had no room to criticise her – he should worry more about his own wife. Tip had accused Joan of sleeping around. He'd actually described her as a slut. Jim must have been aware of her reputation. Was Jimmy even his son? She knew Helga had had doubts.

Alice sighed. Jimmy's parentage was one thing neither she nor Helga could seriously doubt, as soon as they'd met the boy. He was one hundred per cent Armstrong. If anything, he looked more like Walt than Jim. Alice gasped. What was she thinking? No. Not possible. Walt would never have gone with another woman. Never. Never. Never. Besides, Joan wasn't his type. Too dark and sultry for his tastes. She felt guilty for allowing herself a moment's doubt about her dead husband. Her guilt led to shame for allowing herself to be seduced by Tip.

It would never happen again. Alice was determined. She didn't even like Tip. War hero or not, he was not the kind of man she was attracted to. Not at all good looking. He'd never been popular at school. Walt had been his only friend and that had been more out of pity than anything else. Walt had always been affable and when Tip attached himself to him he'd been too kind to brush him off.

Alice tightened the girth of her horse and swung herself up into the saddle. No. Much as it would give her satisfaction to go against Jim, she just couldn't have anything more to do with Tip Howardson.

Cantering across the field, she saw a figure standing near the fence that bordered the eastern side of the farm. Alice turned her horse and headed in that direction. She was going to have it out with Jim.

Jim was leaning on the fence, looking over into the neighbouring field where the corn had already been harvested. He looked up as Alice approached and grinned.

'I was just thinking that once I've got this place sorted it might be a good idea to make an offer on some of the thirty acres Ned Harris has here,' he said. 'What do you think?' His tone was so affable and his smile genuine, so she hadn't the heart to pick up their quarrel again.

'Ned's not so young and may be happy to get a reasonable price for this parcel of land. The future is in bigger acreage. Hard to make a dollar from a couple of quarter sections these days.'

Alice climbed down from her mount and went to stand next to him. 'The Harrises have a daughter in Toronto. They could well be interested in selling up altogether. Their house might suit you and Joan.'

'That's not a bad idea. Thanks, Alice.' He turned and

looked at her. 'I'm sorry for getting angry last night at supper. I should have kept my trap shut. What you choose do is none of my business.'

Glad she'd chosen not to confront him, she said, 'Apology accepted. I think you've been too hard on Tip, but anyway I'm going to keep out of his way. He's interested in more than friendship with me and I don't want that.'

Jim frowned. 'You haven't...'

Alice shook her head. 'No. It's just a feeling I have that he might want to try at some point, but I'm not looking for anyone. Never will be.'

'Never say never.' Jim gave her a rueful smile. 'Maybe one day you'll feel differently if the right man comes along. But that's not Tip Howardson.'

'The right man did come along and he's gone.'

They started to walk back towards the farm together, Alice with the bridle over her arm and her horse following behind them.

'Can I ask you a question?' said Alice.

Jim shrugged. 'Depends what it is.' He looked sideways at her and smiled.

'It's just something Tip said to me. He told me he knew Joan. Back in England. Is that possible?'

'I suppose it's possible. He was in Aldershot before I was. What did he say?' Jim stared ahead, his jaw hardening.

'Just that...oh... he was probably thinking of a different woman.'

'What did he say? Tell me.'

'He implied she was a bit free and easy with herself, if you get my meaning.'

Jim stopped dead. 'He said he'd had a thing with Joan?'

Alice gave a little embarrassed laugh. 'No. Quite the contrary. He said she wasn't his type.'

'Well, what?'

'As I said he was probably thinking of someone else.'

Jim stopped. 'What exactly did that bastard say?'

Alice took a deep breath. 'He said she was a tart. Slept around.'

'And you believed him? I told you he's a lying bastard. That's the proof. Joan's never met him. Until we mentioned him that night, she didn't even know his name or that he was the man responsible for Greg Hooper's death. And one thing I'm absolutely certain about is that my wife has never slept around, as you so delicately put it.' He spat the words out at her.

Alice swallowed. It was a bad idea to have raised this with him. 'As I said, he must have mixed her up with someone else.'

'More likely he's stirring up trouble, trying to trash my wife's good name, the son of a bitch. All because he hates me. Always has. I've never figured out why.'

Alice could see the muscles on Jim's neck tensing. She toyed with telling him Tip had been jealous of Jim's relationship with her since school but decided there was no point.

'Have you told any of this crap to my mother?'

Alice shook her head.

Jim gripped her arm. 'You'd better not have. If I find out you've been stirring up trouble between Joan and Ma, I swear to God, Alice, I won't answer for the consequences. And if you know what's best for you, you'll keep away from Tip Howardson.' He dropped her arm and throwing his hand upwards in an angry gesture, he walked away. Alice got back on her horse and started to trot towards the farm buildings.

As she approached the paddock, she pulled up, turned her horse around and pushed him into a canter, heading towards the track that led into town.

Tying the mare up outside the grain store, Alice crossed the road to the café. As she had expected, Howardson was sitting on a high stool by the bar, the newspaper spread out before him. Did the man never work?

'You seem to spend a lot of time in town, Tip. Doesn't your father have anything for you to do on the farm?'

'Farm's up for sale. When my brothers were killed Dad decided to give up. Knows I never had much of a liking for farming.' He flicked a cigarette to the top of the pack that lay on the counter top beside him and offered it to Alice. When she wrinkled her nose, he said, 'I forgot. You don't.' He drew the cigarette from the pack with his mouth and flicked open his Zippo to light it. 'Bring us a couple of coffees, Freddo,' he called to the owner. 'We'll be sitting over there.' He gestured to a booth at the rear of the otherwise empty room and took Alice by the hand to lead her there.

When they were seated with their coffees, Alice asked herself why she'd come. As Howardson smoked, she studied his face. There was nothing in his features to commend him. His flattened nose looked as if it had been broken in a fight. His hair was thinning on top and his lips were thin and made him look mean. His cheeks were gaunt and when he opened his mouth his teeth were jagged and misshapen. But as she looked up at his eyes she felt a little tremor of excitement. They were cold and narrow like his mouth but the expression in them made it clear that he wanted her. He looked at her and his mouth curled into a smile that echoed the same message. A message that shouted desire.

Her mouth was dry and she tried to sip her coffee. His intentions were clear even before she felt his hand on her leg. She made a small, involuntary sound.

'I knew you'd be back for more,' he said. 'Can't help yourself, can you?'

Alice stuttered. 'I...I didn't...I mean. Look, this was a really bad idea.' She started to get up but the hand under the table moved to the top of her inner thighs and she felt his fingers stroke her through her underwear. 'Please. Don't,' she said.

He withdrew the hand, smiled and leaned back against the wooden banquette. 'You sure about that?'

Alice's stomach clenched as she felt a wave of desire. She hated him, hated herself even more, but had to acknowledge that she liked how he made her body feel. She slipped her foot out of her shoe and lifted it, rubbing her toes against the crotch of his jeans. This time it was Howardson who gave a little gasp. He reached in his pocket, flung a dollar bill on the table and grabbed her arm, pulling her to her feet and pushing her through the door that led to the yard at the back.

Later, as Alice rode home, she knew she was not going to stop seeing Tip. He was like an itch she couldn't stop scratching. She felt a mixture of self loathing and excitement as she thought about what they had just done. Now she had started, she knew she couldn't stop.

WHEN ALICE GOT BACK to the farm she walked into the kitchen to find the family assembled.

'What's going on?'

It was Jim who answered. 'Doc Robinson's upstairs with Pa. Seems Joan managed to persuade Pa to see him.'

Alice looked at Joan. 'Well done. That must have taken some doing.'

She turned to look at Helga, who appeared to be anything but pleased. Evidently Joan's success where she herself had failed was cause for more resentment.

The door that gave onto the stairs opened and Doctor Robinson came into the kitchen. All heads turned to him.

'I've given him something to help him sleep. He should last through till morning. We need to get him back to a normal cycle of sleeping nights.'

'And the cancer?' Helga's face was anxious.

'I'm going to do some tests, but I'm practically certain it isn't lung cancer but emphysema.

There was a collective gasp of relief around the room.

'Now don't get too excited. Emphysema's no picnic and he's still a sick man. The damage to his lungs is permanent, but we can try and stop it getting worse. He's probably got a good few more years left in him as long as he stops smoking that pipe. Smoking doesn't help his shortness of breath.'

The doctor turned to Helga. 'He'll need to use a nebuliser. I'll send the nurse round to show you how it works. You'll need to make sure he uses it, Mrs Armstrong. Your husband's a stubborn man.' He smiled. Inhaling with that will help keep his air passages open. The nurse will fill you in on all the details.'

Refusing the offer of refreshments, the doctor departed, leaving the Armstrongs united in their relief. Helga, overjoyed that the death knell of cancer was gone, forgot her irritation at her daughter-in-law's intervention – although this did not extend to offering Joan her thanks.

GIFT OF RINGS

Joan was washing the dishes in the kitchen.

Don was asleep in his chair by the stove as usual. The wireless was on – she'd discovered that once her father-in-law went off to sleep, nothing seemed to wake him – unless there was something he chose to hear. Perhaps he never really slept at all, just closed his eyes and shut out the world. Who could blame him?

She hummed along to Bing Crosby singing *Don't Fence Me In* with the The Andrews Sisters. She knew the tune well but today found herself listening attentively to the lyrics. As she listened she wondered if Jim had moved back to Aldershot with her, like the song, he would have felt fenced in. While living in close quarters with his family was a constant struggle for her, Joan had begun to appreciate how Jim felt about the land and the farm. Living in Aldershot again would have been a kind of prison to him and she could see why, when here at Hollowtree Farm they were surrounded by fields, gentle rolling hills, quiet and calm. He'd never liked the infertile heathland around Aldershot, with its gorse bushes and thin sandy soil.

Lost in thought, she jumped when Jim appeared behind her, kissed the back of her neck and put his arms around her waist. Joan leaned back against him, surprised. It was the middle of the afternoon and he should be out in the fields until supper.

'What's up?' she asked.

'I had a sudden urge to make love to my wife.'

Joan laughed. 'Don't be daft!'

'What was it you once said to me? Where's your sense of adventure?'

Jim turned her to face him and kissed her.

'Watch out,' she said, 'I've got wet hands.' She held them out.

He pulled her arms down and drew them behind him, heedless of the damp soapy water on his shirt.

'But your mother? And Jimmy?'

'In town. I suggested she take him for a milkshake and keep him out of our way for a while.'

Joan moved her arms around his neck and kissed him and he lifted her up and carried her upstairs.

Later, when they were getting dressed again, Jim fished in his trouser pocket and pulled out a small box and handed it to her.

'For me?' she asked, her hands trembling.

'Who else?' He looked around him and laughed.

She gave him a playful slap and opened the box, which was tied in ribbon. Inside was not one, but two rings. One a simple plain gold band and the other identical but for the addition of a single small diamond. Joan gasped.

'But you can't afford this, Jim.'

'Hell, yes, I can. The cultivator can wait 'til spring. Not a lot of use over the winter. We didn't have time to get engaged but I don't see why you shouldn't have a ring just the same. And I've been long overdue with the wedding ring.

My wife shouldn't have to wear a cheap ring she had to buy herself.'

He reached for her hand and twisted the utility ring off her finger. Then he bent his head and ran his tongue over the green coppery stain and rubbed the mark off with his handkerchief. 'That's better,' he said, as he slipped the engagement ring on her finger. 'Still want to be married to me, Mrs Armstrong?' Without waiting for her answer he bent his head and kissed her softly. 'With this ring I thee wed.' He slid the wedding ring on. 'I'm glad you married me, Joan.'

Joan extended her hand to admire the rings. 'They're beautiful. Thank you, my darling.'

'I have one small request to make.' Jim reached for her hand and held it in his as he looked into her eyes.

'Anything.'

'Please don't ever ask me again if I still love Alice.'

'I won't. I'm sorry. It was stupid. Sometimes I just–'

Jim cut her short. 'Only it made me feel as if you don't trust me.' He looked into her eyes. 'The guy who was engaged to Alice Ducroix isn't me. He was from another life, another world. Long gone. Yes, once upon a time I thought I loved Alice, but it was a puppy love. A shadow of what I feel for you. And...'

'Yes?'

'I want you to know I never made love to Alice. Never. I won't deny that at the time I wanted to, but not any more. You were the first, Joan.'

As he said the words, Joan stiffened, a cold shiver running down her spine. 'The first? But not the last?'

Jim closed his eyes. 'I didn't mean that.'

'Answer my question. You're the *only* man I've ever been with. But you're telling me that I'm not the only woman?' She asked herself why she was doing this – but she had a compulsion to know, to push him, to force the truth from him. 'Was it some Italian girl? You went with someone after we were married. I know three years is a long time but...' Her voice was choked. 'I thought you'd have waited for me just as I did for you.'

'No!' He spoke loudly. 'I swear to you, Joan. I've never been with anyone else since we married. How could I? How could you think that?'

'You said I was the first. Just now and that night in London. So answer my question.'

Jim exhaled. 'There was a woman. When I was stationed in Eastbourne.'

Joan moved away, leaning back against the bed head, her knees drawn up in front of her.

'It was a brief affair. You'd told me you didn't want to have anything more to do with me. Dammit, Joan, you'd slammed the door in my face. You said you were still going to marry that Pete guy. Despite what had happened between us.'

Perhaps she had sensed something all along. A feeling that Jim was holding something of himself back from her. There had been a barrier between them ever since she had come to Canada. His refusal to talk about the war. That implied he didn't trust her enough. Worse – didn't love her enough. Joan sensed that she was playing a dangerous game but she couldn't stop. She had to weed out the truth. Otherwise it would always be between them, festering away.

'Tell me her name.'

Jim was sitting on the edge of the bed, bent forward, his elbows on his knees, head in hands. 'Gwen. Her name was Gwen.'

'Did you love her?'

'She was married. I told you, it was a brief affair.'

'That's not what I asked you.'

Jim was silent.

'I want to know everything. No secrets. What kind of marriage is it if we have secrets from each other? If we can't be honest? Why didn't you tell me this back in Aldershot before you went to Sicily? Why were you afraid to tell me?'

'Look, Joan, don't do this. Please. It's all in the past. I married you. I chose you.'

'Because you couldn't have her.'

He gave a long sigh in exasperation.

'Answer me. Were you in love with her?'

Jim turned to face her. 'Yes. I fell in love with her. But it's over. It was over even before I found out about you having Jimmy.' He paused then reached for her hand. 'In fact she told me I shouldn't give up on you. She told me to go and see you before I went overseas.'

Joan jerked her hand away. 'You told her about me! You talked to her about *us*.'

'Yes. I told you wanted nothing to do with me and she told me not to give up on you. Don't you see, Joan?'

'I see. But what I see is that if she hadn't been married, you'd have gone back to her. And I see that if she hadn't told you to come and find me you wouldn't have bothered.'

'How can you say that? What on earth makes you think that?'

'Because it's true, isn't it? Isn't it?' She pushed him away and ran downstairs and out of the house.

JIM LAY back on the bed and stared at the ceiling. His carefully planned afternoon was ruined. How had he managed to mess things up so badly? It had all been going well. Joan had loved the rings. Why the hell had he gone and opened his big mouth like that?

He knew Joan had always been insecure – even though when they'd first met he had believed the opposite – that she was trifling with him. Over the time they'd been together he'd come to realise that this was a facade, a means of protecting herself from getting hurt.

How could he have been so stupid? What was the point of confessing about Gwen? There had never been any hope of a future with Gwen, so why had he felt compelled to tell Joan about her?

But inside he knew Joan was right. Even though he never expected to see Gwen again, he still thought about her. Thought about what might have been. Thought about how he'd felt with her. About her. He conjured her image now and felt his stomach flip.

He was ashamed. Angry with himself. He'd hurt Joan. Driven a wedge between them. Ruined a beautiful moment. He'd shot his own foot off and for what?

Jim got off the bed and moved to the dormer window. He could see Joan in the distance, walking past the barn yard, down the track towards the woods. He was about to go after her – but what was the point? How could he possibly retrieve the situation? How could he make her believe that he loved her, not Gwen? He knew he couldn't. Because it wasn't true.

MAKING PEACE

It was Alice who found her. The family had sat down to supper and there was no sign of Joan. When it became obvious that Jim wasn't going to go looking for her, Alice took it upon herself. She knew what it was like to feel lonely, isolated, friendless. Perhaps it was time to mend some fences with Joan.

She found her by the pool, sitting in the gloom under the tree.

'Hey, Joan,' she called. 'You missed supper. Pumpkin pie. I saved you a slice.'

'I'm not hungry.'

Alice hesitated then dropped down to the grass beside her.

They sat in silence for a while, then Alice said, 'Judging by the look on Jim's face just now, you two have had a falling out. He's acting like a bear with a sore head.'

Joan said nothing.

'Look... I know things haven't been great between you and me, but I really like you, Joan. I didn't think I was going to and I'm sure you felt the same. Probably still do.'

Still Joan was silent, but she was listening.

'Okay. I'm going to be honest with you. I was jealous of you and Jim.'

Joan turned away. She didn't want to hear any more confessions today.

'Not because you were with Jim.' She gave a little laugh. 'I don't think that way about Jim. I love him like a brother. No, I was jealous because you seem so happy together. The way you look at each other. It made me think all the time how much I've lost with Walt dying.'

Joan frowned, unsure whether to believe Alice.

'I've always thought there's one true love for everyone in this world – but some people never find it and others, like me, have it only briefly before it's taken away from them.' Alice's voice was low.

Joan gave a little sob. Alice shuffled over and put her arms around her. 'Everyone has rows now and then. It doesn't mean you don't love each other. I wish Walt was here to have a good row with me now. Worth it for the pleasure of making up.'

Joan began to cry.

'I don't expect you to tell me what it's about – but you can if you want.'

Joan looked up, wiping her hand across her face to brush away the tears. 'No. Tell me about Walt. Jim never talks about him. That's one reason why I thought–'

'You thought Jim still had feelings for me? No need to worry on that score.' She pulled at a clump of grass. 'We were always more like brother and sister than anything more. I had a schoolgirl crush on him from when I was thirteen and he rescued me from a bunch of boys who were bullying me.' She gave a wry laugh. 'One of them was Walt!'

Joan sniffed her tears back and watched Alice intently.

'We started going out together when I turned sixteen. Jim

was always so darned nice to me. But to be honest, Joan, it was like a habit. We got on really well. Still do – most of the time. Everyone assumed we'd get married. Helga was made up when we got engaged. Walt ignored me. Behaved like I didn't exist. And then one day... well, one day it all changed. Jim never really *wanted* me. Not like Walt did. When I saw him for the first time that way it was a shock to my system. It rocked me to the core.' Alice's eyes stared into space. 'I realised then what love is. Jim never felt that way about me and I never felt that way about him.' She paused and looked at Joan anxiously. 'Is it all right me telling you this? Only there's never been anyone I could confide in. Not Helga – she'd never have understood – she had it fixed in her head that I should marry Jim. She always preferred him to Walt. She'd deny it, of course – and I'm not saying she didn't love Walt. It near broke her heart when he was killed. But she never understood why I chose him over Jim.'

Joan plucked at her skirt. 'I was engaged to someone else when I met Jim. He lived in our street and we grew up together. His name was Pete. Just like you and Jim, everyone expected us to get engaged. I knew I didn't love him, but after war was declared and he was about to be shipped off to North Africa, he asked me to marry him. He looked so eager and optimistic and I didn't have the heart to say no. Not when he was going off to risk his life and might never come back – so I agreed even though I didn't love him. And I didn't believe in love anyway.'

She touched the rings on her finger. 'My father ran off when I was a baby. If you spend night after night hearing your mother crying herself to sleep, love isn't something you aspire to. Mum eventually married my stepdad and while I don't believe for a moment she's ever been in love with him, she's happy. They look after each other. No passion but lots of affection. That seemed the best choice for me too. Pete loved me and would never walk out on me, so I said yes. I never doubted it was the right decision until one night I was sitting having a quiet drink in a pub with my cousin and Jim Armstrong walked in and everything turned upside down.'

Alice reached out and took Joan's hand and squeezed it. 'I wish we'd talked before. We have so much in common. Look, Joan, I don't want to pry or ask what you and Jim have argued about but it's clear to me he loves you. Make up with him. Forgive whatever he's done. He wants the best for you and Jimmy. Just the other day we were talking and he was so excited about the future. I'm probably talking out of turn and it may never happen, but he's thinking of making an offer on the Harris place next door. He wants to expand the farm and they have thirty acres – and a little house. He was so excited about the idea of living there with you and Jimmy. Don't let on I told you – but believe me, he was.'

'Thanks, Alice.' Joan looked towards the horizon, where there was a roseate glow meeting the inky blue-black sky. 'It's almost dark.'

Alice said, 'I love this pool. It was here under this tree that I kissed Walt and my life changed.'

'Yes and it was here you threw a bucket of pond water over me.'

'Sorry about that. I told you I was jealous.' She gave a little laugh. 'But I wasn't lying. It *is* a family tradition.'

The evening darkened – they were two silhouettes in the gloaming.

After a few minutes Alice broke the silence. 'I had sex yesterday.'

Joan, surprised, waited for her to go on.

'It was the second time.' Alice hesitated. 'I don't know why I'm telling you this, Joan. Please promise me you'll keep it to yourself. I beg you.' Her face was anxious.

'Of course. I wouldn't dream of telling anyone.'

'I feel nothing for him. In fact I think I even dislike him. But I'd forgotten what it was like to be wanted. To have a man desire me. And I'd forgotten how much I like sex.' She exhaled slowly. 'You probably think I'm a tart.'

'No. I'm not judging you.'

'I *felt* like a tart afterwards. But do you know, Joan? At the time I didn't give a damn. I wanted to be wanted, to be … you know what I mean. I can't say *making love* as there was nothing about love in what we did. Lust. Pure lust.' She sighed again. 'But oh, my goodness, it felt good.'

'After so long. I can imagine.' Joan picked up a pebble and pitched it into the pool. They both listened to the splash and watched the ripples fading away in the half light. 'Until I came here I'd only had sex once.'

Alice gasped.

'Yes. Jimmy was the result of a one night stand. An accident, I suppose. But he's the best thing that ever happened to me.'

'But how? Why?'

Joan drew her legs up in front of her. 'Jim and I were hardly an item. We weren't even going out.' She bit her lip. It was so odd confiding all this to Alice of all people, yet she found it therapeutic. She'd been so lonely without Ethel and missed having a friend. 'All the way here from England I was terrified that Jim didn't want me; that I'd arrive and he wouldn't be there to meet me; that he'd wish he'd never married me.'

'That's daft. He was so looking forward to you coming. He was pacing up and down the kitchen all afternoon and evening until it was it time to fetch you. Even then, he left a couple of hours early.'

'Really? But he was late. At least I thought he was. He wasn't on the platform when we got off the train.' She gave a dry laugh. 'I'd made up my mind he wasn't going to turn up. And then he just appeared.'

Alice touched Joan's hand. 'You're so hard on yourself. I expect it was because he was just as terrified that *you* weren't going to turn up.'

Joan leaned her head back, breathed out and said, 'There's more. Jim told me tonight that he had a relationship with a married woman. I asked if he'd been in love with her and he didn't deny it.'

'When was that?'

Joan told her. 'But it doesn't matter what he said, I could tell. I've known all along that there was someone else. It explains why he's always holding something back, why he never wholly confides in me, why he won't let me in.'

She began to cry again then brushed the tears away impatiently. 'He has terrible dreams and sometimes he's so withdrawn I can't reach him at all. He calls out in his sleep, thrashes about as if he's trying to run away from something. I've no idea what he went through in Italy and I wish to God he'd tell me but he won't. He shuts me out. Can you imagine how that feels?'

Alice reached for her hand again.

'Don told me I needed to be patient with him. Said he was the same after the other war. Said he saw things he could never ever speak of to anyone. I know Jim is suffering but he won't let me help him. It's because he doesn't love me. He loves her.'

'If he loved her, why didn't he go back to her?'

'Because of Jimmy.'

'Is that what he said?' Alice sounded horrified.

'No.' Joan shook her head. 'He said it was already over when he found out about Jimmy. I'm sure it only ended because she was married.'

'Stop torturing yourself, Joan. He's with you, isn't he? Not her. Do you want to give up on him so easily? Why? What about Jimmy? You both love that boy. What good would it do any of you if you give up on Jim now? That woman, whoever she was, is on the other side of the ocean and as far as you know living happily ever after with her husband. Forget about her. Put the row with Jim behind you. Get yourself back to the house and make up with him. I swear to God, Joan, if I were in your shoes, no matter what Walt had done, I'd be running up that hill back to him.'

Joan said nothing.

'You know I'm right, don't you?' Alice gave her a gentle poke in the ribs. 'Admit it.'

'Thank you,' Joan said at last, biting her lip. 'Talking to you has helped.'

Alice leaned in and gave her a hug and planted a kiss on her cheek. 'I'm just sorry I was such a cow to you, Joan. I'm glad we've cleared the air.'

'Me too.'

'It's getting late. We should go back.'

They got to their feet.

'Tell me about this man of yours,' Joan said as they walked. 'Do you think you could have a future with him?'

Alice gave a snort. 'No. Absolutely not.'

'Why not? Give it time. If he makes you feel good.'

'But that's it. He doesn't. The sex is good but the feeling is bad. It's as if he's using me. Using my body.' She thought for a moment then laughed mirthlessly. 'I suppose the same's true of me. And I'm not interested in a relationship – I'll settle for occasional sex.'

'Well if you're both happy with that.'

They parted in the farmyard with another hug.

'I hope Helga settled Rose down for the night,' said Alice.

'Good luck – and keep telling yourself it's the future that matters, not the past.'

Joan hoped she was right.

ANOTHER RECONCILIATION

JIM SAT at the kitchen table, feeling wretched. He'd made a real mess of things. Why had he blurted out that she'd been his first? Where had that come from? What possessed him? And then why hadn't he solved it with a good old-fashioned lie? But lies always led to more lies – and he couldn't bear the thought of lying to Joan. The way she'd looked at him, as though she could see right through him – she'd have known the truth at once and if he'd lied it would have made matters worse. Besides, lying wasn't in his nature.

He should have gone to find her, but had been afraid of how she'd react. Better to give her time. He'd behaved badly. Not just now but in everything – breaking his promise and bringing her to Canada and then failing to lend enough support to her once she got here. Joan was trying so hard: working in the fields, putting up with his mother's unwelcoming behaviour, living in cramped conditions without a word of complaint. Because of him she'd changed the way she dressed. He bent over the table, his head in his hands. Even in her ATS uniform Joan had always looked her best. Hair and makeup immaculate, making the most of what she could procure despite rationing. Now she was wearing heavy boots and overalls, hair scraped up under a scarf. It was as if he'd captured and caged an exotic bird and as a result she was losing the brightness of her plumage.

The kitchen was in near darkness so he got up and lit the oil lamp. Helga and Alice had been talking quietly as they washed up after the meal then Alice had slipped out and Helga had taken Rose and Jimmy over to Alice's place while Don went up to bed. He guessed Alice had gone to find Joan and he hoped she wouldn't make matters worse. He'd said nothing about what had happened to anyone but in Joan's absence at the table the atmosphere had been tense. He was grateful to them all for not asking him.

He did still have feelings for Gwen but it was pointless. Gwen was history. He had to make the best of things with Joan. And he did love her. He felt bad having to lie when he'd said he didn't care any more for Gwen. But what choice did he have? He hated hurting Joan. He couldn't make it any worse.

It was all so hard. Jim wondered if he'd taken on too much with the farm. Was he crazy to be considering buying more acreage? But with veterans' loans for investing in machinery it could make a real difference – allow him to transform the place. Mechanisation was the future and so was scale. Wasn't that what the guy from the ministry had said? If he could just get through the next year. Things had been easier in the ten months or so before Joan and Jimmy had arrived. All he had thought about then was getting the work done. Now his head was buzzing with so much else. But underneath it all was the unanswerable question – why had he lived when so many around him hadn't? So many dead whose lives were probably worth more than his. He felt the burden of responsibility to those dead men as well. Since he'd been given a life he had to make the best use of it. Maybe it would have been better if he'd been blown up in a mine-field – and that fellow Pete who Joan was supposed to marry had survived. She'd have been in her own home town, surrounded by her own family. She'd said she never loved Pete, but at least he wouldn't have made her unhappy the way Jim had.

He looked up as Joan walked into the house. He saw at once that she'd been crying. She looked at him with what he took to be uncertainty, nervousness. Agonised that he had been the cause of her distress, he got up and moved around the table towards her. He saw her hesitate and then she was in his arms and he held her hard against him.

'I'm sorry, Joan. I didn't mean to hurt you. I hate to see you unhappy. Forgive me?'

She leaned into him, avoiding his eyes as she spoke. 'After tonight I don't want to talk about it any more. I want to try and forget what was said.' She gulped. 'But I've been thinking about it and I had a talk with Alice. She said the future is more important than the past. Do we have a future, Jim?'

He gasped, overcome that he had caused her so much pain, so much doubt. 'Oh my darling, of course we do. I love you. I love Jimmy, and all I want is to make a decent life for us all. That matters more than anything to me. Please believe me.' He looked into her eyes. She seemed so frail. Like a flower whose petals had been crushed in heavy rain. He ran his thumb down her cheek and she turned her head so that her mouth was against the palm of his hand.

'No more secrets?' she asked.

'No more secrets.'

'Then there's something I need you to know. I was going to tell you the other day but we were having such a lovely time with Jimmy down at the pool and I didn't want to spoil the mood.'

Jim frowned, uneasy. 'Sit down.' He took two glass

tumblers off the shelf and poured them each a large slug from a dusty bottle of rye whisky that he extracted from the back of a cupboard. 'I think we both need this.'

She took a sip, pulled a face, then sipped it again slowly. 'Before I met you, before I joined the ATS, something bad happened to me.'

Jim leaned across the table and took her hand.

He tried to hold her eyes as she spoke but she looked down at the table. 'I was attacked by a Canadian soldier on my way home from work. He was going to…it was horrible. He tried to force me to… He was so big and heavy and too strong for me.'

'He raped you?' Jim felt a cold sweat on his face and the muscles in his neck tightened. He slugged back the whisky and reached for the bottle to refill his glass.

'No – he didn't get that far. Some other soldiers came along and I managed to run away.'

'Do you know who he was?'

'All I know is he was called Bill.'

'Rank?'

She shook her head.

'Did you report him?'

Joan shook her head again. 'I was too embarrassed. And afraid. I couldn't face talking about it. People asking questions. I packed in the job and joined the army. Never saw him again.'

Jim leaned across the table and put his hand on hers. 'I wish you'd told me when I was in Aldershot. I'd have found the bastard and punched his lights out.'

'He's here.'

It took a few seconds for Jim to realise what she was saying. 'Here?'

'I saw him in town.'

'You saw him in Hollowtree?'

She nodded. 'And he recognised me. I was alone in the café and he came to my table and he...' She hesitated, avoiding Jim's eyes. 'He touched me. Underneath the table. He put his hands on my legs. It was horrible. I was terrified.'

Jim moved round the table to sit beside her and wrapped her in his arms. He wanted to go out now, into town, walk the streets, hammer on doors until he found the man.

'You don't remember the rest of his name?'

'I never knew it.'

'What does he look like?'

'Tall, big build. Piercing eyes. Back then when he came into the chippy he'd seemed quite a pleasant guy. Not bad looking. Always polite. Friendly. But now he looks mean.'

'That's not a lot to go on. With so many men back from the war and half of Canada stationed in Aldershot at some time, it could be anyone.'

He clenched his fist. 'I swear to God, Joan, I'm going to find that snake and when I do I'm going to make sure he never comes within an inch of you again.' He ran his hands through his hair. 'I wish you'd told me right away as soon as you ran into him.' He frowned in concentration. 'Bill? I can't think of any Bills round here. Maybe he was just passing through.'

Joan shook her head. 'I hope so. But I'm afraid. He said he had unfinished business with me.'

'Hell, Joanie, that means he threatened you. Why didn't you tell me before now? We should talk to the constable.'

'I was ashamed.' She looked away. 'And I don't want to involve the police.'

'Ashamed?' He was getting louder. 'You had nothing to be ashamed about. You'd done nothing wrong.' He thumped the table.

Joan closed her eyes. 'I shouldn't have told you. I hate for you to think of me that way – to know that he tried to do things to me. He made me feel dirty.'

Jim held her hands again. 'Don't, Joan. Don't let him make you think like that. I'll never think of you like that.'

'Better that I just make sure I don't go into town alone.'

'For sure. But I want to find this guy. Hell, Hollowtree is a small town. I'll ferret out that bastard wherever he is.'

Joan gave him a quick smile and got up from the table. 'Enough of him. Take me to bed, Jim. We still have a lot of making up to do.'

Jim needed no more encouragement.

INTO THE WOODS

'HEY, ALICE!' Jim called to his sister-in-law as she cycled past on the track to town. 'You off to the library?'

'Sure am. Want me to pick something up in town?' She slowed down and waited as he walked across the field he was clearing.

Jim wiped his hands against his overalls. 'You know anyone called Bill?'

She frowned. 'Isn't the old blind fellow who lives with Mrs Murphy at the grocery called Bill? I think he's her uncle.'

'No one else?'

She shrugged. 'Can't think of anyone. Why?'

'Oh nothing. Must have got the wrong name. See you later.' He turned and walked back across the field. After a few paces he turned back. 'Alice!'

Alice waited as he returned, her feet planted either side of the bike, hands on the grips, ready to push off.

'I just want to say thank you. I don't know what you said to Joan last night or she said to you, and I'm not going to ask either of you, but whatever it was, I'm grateful. It was good of you to do what you did. Joan needs a friend here.'

Alice smiled. 'She's a nice woman, once you get to know her. I think I was a bit quick to judge when she first arrived. But now I'm glad she's here.'

Jim nodded and stood watching as Alice mounted the bicycle and pedalled away.

ALICE'S DAY at the library dragged. The woman working with her today was not the most talkative of companions and anyway was a strict believer in enforcing the requirement for silence, speaking only when essential to assist a customer and then in hushed tones. Alice took herself off to the stacks at the back of the building, re-shelving books for most of the morning, leaving Miss Simpson to rule from the front desk.

When she came down the steps she was relieved that Tip wasn't there, but the relief was tinged with disappointment.

She'd cycled about half a mile and was approaching an area of the road surrounded by dense trees, when she almost lost her balance as Tip stepped out in front of her, causing her to brake hard and skid to a halt. He stood square on to her in front and steadied the bike by gripping the middle of the handlebar.

'Tip Howardson, you made me leap right out of my skin. What do you think you're doing here?'

'Meeting you, of course.' He took a step back and watched her while he lit a cigarette. 'Surely you didn't think I'd miss a chance to see you when you're in town?'

'I've got to get home,' she said, grinning. 'We made no arrangement to meet.'

'Soon enough, angel. But there's time for a little diversion on the way.' He dragged on his cigarette and jerked his head to signal her to get down.

Alice, excited, did his bidding and followed him as he headed into the woods, leaning her bike against a tree. As he strode deeper along a path through the undergrowth Alice remembered what she'd said last night to Joan – that being with Tip made her feel bad about herself, but right now she felt only desire. Little leaps and eddies of pleasure were already rushing though her stomach and between her legs. What was it about this man? His aggression, hardness, his sense of entitlement were so different from Walt. Maybe that was the attraction. His very difference. It helped stop her from feeling she was being disloyal. Made it clear that it was only about sex, not love.

He was walking fast and she had to half run to keep up. He was wearing a woollen check lumber jacket and his neck emerging from the top of it was thick like a tree trunk. That was different from Walt too. Walt had been slim, fit, lithe, whereas Tip was an ox of a man. Not fat at all, just big, powerful. Scary. But wasn't that part of the appeal too?

He halted suddenly and took her by the shoulders, pushing her up against the trunk of a tree, then his mouth was on hers and his hands all over her. Before Alice had time to draw breath he was inside her, his only concession to foreplay being the walk of anticipation through the wood. To her surprise she was ready for him, hungry for him, the thought of what they were about to do sufficient to arouse her. He paid no attention to her at all, so that she felt like a piece of wood, a part of the tree – a vessel for him to slake his desire.

'Hey, slow down a bit, Tip. You're hurting me.'

He ignored her.

'Tip, I said you're hurting me.'

He reached down and grabbed her left leg behind the knee, jerking it up and lifting it high behind his back. She cried out.

He grinned at her. 'Relax, babe, you know you like it rough. Come on. Go with it. Don't be a bitch.'

When he had finished, he buttoned himself up and lit a cigarette, leaning against another tree watching her. Alice slumped down into the pile of leaves on the forest floor, leaning back against the trunk, exhausted.

'That was great, angel. You are one hell of a good fuck.'

'Don't be so vulgar. I can't abide that kind of talk.'

Howardson stretched a foot towards her and poked at her leg lightly. 'Come on, Alice, you know you loved it.' He squatted down beside her and pulled a silly face. 'Let's have a little smile then, for Uncle Tip. Come on, girl.' He grinned at her and pulled another face. Alice gave a reluctant smile. 'That's better,' he said. 'That's my girl.'

Gratified, he sat down beside her, stretching his legs out in front.

'How are things up at Hollowtree? Jim know you're seeing me?'

'I'm not *seeing* you.'

'Well fucking me then.'

She swatted at his arm. 'I told you to stop that filthy talk. Of course not. He hates you for some reason. And he still doesn't believe what happened to you in France.'

Tip snorted. 'I'm not really surprised. You have to understand, Alice, I was Jim's NCO. He reported to me. I often had to punish him. That didn't sit well with him, knowing me from home and the fact I was in his little brother's class at school. Natural resentment. Some men just can't deal with authority and military discipline. Jim wasn't cut out to be a soldier.'

Alice frowned. 'That's not true. He was decorated in Italy. He had two promotions and finished as a corporal.'

'Buggins' turn, as the Brits put it. The battlefield necessity. When truly brave men, men like *Walt...*' He looked at her intently and took hold of her hand, stroking his fingers along it. 'When brave men sacrifice their lives in battle, their inferiors, men skilled only in surviving at any price, reap the benefits. It's a sad fact. A lot of good men died in Italy. Some of the best. A lot of others were unfairly promoted in their place.'

'Jim's a good man.'

Tip thought for a moment. 'I didn't say he wasn't. He's not a bad man – but he's a weak one. A bit windy, as our British pals used to put it.'

Alice couldn't square what Tip was saying with her own knowledge of Jim. She felt disloyal. But she knew nothing of the army. And Tip had been his senior.

Tip let her hand go. 'So what is old Jim up to these days? Realised at last that that farm's too much for him?'

'Certainly not. In fact, he's thinking of expanding. Hoping to make an offer for the place next door.'

'The Harris farm?'

'Yes. It's about thirty acres. He wants to plant apple trees there. And then there's their house. Moving in there would save him having to build a home for his wife and child. Right now it's all a bit cramped at Hollowtree and living with Helga can be tricky. Poor Joan has a hard time of it.'

'Interesting. Good for Jim.' He smiled at her and patted her lightly on the arm.

Alice got to her feet and brushed pine needles off her skirt. 'I'm cold,' she said, 'and it will be getting dark soon. I have to go.'

Tip reached for another cigarette. 'So long, angel. I'll be seeing you, babe.'

She nodded goodbye.

As she was walking away, Tip called after her. 'I did remember to tell you, didn't I? That you're one hell of a good fuck.'

SNOW

THE SUN HAD ALREADY RISEN when Joan woke. The bedroom was filled with white light, filtering through the threadbare curtains. Damn. Yet again she'd failed to waken when Jim did. She'd asked him to wake her when he rose, but he never did. He probably thought it a kindness, but it made her feel lazy and lacking in effort. Hard to break the habits of a lifetime though – even after almost five months in Canada.

She sat up in bed and rubbed her eyes. It was so cold. Jim had warned her yesterday that it would get a lot worse soon. But at least today the sun appeared to be shining. Then she realised there was something strange about the morning.

The silence.

The countryside was always quiet compared to the street where she'd lived in Aldershot – but there were usually noises underlying the quiet: the distant sound of the tractor, neighing from the horses, the lowing of the few cows still kept on the farm, the call of birds, the clank of milk pails. But this morning there was soundlessness that seemed different from quiet, from silence. It was as though there were a vacuum into which sounds had been sucked, to create an absence of sound altogether.

Shivering, she threw back the covers, got out of bed and went to the window.

The farm was transformed. A world of whiteness. So bright that it made her blink. Opposite, the iron roof of the barn was covered in a thick eiderdown of snow. The yard and the fields merged into one large white carpet and the fencing was piled high with drifts. Through the middle of the yard she saw large footprints marking Jim's passage from the house to the biffy and thence to the barn.

Pulling on her clothes and adding an extra jumper, she hurried downstairs. Her boots and coat were beside the door. The boots were freezing cold as she slipped her feet into them and went outside. She traced her way using the cavities made by Jim's footprints, stretching her legs to match his stride and trying to keep her balance. It must be nearly a foot deep. Snow was no longer falling – the magic had been wrought entirely under cover of night.

When she pushed open the barn door she saw him at once, raking straw across the floor of the extension built onto the rear of the barn close to Alice's cabin.

Jim looked up as she came in. He grinned. 'Got you some snow at last.'

'At last?' she said. 'It's only November.'

'Better get used to it as it'll be here until April.'

Six months. It was hard to imagine. 'How will we get by all that time?'

'What do you mean?' He carried on spreading the straw.

'Well, you can't do any farming in the snow, can you?'

Jim laughed. 'There's more to farming than planting and harvesting. Plenty to do all winter. Just different things. For a start, what I'm doing now. I should have already had this hay down for the cows to come in. They need hay and water and straw to lie on. And there's the yard to be cleared. I need to dig out a path from the house to the biffy and to Alice's door. In fact I'll probably try rigging the snowplough up to the tractor rather than shovel it all.'

Joan stood with her back against the wall, watching him work. She never tired of looking at him. She'd never imagined, that night in The Stag pub in Aldershot, that one day she would be leaning against a barn wall in Canada watching him rake hay. Her eyes welled up at the memory of how, for her, it had been love at first sight and how she had tried so hard to conceal her feelings from Jim – and to tell herself they weren't real. Yet now she was here, married to him and bringing up their child.

Jim was still talking. 'There's grain to be hauled. Corn to be taken down to the granary, other side of town. Beans to bag up. Machinery to be cleaned, mended, maintained. Seeds ordered. Fertilizer to buy. Cows to be milked. Chickens fed. Then when the weather permits I'll be clearing the tree line – cutting back overhanging branches. Otherwise they get in the way of the tractor.' He looked at her, his words coming in rhythm with his strokes of the rake. 'Lots of planning too. Paperwork. Taxes. Applying for grants. Plenty to keep me busy.'

'I'd like to help with that,' she said. 'With the paperwork. You could show me.'

Jim raised his eyebrows, but nodded. Then he grinned at her. 'And there's the little matter of a bathroom to be fitted. But this afternoon there's one thing that I absolutely have to do. Top priority.' He jerked his head towards the wall behind him. Joan followed his eyes. Hanging from hooks on the slats were several wooden contraptions. Sledges. 'I've got to introduce you and Jimmy to the joys of speeding down the hill behind the house.'

'Oh no,' she said, backing away and laughing. 'You won't get me on one of those things.'

'Now I never thought you'd be a chicken, Joan Armstrong. That's not the woman I married.' He dropped the rake and pulled her into his arms. 'You're going to love it.' He kissed her.

Joan looked up at him, happy as she always was when he held her like that. 'But Jimmy? He's awfully young.'

'He was four last week. Besides I've promised him.'

'You did what?'

He kissed her again, lightly on the mouth. 'He can't wait.'

Joan batted his arm. 'You'll have me in an early grave, you, with worry about that child.'

'I told you, he's a farm boy now. I can still remember the first time Pa took me down that slope on a sled. I was prob- ably no more than two-years-old. Walt too. As soon as we could sit up.' He turned away, his face darkened by the memory of times that were now lost for ever. 'Pa won't be sliding down any more hills now. I just hope he survives the winter.'

'But the doc said if he took his medication…And it's not cancer. Emphysema he said, didn't he?'

Jim nodded. 'Yes, we have that to be thankful for – and ruling out tuberculosis too. But while the emphy-thing is not necessarily going to kill him – at least for a long time, it's certainly not going to get better and it saps his ability to do things. That in itself is a death sentence for my father – I'm afraid he's already lost his will to live.'

'No. No. Don't say that, Jim.' Her eyes filled with tears. 'I love your pa. I really do. I've only known him a short time but I feel as though he's… he's my friend. I never knew my father, and I got on with my stepdad well enough, but we were never close. But Don…'

'I know. He loves you too, Joan.' He stroked her hair.

Then he held her away from him, grinned and said, 'But you ask him – ask him whether you should be letting me career down the hillside with Jimmy in front and I can bet you ten dollars what he'll say.'

She smiled and shook her head. 'I know when the odds are stacked against me. You win – but be careful!'

JIMMY WAS BUBBLING over with joy and readiness for the planned tobogganing expedition and at the prospect of playing out in the thick snow. He was too excited to bother with his food until Joan insisted that without a hot breakfast inside him he wouldn't be playing outside and that unless he ate his lunch too there would be no toboggan rides later on. He lifted his head, eyes wide, then dropped it down and began shovelling sausage into his mouth and chewing rapidly.

'Easy, boy,' said Don. 'If you gobble it down that fast, you'll get indigestion, then you won't be sledding at all.'

Jimmy dropped his fork and looked between one and the other, as if to say he couldn't win.

Helga tousled his hair. 'Slow and steady does it, sweetie.'

After the meal, Alice and Joan did the dishes together, watching the two children through the window as they built a snowman, the dog gambolling around them.

'Jimmy's so happy here,' Joan said at last.

'Didn't you think he would be?'

'I thought he'd miss home more. His granny. His Aunty Ethel. I thought he'd find it strange here, but the moment he stepped off that ship and saw the train we were going to ride on, he fell in love with Canada.'

'Kids adapt fast,' said Alice.

'This is a much better life for him than being stuck in a town. And although it's my home town, so I have some affection for it, there's not a lot to commend it. It's basically one huge military barracks.'

'Plenty of men then?' Alice gave a little giggle.

Joan smiled. 'It only takes one.'

She saw Alice bite her lip and wished she hadn't said that. Passing her a wet plate she added, 'Best thing about Aldershot was the swimming pool. A big outdoor pool in a park. It was my favourite place.'

'So that's how come you swim so well,' said Alice.

'I used to go almost every day when I was at school. It was open all through the war too. Only in the summer, of course.'

'Did you take Jim there?'

'No. It was winter when I met him. He was gone to his next posting before summer came.' She dried her hands. 'You still seeing that fellow? The one Jim doesn't like.'

'Not a lot of chance, with Rose and work and everything. But yes. Every now and then.'

'Does Jim know?'

Alice shook her head. 'No. Unless you've told him.'

'I wouldn't do that. It's none of our business and you told me in confidence. But are you serious about him?'

'I can't imagine marrying anyone after Walt, but sometimes I think it would be nice to have a proper home – and for Rose to have a father.' She gazed out of the window, to where Rose was helping Jimmy to his feet after he had fallen over in the snow. 'I'm not sure Tip would make a good father though. Or a good husband for that matter. I think he's really only interested in one thing.' She gave a little laugh. 'He's pretty good at that, mind.' She put the tea towel down. 'Listen to me – telling you all my guilty secrets. You probably think I'm terrible talking about such things.'

Joan smiled. 'I don't at all. I'm pleased you can confide in me. Has he mentioned marriage?'

'Yes. Once. The first time…'

Joan nodded.

'I know what you're thinking. That he only did to get me to...you know...but I think he hasn't mentioned it since because I was pretty clear with him that I didn't want that. And I don't. Well I didn't.' She touched Joan's arm. 'Look, it may be nothing, but I think I might be pregnant.'

Joan gasped. 'Alice! Is that what you want?'

'I don't know. Oh lord, Joan, I'm so confused. I've tried not to think about it because it could be a false alarm, but it's several weeks and I'm usually so regular.'

'Didn't he take any precautions?'

Alice looked sheepish. Sometimes. Not always. He didn't like wearing those things. He wanted me to get some kind of device fitted. A diaphragm I think he said. I didn't know what he was talking about. I've never heard of anyone round here using anything like that. How could I go and ask the doctor? What would he think? It would be all over town.'

'Doctors aren't allowed to talk about patients. And isn't it better to talk to the doctor than risk getting pregnant? Won't the whole town know then anyway?'

'I know. But if we get married it'll be all right. Won't it?'

'When are you going to tell Tip?'

'I keep putting it off.' Alice sat down at the table and Joan sat down opposite. 'He usually waits to see me outside the library when I leave work but I haven't plucked up the courage yet.'

'How do you think he'll react?'

Alice shrugged. 'I don't know.' She picked at the cuff of her sweater. After a few moments, she looked up at Alice. 'But I have my suspicions.' She looked away again.

'You must tell him. No point in torturing yourself. Better to know. I'm sure he'll do the right thing.'

Alice took a long breath. 'You're right. And after all, he did tell me he'd always wanted to marry me. He'll be at the barn dance next week. I'll tell him then. Find the right moment.'

'Barn dance?'

'Hasn't Jim told you about it?'

Joan shook her head.

'Every year there's a barn dance in late November to mark the start of the winter. Over at the Lonsdale place. They've the biggest farm in the county. Everyone in town will be there.'

THE MORE JIM thought about buying the Harris place the better the idea seemed. He bounced it off his father, who agreed the plan made a lot of sense. It would give him and Joan a home of their own without the delays of building from scratch. Being away from the Hollowtree farmhouse might ease the tensions between his mother and Joan, but they would be only a fifteen minute walk away – a consideration given his father's poor health. Jim could use the new bathroom kit and install it in the Harris place – his mother had never wanted to embrace that change and now she could have unrestricted use of the room they had designated to be the bathroom as a pantry and storage place for her canned vegetables and maple syrup. The additional acreage he could dedicate to apples. Once the trees were planted, he believed the maintenance would be significantly lower than for other crops. Getting them planted would be a challenge, but the coming summer would see a new batch of youngsters graduating from the local school, and with no war to lure them away they would be available for hiring. Jim reckoned with two strong lads he could transform the whole of Hollowtree in just a couple more years. He'd already made huge progress compared to the state it was in when he had returned the previous year.

He wouldn't tell Joan yet. He didn't want to risk disappointing her if Harris wouldn't accept an offer. Maybe he'd tell her once Harris agreed the deal – or perhaps he'd wait until he'd completed the purchase and put in the new bathroom. It would be a wonderful surprise. Joan had reason enough so far to be sceptical about his promises on the home improvement front, so better to wait until he'd delivered on one.

Anxious to make a good impression, he put on his demob suit and a tie and drove into town to see the bank manager. Under the Veterans' Land Act there were cheap loans available for land and machinery and Jim was optimistic he could make a good case. He carried a folder in which he had prepared detailed projections of the forecast yields on a five acre commercial apple operation.

Forty minutes later, he emerged from the bank, buoyed up by the reception he had received. The loan was his – now all he needed was Jed Harris to agree a fair price.

He found Mr Harris in his barn. The old man was bent over the engine of his tractor, wrench in hand. He wiped his hands absently with an oily rag when Jim approached and stretched one out in greeting.

'What can I do for you, Jim? How's Don? Haven't seen him in months.'

'Not too good, sir. Bad chest. Doc says it's emphysema. Least we know what it is now. Took me and Ma more than a year to convince him to see him.'

'He's like me,' said Harris. 'Doesn't hold with quacks.' He chuckled. Then, looking serious, he added, 'Don't know what emphysema is but it doesn't sound too good. We're getting old, him and me. Me more than him, in fact. Every day's more of a struggle. Weak heart, they tell me. Have to take so many darned pills I rattle! But you didn't come over here to talk about me and my ailments.'

'Well, maybe it's not unconnected. Have you ever thought of selling up and retiring, Mr Harris? I'd be ready to give you a fair price for this place. I could do with your acreage to add to ours. I'm thinking of putting in an orchard and growing apples. And things are a bit crowded over at Hollowtree now I've a wife and child. I was thinking my family could move over here and let Ma and Pa have the place to themselves.'

'That sounds like a hell of a good plan, son. Funny though, how out of the blue everyone seems to think I should be upping sticks, downing tools and moving house. My son, both my daughters and their husbands, have all been on at me to retire, sell up this place and move over to the city, nearer the grandchildren.'

Jim grinned, relieved that his proposal appeared to chime with Harris. 'So you'd be willing to discuss the idea further with me?'

Harris folded his arms. 'I certainly would have been. But not any more.'

Jim's stomach sank. 'Is it Mrs Harris? Doesn't she want to move?'

'Mary would have gone years ago. Can't wait to be near the family.'

'Then what?' Jim struggled to contain his disappointment and frustration.

'Shook on a deal just two days ago. It was a hell of an offer. You couldn't have bettered it, Jim, I'm sorry. He's paying me over the odds to guarantee I won't consider any further offers. Mary's beside herself. She's over in Kitchener now, house-hunting with the girls.' He shook his head. 'If you'd come by sooner, Jim, we might have had ourselves a deal. Sorry, son, you're too late.'

'Can I ask who you're selling to?'

'No secret. It's the Howardson boy. Reckons his folks want somewhere smaller and more manageable. He's planning to live here with them. Since the two brothers were killed, the Howardsons lost the strength to cope with that huge place. Tip reckons this place is just the right size for them. Seems he's done very well for himself. In the States apparently, but I didn't ask questions as he's not the easiest fellow to talk to.'

Jim nodded, his fists curled tightly inside his pockets to contain his anger.

When he reached the door, Harris called after him. 'Give my best to Don. Tell him we'll have him and Helga over for supper before we leave.'

As he walked back to Hollowtree, Jim cursed Tip Howardson. The timing couldn't possibly be coincidental. Alice must have told him about Jim's idea to buy the Harris place. There was no other explanation.

THE BARN DANCE

ALICE WAS NERVOUS. She would never have a better opportunity to tell Tip about her pregnancy than tonight, but she couldn't help dreading the moment. Since his avowal that he wanted to marry her when he first returned to Hollowtree, there had not been another indication from him of any desire to rush into matrimony. Indeed he had been rather evasive about all of his future intentions. She'd asked him about his work plans – apart from re-stating his determination not to have anything to do with the family farm, he had told her nothing. The Howardson place was supposedly on the market and, in the meantime, Tip appeared to have no gainful employment. Perhaps he was waiting on receiving a payout when the sale went through.

There was no longer any doubt that she was pregnant. She hadn't seen the doctor – hadn't needed to; as well as the missed periods she had been sick almost every morning for the past weeks and had developed an inexplicable desire to eat pickled vegetables. There was something about the tang of the vinegar that eased her nausea, but she was having to be careful to avoid Helga spotting her frequent raids on the pantry shelves.

As to marrying Tip, Alice was no keener now than she had been when he'd asked. Marrying him would be a betrayal of Walt in a way that having sex wasn't. It meant admitting him into the rest of her life, into Rose's too, and Alice wasn't sure she was ready for that. It would also mean leaving the farm and the Armstrongs, severing the last ties with Walt and his family. Every time she thought about doing that, Alice felt desolate. They meant more to her than her own family. Yes, she got on with her mother, but the tense atmosphere in the Ducroix home, due to her father's drinking, had made living under the same roof uncomfortable. For most of her childhood Alice had felt lonely, lacking siblings and witnessing her father's drunken outbursts. He'd never hit her or her mother, but his sudden rages were as bad as physical blows. Finding a safe haven at Hollowtree Farm had been one of the reasons she'd started going out with Jim.

She arranged her dresses on the bed, wondering which one to wear to the barn dance. She didn't really want to go because dancing would make her wish all the more that Walt was the man she was dancing with. It had been as they were leaving the Lonsdale's party in November 1940 that he'd told her he was following in Jim's footsteps and joining up – a bitter end to what had been a beautiful and happy evening.

Rose came into the bedroom, climbed up on the bed and said, 'Wear this one, Mommy. Please!' She held up a buttercup yellow dress with a sweetheart neckline.

Alice groaned. The waist had been tight when she last wore it months ago – in her current state she doubted she would be able to squeeze into the tightly gathered waistline.

'I don't think so, darling.'

'Please, Mommy! It's so pretty.'

Alice reluctantly agreed to try the dress on. As she'd

suspected, it was straining at the seams. A cornflower blue dress was no better. Finally, she put on the yellow one, covered the gap where the fastening wouldn't do up, with a belt, and hoped that no one would notice under her cardigan. She certainly wouldn't be risking dancing tonight.

When Alice walked into the kitchen of the main house, Jim was sitting at the table, waiting for Joan to come downstairs. 'We're going to be late,' he said. 'My wife is still getting ready.' He scowled at Alice and she frowned in surprise.

'What have I done now?'

'Only told Tip Howardson I was planning on buying the Harris place.'

'So?'

'He's only gone and made an unbeatable offer to Harris. Shook on the deal two days ago. Something of a coincidence, wouldn't you say, Alice?'

She blushed. 'I had no idea. He told me he had no interest in farming.'

'Yet another example of the tissue of lies that bastard tells.'

'Jim!' Helga turned and glared at her son. 'How many times have I told you I won't have that kind of talk under my roof.'

At that moment the door to the stairway opened and Joan came into the kitchen. Jim's anger dissolved and he gave a long whistle of appreciation. 'Wow! You look a million dollars.'

Joan was wearing a new frock she had made herself for the barn dance. She'd bought the fabric at the general store in town and had run it up on Alice's mother's sewing machine – which Alice had neglected to return, saying it was better Joan use it than it gather dust in the attic at home. The dress was red with white polka dots and was full-skirted with a neat v-neckline. Joan had made a special effort with her hair – big soft glossy rolls framed her face. Usually, these days, she left it to fall in a long straight bob, scraped it into a scruffy plait, or stuffed it under a scarf. Red lipstick, that perfectly matched her dress, completed the picture. Alice experienced a stab of envy, feeling dowdy in comparison.

Helga looked up and said, 'It's only a barn dance, not the Royal Winter Fair.' Then seeing the looks of disapproval from both Jim and Don, added, 'Very nice.'

Alice swallowed and forced herself to speak. 'You look stunning, Joan.'

'So do you.'

Alice didn't feel that way. The yellow dress was cutting into her waist and the knitted cardigan was hardly the stuff of glamour. Before long she might have to ask Joan to help her make some maternity dresses. She wished now that she had disappointed Rose and put something else on. But whatever she'd have worn she'd be a pale creature next to the vision that was Joan. Strange – Alice had never thought Joan particularly pretty before. She supposed she wasn't – pretty was the wrong word – not beautiful either – but tonight she had an innate quality that made you want to look at her, that commanded attention. Helga's comment about the Royal Winter Fair was not far off the mark. Joan would not even look out of place in a Hollywood movie.

When the three of them arrived at the Lonsdale place, half the town was already there. Cars, trucks, and horse-drawn carts were drawn up in an adjoining field, where the snow had been cleared and the area outside the barn was ploughed and gritted. A pool of light spilled under the heavy oak doors of the barn. The sounds of a country reel, the buzz of voices, thumping of feet and squeals of laughter greeted them as they approached.

Once inside, Alice watched Joan slip her feet out of her boots and put on her high-heels. She herself was still wearing stout boots like most of the other women. All around the cavernous barn, eyes turned to examine the exotic English creature.

Men and women were twirling each other around while the fiddlers and the accordionist played. Others crowded round the walls watching, or gathered at the far end of the room where there was a makeshift bar set up on a long table.

Joan turned to Alice and whispered, 'I haven't done country dancing since school.'

'Don't worry. They call all the dances. And it's all just a bit of fun. Hey, Jim, why don't you get us some fruit cups.'

Jim disappeared and Alice led Joan to a seat on one of the hay-bales encircling the perimeter of the barn.

'I'm definitely going to tell Tip tonight.'

Joan reached for her hand and squeezed it. She looked around the room. 'Is he here? Which one?'

A large group of men were gathered around the drinks table, some of them swigging beer from bottles, although the table appeared to hold only jugs of the innocuous fruit cup.

'Not yet. I've arranged to meet him in the tack room next door. Quiet and away from everyone else.' Alice smiled then swallowed, feeling her throat constrict with nerves. 'Oh gosh, I do hope I'm doing the right thing.'

'What do you mean?'

'Marrying him when I don't love him.'

'Look, Alice, if you have doubts, don't do it. You could have the child adopted.'

'I can't give up the baby. I just couldn't.' She put a protective hand over her stomach.

Jim returned, holding the cups of warm punch and sat down beside them. Joan gave a tight-lipped smile of apology to Alice, who got up. 'I'll see you two later.' Before they could reply she moved away, grateful for the crowds gathering to get ready for the next reel.

Tip was leaning against the wall in the empty tack room that adjoined the barn. 'You took your time,' he said. 'I've been waiting here like a lemon for half an hour.' He pulled her towards him, dropping his cigarette butt on the concrete floor and grinding it out with the toe of his boot, before pressing himself against her.

Alice pulled away. 'No. Not now. Not here.'

'What's wrong with here?' Tip reached an arm behind her and gathered her skirt up, grabbing her bottom to draw her towards him. Alice felt his erection pressing against her and tried to pull back from him.

'See, he's already standing to attention for you, darling.' His hand took hers and placed it against the swelling in his groin.

Alice pushed him away. 'I told you. Not now. Not yet. There's something I have to tell you first.'

Tip scowled. He leant back against the wall, standing between two wooden saddle horses, his left arm resting on one saddle. He lit another cigarette. 'What's so important it can't wait?'

Alice closed her eyes, took a deep breath. 'I've changed my mind,' she said at last, forcing a smile to her lips.

'What about?' He watched her through narrowed eyes as he drew on his cigarette.

'About getting married.'

'So who's the lucky fellow?'

Alice gave a nervous laugh and moved towards him. 'I'm looking at him right now.' She smiled again but there was no smile in response.

Tip gave a snorting laugh. 'I don't think so.'

'But you said…'

'Said what?'

'That you wanted to marry me.' She felt dizzy. It was not going as planned.

Tip said nothing. He drew deeply on his cigarette and blew out a series of smoke rings.

Alice's stomach felt hollow and she hoped she wasn't going to be sick. 'You said you'd always wanted to marry me. That you were patient and would wait until I felt the same. Well, I do now.'

'That was when I thought it was the only way I'd get you to put out for me again.' He plucked a strand of tobacco from his lip and flicked it away. 'You must know, Alice, I'm not the marrying kind.'

'I'm having a baby.'

His eyes narrowed. 'So?'

'It's yours.'

'I think you'll find it's yours.' His eyes fixed on her stomach.

'Stop joking around, Tip. I'm serious.'

'You always said you didn't want another relationship after poor old Walt copped it. Well, you haven't got one.'

Alice felt the panic rise inside her. 'But this makes everything different.'

'Who says? Different for you maybe. But not different for me. You should have thought about that possibility.'

'Don't you get it?' She clutched at his shirt. 'Your child? Don't you even care?'

'I already got a child and I don't want another. Didn't even want that one.'

Alice backed away, afraid that her legs would give way. 'What are you talking about? A child?'

'Two-years-old. Never seen it so why would I want to see yours either?'

'Two years? But you were in France. It was war. Things were different then. That doesn't mean you can't have a place in *our* child's life.' She put her hands over her stomach. 'Was it with the woman who was killed?'

Tip gave a laugh and ground out his cigarette, spitting on the floor after it. 'Don't tell me you believed all that bullshit about me being in France?'

Alice gasped.

'That's the best thing, you know. It's made my day – that you chose to believe my cock and bull story rather than listening to that arsehole, Armstrong. Hell, Alice, it's even better than fucking you – although I will admit that fucking you was pretty damn good. But you swallowing my story. That's my finest moment.'

'Where were you if you weren't in France?' Alice's voice was barely a murmur.

'In the mighty USA. And that's why, as it happens, my dear Alice, I couldn't marry you anyway. I already got me a wife down there. Not that I have any intention of going back to her. Once she told me there was a kid on the way it was time for Uncle Tip to hit the road. I guess that time has come around again.'

Alice slumped down the wall and sat with her legs pulled up in front of her, fighting the urge to throw up.

'My only regret is that I never managed to fuck his bitch of a wife. Must admit I underestimated her – but not you, Alice. You were exactly what I expected – ice on the outside and a volcano underneath. I'll give you that, girl, best fuck I've ever had. But at the core you're just a piece of ass. Just another slut.'

Alice started to cry.

Howardson squatted on his haunches in front of her. 'Maybe I only wanted what I couldn't have. Once you offered it on a plate I lost my appetite. And once I knew Jim Armstrong didn't want you any more, I didn't either. Joan on the other hand…' He licked his lips. 'Different story. She's a piece of work. An A-Number-One Bitch. I nearly had her one night in Aldershot until we were rudely interrupted.

Now she *is* someone I could get excited about. But you, Alice? Not any more.'

He reached inside his shirt pocket, plucked out his Camels, flicked one into his mouth and left the tack room, leaving Alice weeping on the dusty floor.

JOAN WOULD HAVE PREFERRED her first ever dance with Jim to have been a waltz or a foxtrot – something romantic featuring just the two of them, with him holding her in his arms. But she had to admit that the barn dance was great fun. They had twirled up and down and in and out of the other couples, stripping the willow and doing the do-si-do, until Joan was helpless with laughter from her continuing failure to get the moves right.

A break in the dancing was called for everyone to help themselves to refreshments from a table now groaning with food. Roasted corn, cheese, pickles, beans baked in maple syrup, slices of pumpkin pie, fried chicken pieces and pecan butter tarts. While Joan ate and chatted to neighbours, Jim was drawn into a conversation with the man who farmed the holding next door to Hollowtree. Joan looked around, wondering if Alice had returned yet, but there was no sign of her.

She decided to step outside for some fresh air, slinging her coat over her shoulders. Outside, she had a sudden longing for a cigarette. Hoping to find a forgotten pack in the bottom of her handbag, she rummaged around in its depths. But there was nothing there. Just as well. Jim would not be pleased to catch her smoking again. Not that he'd ever commented on her quitting. Perhaps he hadn't noticed? That wouldn't surprise her. Funny how bad habits annoyed people so much, while their absence was rarely remarked.

Leaning against the barn door, on the concreted slope

above the flattened snow, she shivered in the cold. Above her a million stars twinkled in a clear inky black sky. She tilted her head back, trying to remember the names of the constellations Jim had pointed out to her one night. It was so beautiful. She smiled to herself, content with her lot. Even Mrs Armstrong was behaving better these days. Not exactly friendly – that would be an exaggeration – but civil. All she lacked was her own family. If only her mother and Ethel could be here everything would be perfect.

Caught up in her reveries she didn't hear him approaching, until he was there in front of her, his mean face and narrow eyes looking straight into hers. The man from Aldershot.

Joan gasped in fright, her heart hammering in her chest. He grabbed hold of her arm, his grip shackling her, preventing her escape, and he pressed his body up against hers, his breath hot against her neck.

'Joan, Joan, we meet again. At last we get to finish what we started.'

He jerked her arm and a stab of pain shot up to her shoulder. Then he was dragging her away from the barn towards the stable block next to it, his hand clamped over her mouth to stifle her screams. Joan swung her other arm out, trying to find something to grab onto to anchor her down, but there was nothing there. Her feet dragged over the tightly-packed flattened snow, the soles of her unsuitable shoes causing her to skid and the packed snow preventing her from gaining any purchase to slow their progress.

The man was strong. She remembered that strength from the night in Aldershot, remembered how powerless she had been then against his brute force. He dragged her into the building, which was pitch black inside. Before she could adjust to the dark and try to orientate herself he pushed her and she fell backwards into a pile of straw and he was on top of her, tearing at the neck of her dress. Joan twisted her head sideways to avoid his mouth. She could smell the liquor on his breath, then his mouth was on hers, his tongue forcing its way inside. Nausea mounted in her and she thrashed about, desperately trying to free herself from his hold.

All she could think was he wasn't going to win. She wriggled and squirmed, trying to clamp her legs together. Breath crushed under the weight of him. Whinnying and whickering of horses. Soft scent of hay and manure. Foul stench of his tobacco breath. His teeth biting her lips. Tongue fat and darting like a snake, pushing into her mouth. Hands everywhere. No. No. No.

A loud click and the stable was bathed in the sudden incandescent glow of electric light. Bill turned his head, allowing Joan to see past him to where Alice stood framed in the doorway. Relief swept through Joan's body and she barely registered that the shock and anger on Alice's face was directed at her not at Bill.

'He said you were a slut but I didn't believe him. Said you went with half the garrison. How could you? After everything I told you. How could you, Joan?' Alice started to cry.

Joan was still on her back on the heap of straw, the weight of her assailant's body pinning her down. Before she could answer Alice, Jim came into the room. He lunged forward and dragged Bill off her, hauling him to his feet then landed a punch. A stream of blood poured from the man's nose.

Joan shuffled sideways and scrambled to her feet. The two men were hard at it, exchanging blows, and Jim's face was now bloodied too.

'Jim, stop, please, stop, before he hurts you.' She turned to Alice. 'Get help!'

Alice didn't move. She stood motionless with tears coursing down her face, her expression blank, big gulping sobs taking the place of words. Joan moved towards the door.

Alice snarled at her as she approached. 'You bitch. Isn't Jim enough? You have to have Tip too.'

Joan didn't stop. No time to compute what Alice was saying. She ran into the barn and screamed for help. Half a dozen men rushed out and she signalled them towards the adjoining stable.

When they arrived, Jim had regained the upper hand and was pummelling Joan's attacker as though he wouldn't stop until he'd killed him. Blow after blow, with a violence that shocked Joan to the core. Smashing his fists into the bloodied mess that was the corporal's face.The other men pulled Jim off.

'What the hell you doing, Jim? You trying to kill him?' one of the men shouted.

Another yelled, 'That's enough, Armstrong, or you'll be up for a murder charge.'

The men dragged a still struggling Jim off Tip's bloodied body. They hauled him back and pinned him against the wooden wall of the stall. Joan watched in horror, unable to believe Jim had turned into a savage, intent only on hurting and killing the man who had attacked her.

Alice was staring in horror at Bill, the man Joan now realised was Tip. She was still weeping, her tears near to hysteria. She lurched towards him.

'Tip, Tip. Why? Please.' She turned to Jim. 'He was supposed to marry me. He would have married me but he only wanted her.' The word *her* was a snarl of contempt. 'She lured him out here. I found them, lying there, doing it.'

Tip pushed her away and Alice fell onto the pile of straw.

Tip glared at Jim. 'I've had what I wanted with her.' He jerked his head in Joan's direction, then looked at Alice who was now on her knees, 'With both of them.' He shook his shoulders and pushed past the group of open-mouthed men and went out into the night.

Joan turned to Jim. 'You know that isn't true. He's the one who attacked me in Aldershot. Bill. He said his name was Bill.' She felt a rising tide of panic that Jim, like Alice, might not believe her, but he moved towards her and wrapped her in his arms.

'Nothing happened. You got here in time. Well, Alice did. But it was the same man.'

'I should have known. I should have realised at once that it was Tip. Tip's christian name is William. But no one - not even his mother – calls him anything but Tip. It all makes sense. I forgot when they discharged him there was a vague story going round that he'd attacked a woman but she hadn't pressed charges. My God, Joan. That was you.' He reached for her hand. 'This isn't over. I'm going to kill that bastard. Even if I they hang me for it.'

'Please, Jim. Enough.'

She pulled a handkerchief out of her handbag which was lying open on the floor, and began to mop the blood from her husband's face. She was overwhelmed with relief that she'd had another narrow escape, but this was undercut with horror and disbelief at the savagery she had witnessed in Jim when he attacked Howardson – and a realisation that things had changed irrevocably between her and Alice.

THEY DROVE BACK to the farm in silence, punctuated by sobbing noises from Alice in the back. The tension in the car was palpable – not from Alice, but between Joan and Jim.

Joan's face was expressionless, her eyes fixed on the road ahead as the headlights of the car swept over it. There was a rigidity in her posture. Jim wanted to reach for her hand but sensed that if he did he would be rebuffed.

And who could blame her? He was all too aware of his own savagery, the blind rage that had descended on him like a kind of madness. It wasn't just about protecting his wife's honour – any man would want to do that – but that, having started hitting Tip Howardson, he didn't want to stop. Tip had been asking for it for a long time – of that there was no doubt. But the violent rage sweeping through Jim had been uncontrollable, unconscious, as if he were outside his own body looking down on it.

As soon as the men had pulled him off Tip and he realised that if they hadn't, he would have killed him with his bare hands, he had woken up to what he'd done. Seeing the looks on the faces of the guys who had broken up the fight he knew he'd gone too far. The look in Joan's eyes said it all. Puzzled, dismayed, disbelieving – more than that – she had actually looked afraid of him. And Jim realised that there was a part of him that was afraid of what he might be capable of too.

IN THE LIRI VALLEY

May 1944

The day after the Poles made their successful ascent of Monte Cassino, taking it for the Allies on the third attempt, Jim and his company were camped out in the lower Liri Valley, waiting for the signal to push forward through the breach in the Hitler Line that the Americans and the French Expeditionary Force had made.

If the Canadians thought that the fighting here would be easier than what they had experienced in Ortona, they were soon disabused. Everywhere Jim looked was desecration. In the distance in front of him a tank was blazing after an attack by German bazookas and he watched, helpless, as burning men escaped from it, only to be mown down by machine gun fire.

Though massively outnumbered, the Germans had the advantage of concealment and managed to make the most of their small numbers by causing havoc on the Allied forces exposed on open ground. Dug into bunkers, ruined farmhouses and ditches, often on higher ground, they were well-placed to pick off Allied attempts to advance. In spite of this, the combined allied forces were moving forward inexorably.

Jim moved ahead with his platoon, following the designated route, tramping along amid the smell of exhaust fumes from Canadian vehicles, lined up bumper to bumper in a snake that poured through the gap in the Hitler defensive line. They walked, in single file, along a dirt track between tapes marking the edges of the area already cleared of mines. Now battle-hardened, having witnessed so many men blown apart by a careless footstep or a momentary loss of attention, the men were cautious and concentrating on sticking to the safe path.

They had spent the previous evening preparing for today, honing their weapons of war, cleaning them and testing them ready for the attack. Grenades were unboxed and armed with fuses, magazine clips filled ready for loading into the Bren guns. Every man was conscious, as they had been since arriving on the Italian peninsula, that each day might be their last.

Through the gap in the hills they moved into the upper Liri Valley, the main field of battle, which was a scene of devastation. The valley was a vast dust bowl of earth, churned and ploughed by thousands of military vehicles. Shellfire had cratered the countryside, denuded the trees of leaves and branches, pulverised farm buildings and churned up the earth, leaving a lunar landscape of ghostly ruins and stunted tree stumps, interwoven with barbed wire, reminiscent of pictures the troops had all seen from the previous war. Every town, village and farmhouse in the way of the fighting was destroyed as the Germans retreated and the Allies advanced. Days of May sunshine had speeded up the rotting of flesh and the stench of decomposing corpses polluted the air. Jim saw dead Germans by the side of the road, their grey uniforms gashed, and gaping wounds already home to blowflies and maggots. As well as human corpses, the track was lined with the decaying bodies of mules and horses, used by both sides to transport supplies over rough terrain. The Italian sun had no respect for the dead and their decomposition advanced faster than men could be buried, turning the countryside into an open charnel house. The panorama of death was intensified by the stark contrast with the explosion of scarlet poppies in the fields beyond. This renewal of life was a reminder of those other poppies that had come to symbolise the loss of lives on the fields of France and Belgium less than thirty years earlier. In between the noise of artillery fire, nature continued, with larks singing by day and nightingales by night, oblivious to the brutality of men.

Jim and his comrades marched on, passing dead horses still attached to the gun carriages they had been expected to haul, the gunners lying dead in the sun-hardened mud beside them. Nausea rose inside him as he came upon a motorcycle outrider sitting upright, as if to attention, his body aflame in his sidecar.

Then they were stuck. A temporary dead end. Hundreds of them rammed up against each other, all pushing forward with nowhere to go, caught in a bottleneck of bomb-blasted bridges.

Jim trudged with his section along the track, moving forward, past the stacked up tanks, jeeps and lorries. He paused to drink some water, rest his legs, breathe for a while, sitting down in a spot where the air was fresher. A man from his regiment with whom he had shared a dorm back in Aldershot walked past. Jim called out to him. The man – Jim remembered his name was Rick – looked back and waved in greeting. A sudden blinding flash and something was hurled through the air towards him, like a ball passed in a game.

Reflexively, Jim raised his arm to catch it and found himself holding onto someone's hand. Fingers entwined. The hand had detached from Rick's blasted apart body. Jim's former dorm mate had stepped on a land mine. Jim turned sideways, vomiting onto the earth beside him.

On they marched, under the sun, delayed by blown up bridges, waiting for the construction of Bailey bridges to ford the rivers, vying for space with the British to cross the seemingly endless succession of rivers, tributary streams and narrow gullies. Jim was not alone in thinking that this campaign seemed to be progressing in a haphazard rush forward, lacking a well-thought-out plan and with the mountainous terrain of Italy always against them.

He wandered away from the main track, needing to empty his bowels, preferring to find a private place rather than squatting, pants down, beside the track, as some of the men did. Just off the track he came upon a tumble-down building, a cow byre or shelter of some kind, and he headed towards it. As soon as he entered the ruin he knew he'd made a mistake.

The German conscript was alone. Left behind by his companions, wounded possibly, a boy certainly. No more than eighteen, Jim guessed. Blue eyes, blond hair, fresh-faced. The perfect Aryan specimen – and terrified. Full of the terror that he might not survive this encounter. The boy raised his gun and Jim knew immediately he didn't want to die. For a moment – afterwards he thought it must have been a tiny fraction of a second – they looked into each other's eyes. Locked gazes. Acknowledged each other's existence. One human being meeting another, each facing possible death. Then Jim pulled out his pistol and blasted the boy, shot after shot, six or seven times, until he lay on the ground, his blood staining the grey wool uniform and the hard earth of the stone shack.

As soon as the deed was done, Jim knew that as long as he lived he would never, ever be able to eradicate the memory of that German boy. Of the look in his eyes. It was pointless to think of him as Boche, Gerry, Nazi, Hun, Fritz, Kraut, enemy. In that moment he had been a boy, doubtless loved by his mother, his life ahead of him. Then the realisation that it was all up. Over. *Kaput.* The knowledge in his eyes that he was about to die. The look that said, 'You are the one who will end this all for me.'

HELGA LEARNS THE TRUTH

'WHAT'S WRONG? Why are you home so early?' Helga was knitting in the chair beside a snoozing Don when they entered the kitchen. The smell of baking bread pervaded the room. 'Where's Alice?'

Jim looked over at Joan then said, 'She's gone to bed.' He nodded in the direction of the barn.

'Tell me. What happened?' Helga put down her knitting and folded her arms. Then she saw the side of his face that Jim had tried to keep turned away from her. 'Oh my Lord! What have you done to yourself? You've been in a fight? Tell me what happened.'

'Tip Howardson happened.' Jim leaned against the kitchen door and Joan pulled up a chair at the table.

'You'll have to tell me more than that. I'm not a mind reader. Spit it out, son.'

As she spoke, Don jerked upright in his chair and opened his eyes. 'What's going on?'

'Where to begin?' Jim looked at Joan then took a deep breath and said, 'Howardson attacked Joan. Not for the first time either. He assaulted her in Aldershot during the war. It was only thanks to some other soldiers coming upon them in the blackout that he didn't rape her. Same tonight if Alice hadn't walked in on them.'

Helga's hands flew to her mouth.

'I had no idea Tip was the man who attacked her back in England. Neither did she. Back then, he told her his name was Bill.' He moved towards Joan's chair and stood behind it, his hands on her shoulders. 'Didn't I say to you all that Tip was a complete bastard, a low life? I tried to warn Alice but she didn't want to listen.'

'Alice? Has he attacked Alice too?'

Joan closed her eyes and Jim answered. 'No. She's been carrying on with him.'

'Carrying on? Alice?' Helga's voice was shocked. 'What are you saying?'

Jim looked at his mother. 'She's been having an affair with him for months. God knows where or when or how often, but she's expecting his child.'

Helga gave a small choked cry and reached for her husband's arm. 'That's not possible. Not Alice.'

Joan got up from the table. 'I'm going to bed.'

Upstairs she lay in bed, unable to sleep, listening to the voices rising from below as Jim told his parents the details of what had happened. She could make out the soft sobbing of Helga, the low murmur of Don's voice, his rasping cough and Jim's tones, quiet one moment then angry the next. She couldn't have borne to be in that kitchen any longer, listening to Helga's sorrow that her precious daughter-in-law had betrayed Walt's memory. She didn't expect any sympathy for herself from Helga. Things had gone beyond any hope of that.

Joan turned her face to the wall and pulled the blankets over her head, trying to shut out the sounds of the voices as the Armstrongs went round and round in circles trying to make sense of what had happened that night. Through the wall she could hear little snorting noises coming from Rose and Jimmy as they slept in Helga and Don's bedroom, topping and tailing in the little truckle bed that Jimmy now slept on. Joan tried to concentrate on those innocent sounds but her mind was flooded with the image of Tip Howardson's face close to hers, the memory of his whisky-drenched, tobacco breath and the crushing weight of his body on top of hers.

Worse was the look she had seen in her husband's eyes as he attacked Howardson. That Jim had been a stranger to her. She was grateful that he'd rescued her, but the man who had pummelled Howardson relentlessly, who would have certainly killed him if he hadn't been dragged off by the group of men, had been like a wild animal. She couldn't reconcile this with her Jim. It was impossible to conceive how the man she loved with every fibre of her being could be so brutal, could look that way – like a lion tearing its prey apart, so ready to take another man's life. That Jim was as different from the kind and gentle man she thought she'd married as darkness was from sunlight. Joan didn't know him and wondered if perhaps she was now even a little afraid of him.

When Jim eventually came to bed, Joan pretended to be asleep.

THE FOLLOWING MORNING Alice didn't appear at breakfast. Joan took her place at the table, saying nothing. A stony-faced Helga served up porridge and everyone sat in silence apart from the two children who giggled to each other in a continuation of a game they had evidently been playing the previous evening.

Joan avoided eye contact with her husband. She knew she

couldn't go on like this – at some point she'd have to face up to talking it out with him, but not yet. She wasn't ready.

Eventually Helga sat down. 'Go and call your mother, Rose. Tell her breakfast is getting cold.'

Rose pulled a face but got up from the table. A few minutes later she returned. 'Mommy won't come. She says she's sick.' The child scrambled back into her chair, apparently unconcerned about, or disbelieving, her mother's claimed illness.

Helga frowned but said nothing. When the meal was finished, Jim left, saying he had to go into town. He bent down and dropped a kiss on Joan's head as he left. She felt herself stiffen involuntarily, where she would before have welcomed this display of affection from him.

'You children can stay in here to play this morning,' Helga said, then turning to Joan, added, 'Why don't you help me with the milking, Joan?'

Struggling to conceal her surprise, Joan nodded and grabbing her coat from the back of the door, followed her mother-in-law across the yard to the barn.

'I owe you an apology,' said Helga as soon as they were inside. 'I've not been fair to you since you got here and I'm sorry. I truly am. I've no excuse – apart from the fact that I haven't been thinking straight since we lost Walter. Grief for him blinded me. Especially to Alice. I couldn't have been more wrong about that girl. I'd no idea she had such low morals. But that's no excuse for how I treated you. I couldn't blame Jim for Walt's dying so I took it out on you. I did wrong.' She turned her head away from the cow she was milking and looked steadily at Joan. 'It's not easy to admit that but I have to do it.'

Joan was lost for words. She felt a mixture of relief that at last there was a genuine thawing of hostility, with embarrassment at this sudden outpouring from the woman who had spared so few words on her until now. She mumbled that she understood, struggling to find the right thing to say.

Helga removed her hands from the cow and got up. 'I should have known that if my son loved you then you had to be a good woman.' Her voice was gruff, her words clipped. 'I've known it for a while but was too proud to admit it.' She paused, looking away. 'And as for Alice. I was wrong about her too. There was me thinking she was holding Walt's memory sacred and she was behaving like one of the women who live over the beverage rooms in Kitchener. Common prostitutes. I'd no idea Alice was that kind of woman.'

'She's not. She's just lonely.'

'You knew what she was doing?' Helga's nostrils flared and she took a step away from Joan.

'I'd no idea it was Tip she was seeing. She told me there was a man who wanted to marry her. Then she said she was expecting a baby. She was sure he'd marry her but it turns out Howardson is already married. And knowing who he is now, I'd say Alice has had a lucky escape. That man is evil. If she hadn't walked in on us he'd have forced himself on me last night.'

Helga sat down on the low wooden stool and automatically resumed milking the waiting cow, her head pressed against its side.

'Nonetheless she'd be better marrying him than bringing disgrace on herself and her family and ours.'

'Please, Mrs Armstrong, you can't wish that on her. The man is an animal.'

'You can call me Ma.' She spoke brusquely, as if what Joan knew to be an enormous concession had been offered up lightly. 'You can't want her to have a child out of wedlock?'

'She's done well enough bringing up Rose alone. Alice is a strong woman. She'll manage.'

'You don't know what folk are like round here. They'll

have nothing to do with her. They'll never keep her on at the library. She'll be shunned.'

'Then she'll have to get by without such shallow uncaring people. If they're so judgmental then she's better off without them. She's got us.' Seeing the hard look in Helga's eyes, she added, 'Well, she's got *me*. I'm her friend.'

The door creaked open. Alice's voice was waspish. 'Very cosy. You're best of buddies now, are you? Don't suppose she told you she was trying to steal my man. He was going to marry me until he saw her.'

The sound of Helga's hand across Alice's face was like the crack of a whip on a concrete floor. Alice staggered backwards, holding her cheek.

'Joan's done nothing wrong. You've only yourself to blame. From what I understand Tip Howardson has gone to the bad. He physically attacked Joan back in England and he was trying again last night. How dare you accuse her of behaving badly with him. By saying that, you're insulting Jim as well as her. And you've already shamed the memory of my other son.' Helga kicked the stool out of the way and, ignoring the patient cow, stormed out of the barn.

The two women looked at each other in silence, then Alice burst into tears. Joan wrapped her arms around her and was relieved when Alice didn't resist.

'You know as well as I do, you've done well to escape that man,' Joan said eventually. 'Marrying him would have ruined your life. Things will work out in the end. You're a good mother. You'll cope with another child. And I'm always here to support you in any way.'

Alice pulled back her head and wiped away her tears with the back of her hand. 'I should never have said that. And I know you're right, Joan. I knew Tip wasn't a good man. I just pretended to myself and then when I knew I was having a baby I was frightened. Marrying him seemed the only way.

He said some terrible things to me last night. That's why I was so upset and angry with you. You were an easy target.'

Joan stroked Alice's hair as though she were a small child.

Alice looked up at her. 'I'm going to go away. To Ottawa. I've always wanted to try living in a city. I've an aunt there, my great aunt on my mother's side. She'll take me and Rose in. She's frail and elderly and I can look after her so she doesn't have to give up her house. And I've Walt's pension. We'll get by. No one knows me in Ottawa. As far as anyone's concerned I'm a widow. No one needs to know any more.'

She pulled her lips into a tight smile. 'Now we'd better get these poor old cows milked. I'll show you how it's done.'

WHEN JIM RETURNED from town later that day he announced that Tip Howardson had already left the district. There was word around town that some men from across the border had come looking for him.

'Bunch of low-lifes, according to Freddo in the café. Not the kind of guys you'd want to run into in a dark alley. Told him Howardson owed them money. A lot of money. Soon as Howardson knew they were in town he was gone.'

Don looked up. 'Where's he gone?'

Jim shook his head. 'No idea. As far away as possible I hope. Good riddance.' He looked sideways at Alice.

Alice lowered her head. 'I don't know why I believed what he told me about being in France. I was so stupid.'

'Hindsight's a wonderful thing.' Joan gave her a tight smile.

'He showed me cigarette burn scars on his arms. Said it was the Gestapo. Must have been whoever he was mixed up with in the States.' She sounded gloomy.

Jim said, 'I met up with Jed Harris too. He was mad as hell when he went over to the town clerk's to register the sale of his place this morning and the son of a bitch failed to show up. From what I gather, Howardson never had the money in the first place. Just wanted to screw things up for us.'

He leaned back in his chair and grinned. 'Good news is Jed Harris is keen to cut a deal with me. Now that he and his wife have got their heads round moving house they don't want to hold back. They've found a place in Kitchener and want to go ahead, so I reckon we can get it for less than I thought.'

He looked over at Joan. 'It was going to be a surprise for you – until I found out that Howardson had got in first and made a ridiculous offer. But there's no point in not telling you now, Joan.' He moved over to where Joan was sitting. 'Aren't you pleased? Means we can be in our own place by the time spring's here.'

Joan forced a smile to her lips, but her stomach felt hollow. She wasn't sure she wanted to be alone in a house with a man who had behaved like a crazed killer. She wanted her Jim back, but every time she looked at him all she could see were those angry eyes and those pounding fists.

That night she turned away from him in bed again, feigning tiredness. He stroked her hair and kissed her gently on the temple. 'Tell me what's the matter, Joan. You still upset about what Howardson did? He's gone now. He'll never come back. If he tries, they'll run him out of town. Everyone saw what happened last night.'

She pulled her knees up and edged away, eyes closed, shutting him out. She couldn't face talking to him. Not while she felt this way, as if she was with a stranger, a man capable of killing another man with his bare hands. After a few minutes she heard him snoring gently.

When she awoke next morning, Jim was still lying beside her in the bed. She opened her eyes to see him propped up on his side, watching her.

'What?' she said, her tone sharp.

'Can't a man look at his wife?'

'What time is it?'

'Almost six.'

'Shouldn't you be up by now?'

'I'm going nowhere, Joan, until we've sorted out what's wrong between us. You've barely looked at me in two days. I feel as though every time I come near you, you shrink away. What's going on.' His eyes were fixed on her. She squirmed, wanting to get out of bed and away from him but it would mean climbing over him as her side was against the wall.

'Talk to me, Joan.'

She sighed, resigned to talking. 'You frightened me. When you fought with that man. I didn't recognise you. You were so angry. Violent. I thought you were going to kill him.'

'No more than he deserved.'

'Not like that. If those men hadn't pulled you off him, you'd have torn him apart. You were like a wild animal. I didn't like it. Didn't like seeing what you were capable of.'

Jim rolled onto his back. He looked up at the ceiling as he spoke. 'Maybe I would have killed him. I have enough reason after what he did to you. To Ethel. To Greg. And now to Alice as well.'

'You scared me. I'm not sure I really know you any more.'

He turned his head to look at her. 'Maybe I got a bit carried away. Seeing him there on top of you. Seeing what he was trying to do to you.' He covered his eyes. 'I love you so much, Joan. I couldn't have stood it. So yes, I would have torn him apart if I could.'

Joan turned to face him. 'I don't understand where it came from, Jim. All that rage. That aggression. Can't you see what I'm trying to say? That's not the Jim I know. It was as terrifying as what that man was trying to do to me. Worse in a way. I can hate him. But you? I love you and now I feel as if

I don't know you any more. Where did all that anger and violence come from? Is it because of the war? Because of the things you dream about? What terrible things did you see? Why can't you tell me?'

'Because I want to forget about it. If I tell you, you'll carry the burden of what I saw and what I did and I don't want that. I love you too much, Joan.'

'You've killed people?' Her tone was flat.

Jim stared up at the ceiling again. 'Of course I've killed people. That's what you do in a war. But we're not at war any more and I won't ever kill another human being again. I swear to you, Joan. But the other night I hated Tip Howardson as much as those Germans I killed in the war. More. I killed them because it was my duty. My country expected it. My CO ordered it. But I *wanted* to kill Howardson. I wanted to kill him because he was trying to hurt you. I'll never stand by while anyone tries to hurt you, Joan. I care too much for you to let that happen.'

Joan looked into his eyes and saw what she hoped was love there. Looking at him now she found it impossible to remember that she had been terrified of what he might do the other night. His eyes were gentle, concerned, loving. This was the Jim who made her feel wanted, desired, who gave her the confidence that she could take on the world. But still she was uncomfortable with the thought that there was a part of his life and his history that he was choosing to keep from her. She tried to tell him this.

He stroked her hair and kissed her again. 'Please, Joan, trust me. I want to wipe all that out. Obliterate it, forget it. If I share it with you it's always there. Please try to let it go. Then there's a chance that over time I'll forget the things I saw and did. That's what Pa told me. He never could talk about his war either. He said after a while the memories start to fade; they stop haunting you. When I'm with you that seems possible. When I'm with you, I never think about it. So what I need is more time with you.'

He slipped his hands under the sheets and moved them under her nightgown and up her leg. She gave a small gasp at the touch of his hands upon her skin. Rolling over he pulled her nightdress up and lifted himself over her. Joan pulled his head down so her mouth met his. She hated having secrets between them but the alternative was far worse. Life without Jim was inconceivable. She moaned with pleasure as his hands moved down her body and he entered her.

MAPLE SYRUP

ALICE AND ROSE remained at Hollowtree farm for another month. Joan had hoped to persuade her to stay, but she was obdurate in her decision to go to Ottawa.

Even as Alice was about to get into the car to leave, Joan said, 'It's not too late to change your mind.'

'I can't possibly stay. Not with Ma knowing what I did. She'd never accept me carrying on living here with another man's child. She's made it clear how she feels about what I've done.'

'But she'll come round in the end – she won't want you to take Rose away. She's her first grandchild.'

'Rose can come and stay in the holidays. And I've this one to think of too.' She patted her stomach, where there was now a slight bump. 'If I stay here I'll never be able to forget who the baby's father was. Not with Ma reminding me at any opportunity.'

'She wouldn't do that.' But Joan said the words without conviction.

'Oh yes she would.'

'You'll be lonely in Ottawa. Apart from your aunt you know no one.'

'Joan, please. We've been over this a thousand times. I'll manage. It's a new start. I'll make new friends. A new life where no one knows me as the woman who dumped Jim for Walt, slept with Tip Howardson and had an illegitimate baby.' She smiled. 'No. Much better to be Mrs Armstrong, a widow with two small children.' She laughed. 'They'll see me as a tragic figure rather than someone to sneer at and gossip about.'

She hugged Joan goodbye, opened the car door for Rose to clamber in, then got into the passenger seat beside Jim, who was going to drop her at the station in Kitchener. 'I'll write as soon as we're settled,' she called through the window.

It was only when they were on the train and a tired Rose had fallen asleep against her, that Alice allowed herself the luxury of tears. She stared through the window, unseeing as the fields passed by. She was leaving everything she'd ever known. Leaving the home Walt had built for them. The pool where he had first kissed her. The loft in the barn where they had first made love. They had only had a brief time together. Not long enough to build sufficient memories to last the rest of her life. It wasn't fair.

Rose stirred in her sleep and adjusted her position, her head slipping down onto Alice's lap where she stroked her hair. She had Rose. The living image of her father and the best present she could possibly have hoped for. As long as Rose was with her, a part of Walt was with her too. If only he had lived to see his child. He would have been so proud of his little girl.

Her hand brushed against her belly as she caressed her daughter. What of the other child growing inside her? Fathered by a man she now saw as the scoundrel Jim had always warned her he was. Unwanted by him too. The way Tip had reacted when she told him about the baby, made it easier for her to pretend he'd had nothing to do with its conception. This child would be hers alone. All she had to figure out now was what she was going to tell Rose about her new brother or sister. But she could worry about that later. Rose was too small to understand now.

Alice brushed the remains of the tears from her eyes and turned her head back to look out of the window. A new beginning. She was going to do her level best to make the most of it.

It must have been about three months later, when Joan looked out of the kitchen window and saw a steady drip of water falling from the roof to the ground, joining with the melting snow. Across the yard there was already a patch on the barn roof where a sheet of snow had slid over the corrugated iron and landed in a heap below. The thaw was happening at last. Over breakfast Jim had told them that the sap was rising in the maples and he was going to start tapping the trees.

'You want to come along?' he asked Jimmy and was greeted with a wide-eyed grin.

Jim looked at his mother. 'I checked the kit over yesterday and everything's ready. There's a good pile of wood cut for the fire.'

'I'm ready when you are.'

'Will you show me how you do it?' Joan looked at her mother-in-law, still slightly nervous that she might yet get a knock back, but Helga was smiling.

'Best time of the year. I'd be happy to show you. But if you give away my methods to anyone in town I just might have to kill you.' She gave a little laugh and wiped her hands on her apron. 'But you go along with the boys today and see what happens to get the sap out of the trees. We'll get boiling tomorrow if they collect enough.'

The snow was beginning to turn to slush underfoot and sparkled like shattered glass in the March sunlight. Spring was definitely on the way even though the snow was still thick on the land.

Joan tramped along through the white fields beside Jim, both of them carrying buckets and Jim with a holdall, containing his kit of a drill, a hammer and a number of metal spigots, slung over his shoulder. Jimmy ran up and down in front of them, keen to find out if the syrup on his pancakes did indeed come out of a tree trunk.

There was a small stand of sugar maples: tall silvery trees, enough to furnish the farm with plenty of syrup and some over to give away. Jim explained that one of the neighbouring farmers was a significant producer and was looking at building a sugar shack and installing an evaporator to handle industrial quantities. For the Armstrongs, it was a pleasurable sideline rather than a source of income.

They stopped in front of the first tree and Jim used a small hand-drill to make a hole, then took a metal spigot out of his bag and hammered it into the trunk.

'Won't it damage the tree?'

Jim laughed. 'How else we going to tap them? These trees are sixty or seventy-years-old. We tap them every year.'

'But won't they run out?'

'Sap rises up inside the trunk every year in spring and summer, then falls away when the cold comes. Now the thaw's started it's racing up these trees again. Happens every year. All summer to make new sap and all winter to sleep. We only take one tap from each tree unless it's a biggie.' He turned to grab a pail and attached it to the hook on the spigot. 'Need to tap them on the south side, where the sun hits them.' He stood back to look at his handiwork. 'Should be full by the end of the day. Then it's up to Ma to work her magic.' He moved on to the next tree.

Jimmy leaned over the bucket watching the sap oozing out of the spigot. 'It doesn't look like maple syrup.'

'That's because it isn't yet. It's sap – we haven't cooked it yet. Your grandma has to boil it up and strain it. Sometimes she lets it boil all night. Once these buckets are full we need to get them to her. If we don't get them boiled up same day, the bacteria can get to the sap. You wouldn't be happy if you put maple syrup on your pancakes and it tasted like vinegar.'

Jimmy pulled a face. 'Vinegar's horrible.'

Joan laughed. 'Not on fish 'n' chips it isn't.' She shook her head. 'What have I done, letting him turn into a little Canadian? What about his national heritage?'

'Maybe one day we can introduce him to the cultural highlights of his birthplace.' Jim grinned at her. 'Once we've got this farm back on an even keel, we might have to think about a trip to England.'

Joan put her fingers to her lips. 'Ssh. Don't get his hopes up. He'll be on and on about it. Let's wait until we know it's going to happen.' She paused. 'And don't get my hopes up either.' She gave him a sad smile. 'Now let's get the next tree done.'

She watched her husband and son as they went about the tapping and collecting of sap. She had never felt happier. The long winter was almost over and spring was coming, bringing new hope and life. Not just plant life, she hoped. She still hadn't allowed herself to think too much about the possibility she might be pregnant again. She was three weeks overdue. Years of rationing had made her cycle unpredictable during the war, but over most of the almost nine months she had been in Canada she had been regular. She'd wait a while longer, maybe see Doctor Robinson before she told Jim. Joan smiled to herself as she imagined his face.

In the early evening they began to make syrup. Helga supervised the operation in the open air beside the barn, where there was a makeshift brick fireplace, fuelled by wood. Jim told Joan that maybe next year, with the additional stand of maples they would be acquiring with the Harris place, they would need to build a dedicated sugar shack to boil up the syrup, and maybe even put production on a commercial footing.

'I'm still going to boil up my own from our trees out here. No matter what.' Helga turned to Joan. 'Tastes different when it comes from different trees. Every farm has its own flavour.' She poured the buckets of sap into an big iron pot on top of the fire. 'Need to get it to a rolling boil and let it reduce slowly. That's when it gets darker. We want a nice amber colour. Then we strain it in cheesecloth. I check it's done, like this.' She scooped a ladle of syrup from the tank and flung it over her shoulder onto the snow.

Joan watched, fascinated. Everything had worked out better than she could have hoped. Jimmy was happy and healthy. She herself had adjusted to the different pace of life and to the quiet pleasures of country living. Every day, she loved Jim more and looked forward to at last having a home of her own. As soon as the Harrises moved out at Christmas Jim had been hard at work and had installed the bathroom in the new house. The prospect of indoor plumbing, of running a hot bath and luxuriating in it, of no longer having to trudge through snow and ice to the draughty biffy, filled Joan with pleasure. Jim had painted the interior and put up shelves in the kitchen and she had been busy making new curtains with the sewing machine which Alice's mother had told her was hers to keep. She surprised herself with the thought that she would miss living with Helga and Don and was glad that they would be close neighbours and frequent visitors – but the prospect of sitting down at her own table with just her husband and son was a welcome one. Just the three of them. Or maybe four soon?

She missed Alice and Rose though. Since Alice had left Hollowtree she had kept her promise to write regularly to Joan. Her letters were full of optimism, but Joan couldn't help herself from reading between the lines and imagining how lonely Alice must be.

Her sadness for Alice aside, life was good. The only shadow was the way Jim still volunteered nothing about his time in the war. Only by sharing his pain would she feel he truly trusted her. In the absence of that knowledge she felt shut out, powerless to offer any comfort. Don had told her to give Jim time. He'd also said that some things were too painful to share and better allowed to fade away with the passage of time. But Joan couldn't help worrying, wondering whether her husband was hiding something so bad she wouldn't be able to accept it. Maybe it was better not to know.

She wasn't going to think about it now. The day after tomorrow they would be moving house. A new home and, she hoped and prayed, before long a new baby. Joan smiled to herself and went inside to pack up their clothes and few possessions.

THE MORNING SUN reflected on the melting snow and shone a limpid light through the bedroom window, lighting up the shabby furnishings. Just one more night here in the farm-house. Joan tried to imagine the luxury of a big new bedroom and a proper full-sized bed. She straightened the quilt and pulled her suitcase out from underneath the bed. Once she'd filled it there were still Jimmy's clothes and a few more of Jim's. On top of the rickety wardrobe she saw a khaki canvas holdall, printed with Jim's army number. She hauled it down and folded the clothing inside. It was a tight squeeze and she had to pull hard on the buckled straps to get it to close.

She noticed a small side pocket on the bag. Just the right size for the pair of Jim's socks that she'd missed and were lying in the bottom of the wardrobe. She put her hand in and found an envelope. It was postmarked Eastbourne in December 1942 and the envelope was addressed to Jim in elegant handwriting, care of his regiment at the Aldershot barracks.

Joan sat on the bed, her hands shaking. It must be from *her*. From Gwen. She flipped it over. Inside was another envelope, folded, but also opened. It bore the words *Don't read until the war is over.* She hesitated for a minute. To read it would be a betrayal of trust. But she had to know. She had to. Had to read the words of this woman who Jim had admitted he'd once loved. If he was right and it was just a brief affair the letter would show this. She closed her eyes. It was no good. She couldn't live the rest of her life knowing this letter was here without reading it. She could destroy it – take it downstairs and drop into the stove and watch it burn. That was the best course – wasn't it? But the fact that Jim had kept it was surely proof of his lasting feelings for this woman. And if indeed he had waited to read it until the war was over, by then they were married, so he should have destroyed it afterwards. But he hadn't.

Decision made, she slipped the paper out of the inner envelope and read the contents.

My DEAREST JIM,
I had to write this after you left this morning. I had to say

again what I didn't feel I said properly then. I meant what I said about us not keeping in touch. I know it is the best for us both. But I want you to know that these past weeks have been the happiest of my life, my love.

THE WORDS BEGAN to swim out of focus on the page, as Joan read. She put the letter down and wiped her eyes on the edge of the bedsheets.

I CAN'T POSSIBLY KNOW if Roger will return from wherever he is – but I pray he does and I feel sure he will, even though I've heard nothing from him since he went away in '40. I do love him, even though I know I will never have with him what I have had with you. If I get closer to that it will only be because of you – you taught me how to love, how to feel, how to show love. You opened me up to the possibility of loving and being loved in return. You healed me, Jim, and healed my lonely heart. I had believed myself to be incapable of feeling anything since I lost my beloved brother. I will always love you for doing that, no matter what.

Maybe by the time you're reading this, if, God willing, you make it through this war, you will have found someone else. I do hope so. You deserve to be happy. I see you married – to that girl in Aldershot – or someone else if you're right and she really won't have anything more to do with you. Whoever it is, I hope she values what she has – much as I want your happiness, deep down inside the thought of you with someone else is like a physical pain to me. I know, I know – how can I say that when I hope to be with Roger again? Because I can't help it. I know you feel that way too about Roger and me.

Jim, what I'm trying to say is that even though we can't be together I hope that we both find some approximation of happiness. Meanwhile, no matter what, hidden deep inside me, you will always live in my heart. I will treasure the memory of our time together. Maybe in another life – another universe – our souls can be together.

Your Gwen.

Joan crumpled the paper in her hands and let it fall to the floor. Great gulping sobs came out of her. Eyes streaming with tears, heart thumping in shock, rage, hurt and a terrible all-enveloping sense of loneliness, she hauled her suitcase back onto the bed, pulled out Jim's clothes and stuffed it with Jimmy's.

The cash her mother had sewn into her case as an emergency fund had been untouched. Joan took a pair of nail scissors and unpicked the suitcase lining and released the envelope. She had been intending to send it back as the means for her mother and Ethel to come out for a holiday. But now it meant she could buy a passage back to England for herself and Jimmy.

Leaving Jim's clothes scattered across the bed she kicked the now empty army holdall across the room, grabbed Gwen's letter and the money and bounced the heavy suitcase down the stairs behind her.

Helga was in the kitchen, standing by the stove, stirring a pot. 'I'm bottling the first batch of syrup for you to take with you, Joan. It smells really good, don't you think?' She turned and gasped, dropping the spoon. 'What's wrong, girl?'

'Can you drive me and Jimmy into town? We can get a bus from there to Kitchener.'

'Where are you wanting to go, Joan?' Helga moved towards her, anxiety in her face.

'Home. I can't stay with Jim. Not any more.'

'What's happened? Tell me. You were laughing less than an hour ago. What's got you in this state?'

'I can't stay with him. Not after this.' She flung the letter on the table. 'You might as well read it.'

Helga picked up the crumpled paper and began reading, a frown creasing deeper into her face as she scanned the page. 'Where did you find this?'

'In his canvas holdall when I was packing.'

'Who is this woman?'

'He told me he'd had an affair with a married woman before we were married. Told me that night when I didn't show up to supper.'

Helga squeezed her lips together tightly into a thin line. 'So it was a long time ago. Before you were married. But he chose you, Joan.'

'Because he couldn't have her.'

'Talk to him, please.'

'He had his chance. Back then after we had that argument. We agreed. No more secrets.' Joan took down her coat and buttoned it up. 'Where's Jimmy?'

'Never mind where he is. You need to talk to Jim.'

'How can I possibly stay when I know now that I'm just his 'approximation of happiness'? How do you think that makes me feel? He had his chance when he told me about her – if he really loved me he'd have destroyed that letter – but he kept it.' Joan gave a sob and sank into a chair.

'Maybe he'd forgotten it was there. Because she means nothing to him now. If she did, wouldn't he have wanted to keep the letter from you? He'd have found a better place to hide it. Surely?' Helga wiped her hands on her apron. She bent over Joan in the chair, hugging her. 'He loves *you*, Joan. No matter what he thought about this woman once upon a time.' She looked at Joan. 'I know my son.'

'Yes. Just like you thought he loved Alice, not me.'

Helga looked away. 'I was wrong. And I never thought he loved Alice rather than you – I *wanted* him to love her – but I knew all along he only wanted you. From the moment I came upon you both in the meadow that night. Every time I saw him look at you. I just didn't want to believe it. Just like I didn't want to believe anything bad about Alice.'

She sat down, slumping into a chair. 'But I know for a fact, and I'd stake my life on it, my son loves you, body and soul. Don knows it too. So does Alice. In fact the only person round here who can't seem to see it is you, Joan.'

IT WAS mid afternoon before Jim found out they'd left. His mother had unwillingly taken Joan and Jimmy into town to catch the Kitchener bus. The bus wasn't due for another half hour so she had waited there with them, trying in vain to persuade Joan to change her mind.

Returning at lunchtime there was no sign of Jim. She had promised Joan to give her several hours before letting him know but Helga decided that was a promise she was going to have to break. Now that she had accepted Joan she had become increasingly fond of her. She'd already lost one daughter-in-law and a grandchild and she wasn't going to give up on Joan and Jimmy without a struggle.

Helga ran round the farm frantically looking for Jim. When she returned Don was seated at the table, waiting patiently for his dinner. Joan hadn't let her wake him to say goodbye, saying she was too upset and didn't want to risk Jim returning before she left.

Don looked at her in astonishment when she broke the news. His eyes welled with unshed tears. He shook his head. 'I love that girl,' he said. Then, his voice barely a whisper, 'and Jimmy.'

'Where in heaven's name is Jim? He needs to go after them. They'll be halfway to Kitchener by now. Once they're on that train he'll have a hell of a time catching up with them.

'He's gone over to the Harris place. Wanted to do a last check to make sure everything was ready for them moving in tomorrow. Said he'd be back soon and to leave his food in the oven.'

'Who's talking about me, then?' Jim came into the kitchen, a wide grin on his face.

When Helga showed him the letter his complexion drained of blood and he closed his eyes.

'Why in heaven's name did you hang onto it, son? Why did you leave it where she could find it?'

Jim shook his head. 'I don't know. I'd forgotten it was there. I read it on the ship then stuffed it back in my holdall.'

'You *forgot*? How could you forget something like that?'

Jim shook his head again. He ran his hands through his hair and looked at her with despair in his eyes. 'I didn't want to destroy it. I've never looked at it again. But knowing it was there. In the back of my mind. A connection to her.'

'So she did mean something to you, this woman? This *married* woman?'

Jim looked away but nodded his head.

'And you're saying she still does?'

'I don't know. I don't know what I'm saying. I don't even know what I'm thinking.'

'So your wife and your son have walked out of that door and you're sitting here saying you don't know what to do about it?' said Don.

He put his hands over his face and groaned.

'Don't you love Joan?' Don's voice was incredulous.

'Yes, of course I love her.' His voice was fierce.

'And this woman? This Gwen?' Helga's face was contemptuous.

'It's different. I told Joan about her months ago. Told her it was a wartime affair. Joan and I weren't even together when I was with Gwen.'

'But you kept her letter.'

He looked up at his mother, his face wretched.

Helga went over to the stove, letter in hand, opened the lid and dropped the letter into the flames inside. 'There. What was so difficult about that? That's what you should have done more than a year ago. Or dropped it into the ocean. Preferably without having opened it in the first place.' She looked at him, hands on hips, daring him to challenge her.

Jim crumpled where he sat at the table, head in hands. 'You shouldn't have done that. It wasn't yours. You should never have read it. It's none of your damned business.'

'Don't speak to your mother like that.' Don's voice was angry. 'She's right.'

'Now you need to go after Joan and find her and bring her back.' Helga pulled a chair out and sat down opposite her son. 'If you can't stop her before she leaves the country, you'll have to get yourself on a boat to England and go to Aldershot and bring her home.'

'There's something else he needs to do first,' Don said. Mother and son turned to look at him. 'He needs to go and see that Gwen woman. Needs to find out for sure what he really feels instead of torturing himself and hurting everyone around him…' His words crumbled into coughing. 'No point trying to get Joan back until he believes she's what he really wants. She doesn't deserve to be second best.' Coughing again.

'You're not serious?' Helga looked at her husband in disbelief. 'You're suggesting he goes to England to find this woman. This *married* woman?'

'I am. If Jim really loves her. Loves her more than Joan and Jimmy, he needs to face up to that fact. The married woman needs to face up to it too. And her husb… Better to get it out in the open than live with a pack of lies.'

Helga got up and began to pace up and down. 'I can't believe you're saying that, Don. Why aren't you telling him to

247

forget all this nonsense and get on with his life? Preferably with Joan. But if not, without her. Certainly not going to see a married woman who's already told him the affair is over.'

'Joan, if she's any sense, and I think she has plenty, won't take him back if he's still hankering after this other woman. He needs to face up to it. Confront the situation. Lance the boil.'

'So as well as wrecking his marriage you want him to wreck someone else's as well.'

'If this woman still feels like that about Jim then there can't be much left to wreck.'

'Don Armstrong, I'm shocked at you. You should be telling him to fight for Joan.'

'He can't fight for her until he believes he wants to. I'm not sure he's realised that he does yet.'

Helga looked at Jim. 'You got nothing to say for yourself?'

Jim said nothing, He got up from the table and went up to his room, slamming the bedroom door behind him.

WITH THE PARTISANS

1944, The Apennines, Italy

THE SMALL TEAM of Canadians thought the young woman was a dyed-in-the-wool partisan. So did the partisans themselves. Her infiltration had convinced even their leader, Massimo, who also happened to be her lover. She was called Luciana – Jim never found out her surname. Long black hair, dark eyes and sun-bronzed skin, painfully thin – but then all the Italians were, never knowing where their next meal might come from. Jim had noticed her as soon as the band of *contadini* arrived at the ruined farmhouse. Impossible not to notice her, with her full sensuous mouth and those dark eyes that made wordless promises. The leader of the small Stella Rossa band had made it clear that Luciana belonged to him alone, marking possession by rarely taking his eyes off her, while outwardly projecting disinterest.

They sat around a fire, drinking rough wine, eating their fill of food offered by the soldiers and talking rapidly in dialect-heavy Italian, which Jim, who by now had picked up a smattering of the language, struggled to understand at all. Luciana spent most of the evening in silence. Jim had thought she seemed nervy, unsmiling, almost fearful, so it was a surprise when during a lull in the conversation she began to sing. Her voice was melodic, surprisingly deep and low, a contralto when her appearance might have suggested a sweeter, more fragile, soprano vocal range. One of the men accompanied her on the harmonica. The song was an opera aria, plaintive, melancholy, and she rendered it in a way that seemed to come from the heart. It was a moving performance. Jim mused that in another life she might have been enthralling crowds in an opera house, instead of here outside a tumbledown farmhouse, singing to a motley band of *contadini* and a bunch of homesick Canadians. When her song ended, the Italian men started singing, each starting up a different song which the others joined in. They were a mixture of sad songs and rousing tunes – the kind that men had sung through the ages when going into battle.

None of the partisans noticed when Luciana slipped away. Not even Massimo, who was drunk by now and caught up in the singing, his stomach replete after the meal. Jim watched as she moved into the shadows and passed behind the farmhouse. Something told him he should follow her. He'd never know why – only that it was a compulsion he couldn't ignore.

She was standing on a rocky outcrop behind the farm buildings, a torch in her hands and her slim outline lit by the moonlight. Jim waited at the corner, out of sight. His blood chilled when he realised she was flashing the torchlight into the darkness towards the mountainside opposite. Morse code. He looked towards the dark mass of mountains and saw a faint light flashing back. Three short flashes. Presumably an initial acknowledgment. Parts of the mountain ranges were impassable by vehicles and offered perfect hiding places for German scouts and snipers, republican partisans and local fascists.

Jim hesitated for a moment, not wanting to believe that this young woman was a traitor, a fascist sympathiser. Her torch flashed again into the dark night. He had to stop her. He reached for his gun, took aim and shot her through her thigh above her right knee. She fell, crumpling into a heap, screaming in pain and shock. The sound of the gunshot caused the partisans to stop singing and a moment later they appeared around the corner of the building, the rest of Jim's section behind them.

'What happened?' Massimo's voice. 'What you do to her?' His tone was low but angry.

'She was signalling to someone with a torch. Someone out there.' Jim indicated the mountainside. 'They signalled back.'

'Porca puttana. The partisan leader swore, cursing his former lover. *'Che troia,'* his precious beauty now a bitch and a whore, in his eyes.

'Could you make out the message, Corporal?' one of the Canadians asked.

'No. Just three short flashes. Not enough if it was morse. I thought it better to stop her.'

Massimo turned to the men around him and spoke to them, his dialect and the speed of his words making understanding impossible, apart from a few words – *fascisti* and *tedeschi* among them - fascists and Germans.

While they deliberated, the woman writhed in pain on the ground, clutching her leg, a pool of blood spreading underneath her.

'She needs medical help,' Jim said. 'We have to tourniquet her leg before she loses too much blood.' He ran back to the front of the ruined house and returned with bandages which he tied tightly around her thigh as the

Canadian sergeant stood over them with a gun and one of the other privates searched her and removed her pistol from her belt.

Massimo stretched out his hand to take it. 'We bring her to Santa Prisca.' Massimo pointed in the direction of the valley below. 'To the convent. The sisters will help her.'

As Jim twisted the tourniquet tighter, Luciana looked up at him, her eyes wet with tears, her face contorted in pain, her expression like a frightened animal. She was little more than a girl, probably still in her teens.

The partisans made an improvised stretcher from a blanket and a pair of poles they found in one of the outbuildings and lifted Luciana onto it, ignoring her agonised cries.

'We go now. Before dawn,' said Massimo.

As they passed Jim, two in front, two carrying the stretcher and Massimo bringing up the rear, the girl turned her eyes to look at Jim. He expected anger there but instead he saw only fear and desperation. She stretched a hand towards him, her thin fingers brushing his sleeve.

'Aiutami, signore,' she said, pleading for him to help her. 'Per dio, aiutami!' Then they were gone, disappearing down the stony hillside towards the distant town.

Jim turned to his sergeant. 'I don't think they're taking her to the nuns, sarge.'

The Canadian shrugged. 'Not our problem now. Traitorous little bitch.'

He clapped a hand on Jim's shoulder. 'Well done, Corporal. Well spotted. You might have saved us all.' He turned and snapped out orders to the others. 'Move the Bren gun to cover this side of the building. Someone's out there and we're not going to let them take us by surprise.'

As they swung into action, Jim thought it was unlikely they'd be attacked. Whoever was out there would know the woman had been intercepted. He was proved right when the rest of the night passed without incident. Whoever had been there had faded back into the scrub-covered rocky terrain.

When Jim had joined up he had not expected to fire a gun at a woman. Consumed with guilt and shame he had no sleep at all that night.

Next morning they packed up quickly and made their way down the hillside. Their orders were to meet the rest of the unit in the town below, before merging with other units of the Eighth Army to press on up the valley towards German lines.

It was already blazing hot by the time they entered the dusty little town at around eleven. The place was quiet. Usually when they entered a town or village the people came out of their houses to greet them, cheering and waving and often strewing flowers. But Santa Prisca was silent, almost ghostly. Its people had either already evacuated during the German occupation or had shut themselves indoors. The only sound was the bleating of goats as they picked at the scanty patches of grass and scrambled over the ruins on the perimeter of the settlement.

As soon as they entered the main square he saw her. Her long dark hair tumbled down her back, covering her partly naked body. Her head was bent back at ninety degrees to her body, her overstretched neck broken by the thick rope they'd used to string her up from the lamp post. Her chin was pointing skywards as though she were looking to the heavens for salvation, and her thin body dangled downwards, bare feet with toes pointing at the ground. Her naked breasts were covered by a cardboard placard on which had been painted the words *"Porca fascista"* - fascist pig. Flies were buzzing around her once beautiful eyes and clustering over the gaping wound that Jim had blown in her leg. Her thin muscular arms hung by her sides, like a marionette.

Jim pulled off his cap and stared at her poor abused and

broken body. They hadn't even left her the dignity of clothing, leaving her to hang here in the public square like venison in a butcher's. He had seen far too many partisans and innocent citizens strung up from lamp posts by the Germans since he had been in Italy, a warning to the population or in reprisals for German deaths. But he'd never seen a woman killed whom he had known personally. And by her own friends. Her lover. If he had known how brutal war would prove to be, the savagery, the complete absence of mercy, of compassion, on all sides, he would never have signed up. He felt tainted, contaminated, but most of all, consumed with guilt. It was his fault. He had shot her, put her in the position where this could be done to her.

It was no good telling himself that she had betrayed her friends. He knew enough by now to understand that loyalties were complex in this country. Family ties, blood resentments, feuds, allegiances, went back decades, centuries even. Luciana's decision to support the fascists was unlikely to have been carefully thought-out, the result of a measured decision as to which side deserved her allegiance. No. She was most likely obeying orders. From her father or brothers, a local priest, a lover, or avenging a past wrong. He remembered the look in her eyes as she had gazed into his, begging him to help her. It was like that of the young German he'd shot in that cow byre months earlier. The certain knowledge that death was coming, that her brief life was soon to be cut short, that he was her only hope. And he had stood by and let them take her, knowing he was kidding himself that they would deliver to her to the convent and the care of the nuns.

But what else could he have done? Taking on the partisans would have been foolhardy and would have endangered the rest of the small team. They were expected to work closely with the partisans when they came across them: these bands of locals were deemed critical to the war effort, particularly in this unfamiliar terrain where the Allied armies depended on their local knowledge. If he'd called out to her and tried to arrest her at gunpoint, she wouldn't have hesitated to shoot him first. Earlier that evening he'd watched her as she cleaned her gun with speed and expertise that could only have come with long experience. Should he have warned her and let her escape? That would have been treachery on his part, risking the lives of his team. And even if he'd not shot her, it would have made little difference in the end. Once the *Stella Rossa* knew she was working for the fascists she was a dead woman anyway. No. The only thing he could have done, now wished he had done, was shoot her dead as soon as he saw her signalling with that torch and spared her this rough justice, this undignified, disgraceful death. But to kill a woman, little more than a girl? That was beyond his capacity.

Jim continued to look at the undernourished body as it hung motionless in the heat of the day, its skin drying under the reflected heat from the blinding white flagstones of the town square. A dog appeared and began to lick at the congealed blood that had dripped from her leg onto the ground, where the tourniquet bandage he had so carefully applied now lay beside the her torn-off clothing.

'Forgive me, Luciana,' he said. 'May you rest in peace.'

RETURN TO EASTBOURNE

JIM'S HEART was hammering as he walked up the road, the familiar red brick Victorian pavement beneath his feet. A wave of nostalgia swept through him to heighten his nervous anticipation. He'd stopped off on the way for a whisky at The Ship to give himself Dutch courage. The pub looked the same as it had when he'd last been there in 1943, but was quiet without the buzz of Canadian soldiers clustered round the piano, singing. Apart from a couple of old men bent over their pints of stout and the barman polishing glasses, the place was deserted. This was a different barman. Jim wondered if the man had also returned from war service – but he'd not been in the mood to find out.

Above the tree-lined road of large, late Victorian houses, the Downs swept up to the blue cloudless sky and he thought of the nights he had spent up there, on Beachy Head, transcribing German Morse messages in a cramped hut with a morose RAF man for company.

He arrived outside the house. It looked just the same. Only the front garden was changed – lawns and herbaceous plants where he remembered neat rows of vegetables which Pauline Simmonds, the housekeeper had tended.

The motor car was parked on the drive, so Gwen was probably home. Jim had no idea what he was going to say to her. No idea if she'd be alone or if the husband who had been gone for most of the war would be there with her. Jim hadn't prepared his words. He'd wanted to trust to his instincts, to his feelings, to fate. But now he felt hollow, uncertain, paralysed, and wished he'd made that whisky shot a double.

He rang the doorbell. Heard it echo in the hallway inside. Remembered the layout of the furniture – the mahogany hall stand, the ornate mirror, the stiff-backed chair next to the console table where the telephone sat. No answer. He swallowed and pressed the bell again, jumping nervously at the sound of a voice behind him. He turned to see a wiry man, wearing a colourful fair-isle sweater and a pair of grimy pants, holding a pair of hedge clippers.

'You looking for the Collingwoods?'

Jim noted the plural and nodded.

'They've gone down to Holywell for a walk by the sea. You can sit in the garden to wait for them.'

'I'll take a stroll down there and see if I can find them.'

'Nice day for it. You American?'

'Canadian.'

'Thought I caught an accent. You'll probably find them at the Tea Chalet. It's Saturday, so the lassie's with them.'

'The lassie?'

'Their little girl, Brenda.'

'I see.'

'Well, best get on. They don't pay me to stand and chat all day. Have a good one, mate.'

Jim walked back down the road and took the turning that led down towards the sea.

So he had come back. Roger. He'd survived the war. But

Brenda? Gwen's friend and housekeeper, Pauline, had had two little girls. Wasn't the baby called Brenda? Perhaps the gardener hadn't meant Roger after all, but Gwen and Pauline? But the man had said 'the Collingwoods'. Unsure whether he felt hope or disappointment, Jim increased his pace, impatient to find out.

The seafront had changed radically. Gone was the barbed wire that laced across the top of the beach. No more Bofors guns. No sandbags and tank traps and warning signs. No mines on the shingle and in the sea.

Being April, there were no bathers on the beach, despite the mildness of the weather, but plenty of people were enjoying a stroll, walking dogs or playing impromptu ball games on the shingle. Queasy, Jim started to wish he hadn't come. But what had his father said? 'You need to lance the boil.'

He saw them on one of the beaches in front of the Edwardian bathing-chalets. They were playing a game of catch. A dog, a Labrador, was doing its best to disrupt them, much to the amusement of the little girl. The child was about six or seven and had her mother's blonde curls. Definitely Pauline's daughter. Jim sat down on the edge of the sea wall and watched them playing. Absorbed in their game, they didn't notice him. The man was older than Jim: in his forties probably. Still handsome, but with a slight limp. Then there was her – Gwen Collingwood.

She was wearing a pair of wide-legged pants with a white shirt. A knitted jumper was tied loosely around her waist. Tall and elegant, she looked a little like Katherine Hepburn. She jumped into the air to catch the ball then quickly feinted and made a rapid pass to the little girl, who was caught by surprise and fumbled it.

'That's not fair, Mummy!' The little girl pulled a face. 'You're always doing that to me! Isn't she, Daddy?'

Roger Collingwood bent down, scooped the child into his arms and swung her round in the air as she made peals of laughter.

'Don't make her sick, darling!'

Then the three of them moved close together and Jim couldn't catch what they were saying.

Brenda started to run up the beach and called over her shoulder, 'Last one there buys the ice creams!'

Gwen reached for her husband's hand and the two of them began to run together towards the child. When they caught up with her, they each took a hand and swung her up into the air between them. Brenda's laughter rippled into the distance as they moved away from where Jim was sitting towards the tea rooms. They conveyed the image of a tightly-knit unit. Impregnable. Self-sufficient. Happy.

He knew now for sure. Watching them, he was envious. But not for them. He felt no desire to be there in Roger Collingwood's place, swinging that little girl by the arms en route for an ice cream cone. No wish to be there walking hand-in-hand with Gwen. No longing to put his arms around her shoulders, to pull her into a kiss.

All he wanted was to be be with Joan and Jimmy. His own family. Tears pressed at his eyes as he thought of them and of what he had done to them. What he had put them through. How much he had hurt Joan. All he wanted was to be with her, to hold her, to tell her how much he loved her. To show her. To prove his love to her and wash away all memories of Gwen. He had been such an idiot. Such a selfish lout.

Seeing Gwen made him realise with an absolute certainty that he didn't love her. Maybe never had. Yes, she was a beautiful woman. A good woman. The right person for him to have met when he had, to help heal the pain of what Alice had done to him by jilting him for Walt. But Gwen had no place in his life now, just as he had none in hers. He was happy for her, that she had found love and happiness – there had been no mistaking the expression on her face when she had looked at her husband and daughter. Brenda had called them Mummy and Daddy. What had happened to Pauline and Brenda's older sister? It was not difficult to imagine, given the pounding Eastbourne had taken from the Luft-waffe during the war. Poor Pauline. He'd liked her. Always ready with a smile and a cup of tea for him and the other soldiers billeted at Gwen's house.

Jim got to his feet and turned to walk back along the front towards the town and the railway station, but he found himself running. Running as fast as he could. Running towards Joan.

THE STAG

WHEN JIM KNOCKED at the front door of Joan's mother's house he saw a curtain twitch. Moments later Ethel opened the door and stepped outside, pulling it shut it behind her. Her mouth was down-turned and tight-lipped as though she was trying to force a look of disapproval onto her face. But then, unable to sustain it, she flung her arms around Jim. When she released him she said, 'She doesn't want to see you. She said if you turn up I'm not to let you in the house.'

'I have to see her, Ethel.'

'Look, why don't you come to my house. Mum's out. We can talk there. You look like you could do with a cuppa.'

Jim glanced at the closed door and reluctantly agreed, following Ethel to the house she shared with her widowed mother in the same street.

They were silent until she had made a pot of tea and poured them each a cup. Ethel sat down opposite him. 'Well, Jim Armstrong, I don't suppose there's any point in telling you you've messed up good and proper. I'm sure you know that as well as I do.'

He nodded and studied the surface of his tea.

'I'm surprised how long it's taken you to come here. It's over a week since she's been home.'

'Home?' He sounded rueful. 'I want her to come home.'

Ethel shook her head. 'You've cut her to the bone, Jim. She's in pieces. She worshipped the ground you walk on and you've broken her heart.'

Jim gave a groan of anguish and buried his head in his hands. 'I know I've screwed up. I never wanted to hurt her. You have to make her understand, Ethel. I can't function without her. She's everything to me. It just took me a while to realise that. I was too blind to see what was right in front of me. How can I convince her? There is no one else. No one. Only her.' He looked up at Ethel. 'I've been so stupid. I wish to God I'd destroyed that letter as soon as I read it. I wish I could turn the clock back.'

Ethel reached out and patted his hand. 'I know you love her, Jim. But she's stubborn and she's hurt and she doesn't want to listen. Joan's always had it in her head that she loves you more than you love her. Even before she knew about this Gwen woman. That letter was the last straw.'

'Get her to see me. Please. I've come all this way. I've used up all our savings to get here. I have to talk to her. I have to see her. And Jimmy. Please, Ethel, help me. I beg you.'

She gave a long sigh and reached for a packet of cigarettes, lit one and said, 'I'll try. But I have to warn you, Jim, I've never seen her like this before. She's not even sad any more, she's angry. And I can't blame her. After all she's been through. I don't think it's been easy for her, getting used to life in Canada. It's so completely different from everything she's ever known. Her letters were always cheerful. Putting a brave face on I suppose, but yesterday she told me your mother was very hard on her in the beginning and you didn't stand up for her a lot of the time. You just left her to get on with it.'

Jim's hands formed into fists and he beat them against his head. 'I know. I know. I don't deserve her. I wish I could go back and start all over again and do everything differently. Joan is the best thing that ever happened to me and I've messed up her life and made her unhappy. That's the last thing I wanted. If it would win her back I'd give up the farm, sell the land and move over here. I'll do anything to get her back. I love her so much.'

He sat in silence for a few minutes, breathing deeply, his fingers tapping nervously on the table.

'Drink your tea.'

He drank it down in gulps. 'Tell me. What should I do? How can I get her to listen, to understand? Can't you persuade her? She thinks more of you than anyone, Ethel.'

'I can't promise. She seems very determined. But I'll do my best. Where are you staying? I'll talk to her and get word to you if she agrees to see you.'

THE FOLLOWING AFTERNOON, Jim presented himself at Joan's family home, at the time agreed with Ethel. He stood outside the door, shuffling his feet, straightening his tie and taking a deep breath, before knocking on the door with a shaking hand. When Joan answered it, his heart soared inside his chest. She looked pale, wearing no makeup, her eyes slightly red at the rims – but he had never thought her more beautiful. He wanted to wrap his arms around her and kiss her but she stepped backwards into the hall signalling him to follow her.

'Jimmy's at Ethel's,' she said.

She showed him into the front parlour and Jim remembered the last time he had been there, when he had discovered she had had a child. His child. Jimmy. She had been nursing the baby and Jim remembered how he had felt then, seeing his tiny baby son for the first time, cradled in Joan's arms as he suckled her breast. A lump formed in his throat.

He sat down on the settee, twisted his hat around in his hands, searching for the right words, terrified of making matters worse. Joan was avoiding his eyes.

'I've been a fool. I'm so sorry, Joan. Please come home. Please try to forgive me. I promise I'll make things up to you. I'll do anything if you'll come back to me.'

Joan said nothing, turning her head to look out of the window, through the grimy net curtains.

'I'll give up the farm and move over here if that will make you happy.'

'Don't be daft,' she said at last. 'You couldn't live here. You wouldn't last five minutes.'

'I lived here before.'

'Yes, and you hated it.'

'I don't care. I'll put up with anything if it means being with you.'

'Why did you keep her letter?' Her inflexion was sharp.

'I don't know.' He bent his head, eyes closed. 'You've no idea how many times I've asked myself that question. I wish I'd torn it into a thousand pieces and scattered it overboard as soon as I read it.'

'Did you often read it? When I wasn't around?'

'No!' Horrified. 'Never. Not once.' He paused then added, 'To be honest I'd forgotten it was there.'

'Don't lie to me. I can't have any more lies.'

'It's true. I hadn't forgotten *her* but I'd forgotten the letter was there. I swear it, Joan.' He took a deep breath and decided it was all or nothing and only the truth. 'I went to see her. Two days ago.'

He heard Joan gasp. Jumping up from the sofa, he knelt

on the floor in front of her chair and reached for her hands. 'Look at me. I'm telling you this because you asked for the truth. Pa told me I had to find out what I really felt about her. Get her out of my system. He knows me better than I know myself. He knew when I saw her I'd be sure it was you I loved.'

Joan jerked her hands away but he grasped them again and held them tightly. 'And he was right. I didn't speak to her. She didn't even see me. I saw her with her husband and child on the beach.'

Joan's head twisted away.

'Please. Look at me. I watched her with them for five minutes or so and all I could think was that I wished it was you and Jimmy there on that beach instead of them. All I could think of was you and how much I want you. How much I've missed you – every minute since you left. I didn't want to see her face, I only wanted to see yours. I love you, Joan. Maybe you won't believe me. Maybe you won't take me back – and God knows I don't deserve you. But the only thing in this world that's certain is that I want *you* and nobody else. If I lose you I will *never* get over it. Never forgive myself for what I've done to you. Never forgive myself for my spectacular failure to make you realise that I love you more than life itself.'

She looked at him, her eyes welling with tears. 'It's too late, Jim. I don't love you anymore. I don't love you because I can't trust you. You won't talk to me about the things that matter.'

'What things?'

'What happened in the war. Not just her. Afterwards. What you did; what you saw; what changed you; what made you so angry and so haunted.' She looked at him but he was looking down, avoiding her eyes. 'I told you after what happened with Howardson. You scared me. I don't know you. And it's not because of what you might have done. It's because you can't even bring yourself to tell me about it.'

He rocked back onto his heels. 'I can't, Joan. If I told you there would be no hope of you loving me. And I can't inflict it on you.'

She pushed him away. 'Then I've nothing more to say to you. Goodbye.'

JIM WALKED for an hour or so, trudging through the streets of the small town, running Joan's words over and over in his head. He imagined going back to Hollowtree Farm, the expectant look on his parents' faces, their disappointment when he told them Joan wasn't coming back. The thought of living without her, without their son, was so desolate he couldn't even bear to contemplate it. The little house he had readied for her still stood empty and he couldn't stand to live there alone. Yet the thought of living in the main farmhouse was just as unsettling – sleeping in the bed without her, walking into the kitchen and seeing only his mother and father at the table where Joan and Jimmy would once have been sitting. He remembered the happy days swimming in the pond, sledding down the hillside, fishing with Jimmy in the stream. Was it only two or three weeks ago that they had helped him tap the maple trees? They'd been so happy that morning. He squeezed his fists tight in his pockets, cursing his stupidity, his selfishness, his careless ruination of everything he had held valuable in his life.

What had he got to lose now? She couldn't think any worse of him now so he might as well do what she wanted and tell her what she wanted to know. He went into WH Smith and bought a small pad of Basildon Bond writing paper.

Ten minutes later he was outside the Stag pub. It felt right to come here. It was where he had first met Joan, when he and his friend Greg came upon her and Ethel in the little snug bar at the back of the pub. He pushed the glass panelled door open and went into the pub. It looked exactly the same – apart from the absence of the heavy blackout curtains so that now the windows on the front facade were revealed in their Victorian etched glass splendour. There was an off duty soldier sitting on a stool in the public bar, nursing a pint, a group of elderly men playing a game of cards at a table under the window and what looked like a commercial traveller, washing down his lunchtime sandwich with a beer. Jim bought a pint of bitter and went to the door marked Snug. Relieved to find the room empty, he sat at the little table in the corner and tasted the beer. He'd forgotten how good English bitter was – once you got used to it. Putting the glass down, he opened the pad of writing paper and began to write the story of what had happened in Italy.

He spared nothing in the telling. He began at the beginning with Sicily. It was there he had witnessed the brutality of death on the battlefield for the first time when he watched his friend Mitch take a bullet as they waded ashore, and then after he had dragged him up the beach saw him dying in a vineyard as shells burst around them; the lance corporal whose stomach was ripped apart and his intestines spilled onto the dry earth around them; the young boy from Winnipeg who asked Jim to pray for him as he lay dying. He wrote of the stench of death and how after a while he ceased to notice it. Taking another mouthful of beer, he asked himself why he was doing this. How could he ever give this to Joan? How could he expect her to understand the horrors he had seen? But still he wrote on, filling the pages of the notepad, feeling as he did so that a weight was beginning to lift from his shoulders.

He told her – for by now it felt as though he were

speaking directly to Joan – about the hand-to-hand street fighting in Ortona, the heat and dust of the Liri Valley underneath Monte Cassino. He recounted the day he had stood with his platoon, watching the public shaming of a dozen men from his company who had been caught after deserting the fighting in the Liri. The men were to be sent to do hard labour in the burning heat of the North African desert but first underwent the humiliation of having their badges torn off, their caps removed before they were paraded in front of the entire battalion while drummers beat out the chirpy tune of *The Rogues' March.*

He finished his pint and bought another, drinking it as he wrote. The death of friends, of enemies, the sight of starving Italians in towns, cities and villages, their stomachs bloated with hunger. Young women prostituting themselves in exchange for black market food in the cesspit of crime and poverty that was Naples, when his platoon were sent there for a few days leave away from the battlefield. In Tuscan towns behind the German retreat, seeing women and children shot dead and their bodies strung up from trees or lampposts, or left abandoned to rot by the roadsides as a warning to others against helping the partisans. He told about the men he had killed, some remotely when he had fired on an enemy installation, others when he had been able to see their faces, the fear in their eyes as they faced death. He told her of the young German boy who had been the first, later just one of many. He told her of Luciana and his role in her death and humiliation. The endless days in the mud of the Po Valley; the fear of being blasted into oblivion by a German mortar. The constant need for caution as a moment's distracted attention could lead to stepping on a land mine and getting blown sky high, as happened to his pal, Rick. The smell of corpses rotting in brilliant sunshine. The biting cold of the snow on the plains of the Po. The way that, after a while, death was routine, like eating or sleeping. Killing was something he had done with barely a moment's thought as if he were threshing corn on the farm.

By the time he had drained his second pint, he had finished writing. All but two of the sheets of the pad of writing paper were filled. He stuffed the pages in his pocket, went into the public bar and downed a whisky chaser in one. He would ask Ethel to give the letter to Joan and tomorrow he would go home. It was done. It was over. He realised as he walked back to the guest house, that while his misery about losing Joan was as intense as ever, he felt lighter, less burdened, having got the weight of the war off his chest.

Jim stood on the platform at Aldershot station, waiting for the train to Southampton. He felt sick at the prospect of that long lonely voyage back, but couldn't afford to go by aeroplane. He felt even sicker at the thought of spending the rest of his life without Joan. Without Jimmy too, except for the occasional holiday trip when he could make enough money to pay for the boy's travel and he was old enough to make the journey unaccompanied.

All the previous night he had lain unsleeping in his bed in the guest house, torturing himself over what had happened, desperate at being so powerless, losing control over his own life, messing things up so badly that he had caused so much pain.

The platform was crowded with soldiers off for a few days leave. It had not been so long ago that he had stood here himself, waiting for a train for a few days furlough – but it felt like another lifetime and another person. He tried to distract himself by thinking of the things he'd need to get done on the farm when he returned, all the jobs that had been neglected while he was away, but he had no stomach for it. What was the point of building up the farm when he had no one to share his life there? How was he going to survive the loneliness and emptiness of a life without Joan in it?

He heard the sound of the approaching train and for a brief moment thought of throwing himself in front of it, but he could never take his own life, much as it weighed him down and stretched in front of him like a terrible punishment. That was it. It was his punishment. He would have to endure a life of misery to atone for what he had done. And most of all for what he had done to Joan.

The platform was shrouded in steam as the train swept slowly into the station. He could hear the whistle blowing, his nostrils filled with the acrid smoke from the engine, and he coughed as the crowd of people surged forward. He bent down to pick up his kitbag and saw her feet in front of him. High-heeled black patent leather shoes, shining below a pair of slim ankles. His heart leapt, a vast tidal wave of love and hope and longing rising inside him. The crowds pushed past to board the waiting train and the smoke cleared from the platform. And there she was. Dark glossy hair under a little green hat, mouth with that familiar cherry-red lipstick, eyes brimming with tears and more – with love. Jim dropped his bag and stretched his arms around her, enveloping her, holding her, kissing her, feeling the beating of her heart against his chest.

'I love you,' he said.

'Thank you for trusting me at last,' she answered. 'Thank you for letting me in. Just show me you love me as much as I love you.'

'Every day for the rest of our lives. You're the reason I survived the war. You were my reason for living. You still are. Without you I'm nothing.'

'That's good,' she said, 'as I can't live without you, Jim

Armstrong. Not for another minute. Now, take me and Jimmy home to Hollowtree.'

He held her tightly, breathing in her familiar perfume, the fresh scent of her hair, the sweetness of her face powder.

'We're having a baby, Jim,' she whispered in his ear.

THE END

ABOUT THE AUTHOR

Clare Flynn is the author of six novels and a collection of short stories. An ex-Marketing Director and strategic consultant, she was born in Liverpool and lived in London, Newcastle, Paris, Milan, Brussels and Sydney and is now in Eastbourne where she can see the sea from her windows.

Clare loves to travel (often for research) and enjoys painting in oils and watercolours as well as making patchwork quilts.

Sign up for Clare's newsletter for a free copy of her short story collection, A Fine Pair of Shoes and updates in forthcoming publications, special offers and promotions. To get your free copy go to the Home Page of Clare's website and sign up there

To contact Clare

www.clareflynn.co.uk
Click reply to newsletter after signing up

facebook.com/authorclareflynn

twitter.com/clarefly

ACKNOWLEDGMENTS

Thanks to my critique group, Margaret Kaine, Jay Dixon, Jill Rutherford and Maureen Stenning. You are always a huge support and a valuable source of positive and constructive criticism – as well as laughter.

Jane Dixon-Smith for yet again doing a splendid cover design - the seventh she has done for me. You are a star, Jane.

My editor Debi Alper – I can't begin to express how much I value your input and insights.

Special thanks to Peter Monahan, Adelaide Campbell and Janine Harris-Wheatley of Ontario Canada, for being my personal Canadian Wikipedia, dictionary and fact checkers and to Hilary Bruffel for asking these lovely people to help me. They were always there ready to answer all the questions I put to them via our personal Facebook Messenger group.

Thanks also to Clare O'Brien, Sue Sewell and Lina Negri for pre-publication feedback. Invaluable as always.

Last but not least to my many loyal readers. None of this would be possible without you.

CPSIA information can be obtained
at www.ICGtesting.com
Printed in the USA
LVHW11s0359241018
594536LV00003BA/520/P